THE RESCUE: SANCTUARY'S AGGRESSION 5

A POST-APOCALYPTIC THRILLER SERIES

MAIRA DAWN

SKYLAN PUBLISHING HOUSE

PROLOGUE

One glimpse at the sleepy seaside town, and there was no mistaking the devastation that had rolled over it. It took a second, third, or even a fourth look to see that what it left was truly evil.

The hurricane had hit it hard, and even as the violent storm blasted its way through the town, another calamity was underway.

The AgFlu tore through the population.

Infants to the elderly fell victim to one or the other.

The very strong held on for a while, clinging and crying during the worst of the screaming winds—limp and defeated when they were over—shivering in fear of contracting the dreadful disease.

Even some of these, with time, the AgFlu overtook.

The wounded souls roamed the town's dusty ruins in their sickened condition for weeks, hoping each day would bring their release from the disgusting illness. Until they couldn't hope at all, were just some shell of a person with little sanity, forever roving from one street to another, a danger to anyone left.

1

Even through all this, some fortunate lived, though most doubted the word applied. Their homes destroyed—the world's fate reflected in their once lovely town—they saw only ruined houses open to the elements and streets filled with debris.

Somehow, they had survived the gale-force winds, disease, and attacks of the Sick and Infected, only to be lost at how to continue with the gift they had somehow held on to, the gift of life.

All eyes turned to the only intact building left, a concrete dome once used for enjoyment and education—a safe place.

One by one, the healthy turned up at its doors, and were welcomed into the building.

Once invited in, the healthy newcomers never left.

Newcomers first noted its cleanliness, then as they were led deeper into the center of the building, the pristine white countertops lined with test tubes, beakers, and Petri dishes.

Men and women in white coats, pens in hand, and glasses firmly planted on their faces breathed through masks as they investigated their findings. Their gloved fingers quickly scribbled into notebooks as they checked and doubled checked all their numbers.

The White Coats were convinced that everything they did, good or evil, had to be done, *needed* to be done, to save everyone, or maybe just to save someone.

As newcomers entered the specimen room, they heard the small animals chattering. Mice, hamsters, and rats skittered to the back of their cages in fear. Screeching primates screamed their distress.

The sure feeling of safety cocooning the newcomers since they had arrived fled at what they saw next.

Men, women, and even children occupied the cages.

They moaned and cried as they tried to console one another.

"It's for the good of all humankind," the White Coats told the newcomers as they pushed them into the barred enclosures.

Fear and pain ruled their lives now.

Pain came from the scientists.

Fear from what the cages across them held.

The large human-like beings raged against their imprisonment, wrenching at their thicker bars. With little room to move, they roared their distress until someone came to calm them—either with a needle or a cattle prod.

Everyone trembled when someone new walked into the room, accompanied by two assistants. The attractive, dark-haired man in a suit and a lab coat looked like someone who would set everything right. But they had already learned nothing here was as it seemed.

The man waved toward their cages. "We're going to need more of them. These won't last long."

The assistants cringed.

"There are not many left out there," one brave assistant said.

The dark-haired leader glared at her.

The assistant licked her lips and was quick to say, "Jack's out there. He's been going further afield to find good specimens. He's due back. Perhaps he'll have something.

The leader nodded and pointed to the caged men, women, and children. "Let these go in the usual place."

Then he pointed to the beings across the room. "And do what we usually do with these abominations. Get more as quick as possible—we needed them yesterday. We can't have this holding us up."

The men, women, and children cried in happiness over

their release as they looked across the way and thanked God they weren't those beings.

This was the new normal in the small town of Seaside.

Dread was the companion of every resident. Fear was their ruler.

1

TAKEN

S kye glanced down the hill one last time, praying Jesse would get away. Let him make it home—for his own sake, at least—and hopefully for her and Kelsey, too.

Someone gave her back a light push-just a reminder of what she'd promised.

To stay with Kelsey--and be taken wherever it was Jack that took his victims.

Heaven help them both.

Skye slid into the back seat of the car, a cold quaking in the pit of her stomach. She tested the rope Mark had tied around her wrists. It was not as tight as it could have been, and he'd tied them in front of her.

That may come in handy.

Skye reached for Kelsey, lifting her arms over the girl's head, laying them around her shoulders, and pulling her close.

The girl trembled.

Skye tightened her arms, hoping the embrace would offer some comfort. Since the world had turned upside-down, this poor child had gone through so much—no doubt she imagined the worse.

Skye would be the same except for Dylan's instructions.

Stay alert during turbulent situations. Forget what could happen. Focus on what *was* happening. A way out could come, most likely with a small window of opportunity.

She needed to stay sharp.

Outside the car, two of Jack's men said something to Reed and Spencer and bashed them again with the wooden ends of their rifles.

Spencer dropped to the pavement and stayed there.

Reed held a hand to his bloody scalp as he crouched above him and stared at Skye.

"We will find you," he mouthed to her.

Despite her resolve, tears filled Skye's eyes and threatened to fall.

She nodded.

Maybe a proper leader would tell them not to follow— to keep themselves safe—but right now, she was too frightened to be a good leader.

Skye wanted out of this situation, and if Reed felt he had any semblance of a plan, she wouldn't say no.

The front car doors opened and closed. Skye stared at the leader, Jack, and one of his goons from beneath her lashes as they jumped into the front seat.

Jack sat on the passenger side, dragging his seat belt down his middle, a big grin on his face.

"Safety first!" he said as he threw a glance back at Skye and Kelsey. "Make sure you buckle up. You're precious cargo."

Kelsey glanced at Skye with a question in her eyes.

Skye nodded at her and put her own seatbelt on. As much as she wanted to ignore everything the man said, this wasn't the time to make a stand. The last few moments had just proven that.

Jack's vicious attack on their group showed how far he would go to get what he wanted.

Skye looked back as they drove away. Spencer raised his head and frowned as if trying to get his bearings.

Some tension left her once she saw him up and moving.

For a long while, the car was deathly quiet. For that, Skye was grateful. Her nerves were stretched too thin to listen to Jack's prattle.

She and Kelsey studied every turn the driver took, sharing a look and a nod over directions to memorize. It was critical they remember the way home.

After a while, Jack glanced at Skye and asked, "Have you been out and about lately?"

She compressed her lips into a firm line. There was no way she would chit-chat with the man who was putting mile after mile between her and Dylan.

"Come on," Jack said, eyeing her. "Can't you be civil? It's a simple question."

One eyebrow arched, Skye turned and looked out the window beside her.

Jack cleared his throat. "You know, I've been real nice to you so far. You're just sitting there, pretty as you please, on a seat. I should have hogtied and thrown you in the trunk. But I've been neighborly."

Anger lit in Skye's belly. "Neighborly? You call kidnapping neighborly?"

"I thought we already went over that. Do we need to again?"

"No!" She didn't want to hear his asinine reasoning—that she and Kelsey had "volunteered" to go with him.

"Fine then," Jack said. "Back to my original question, have you been out and about much?"

Skye hadn't realized it until now, but other than her unsuccessful jaunt to retrieve her parents, she hadn't been further than the superstore since she'd started living on Cole's Mountain. "No, I haven't been."

"Umm. It's gotten rough out here. If you think I'm bad . . . well, let's just say, most often, I'm the good guy."

"That's hard to believe."

Jack barked out a laugh. "Kinda mouthy, aren't you? It's okay," he reassured Skye. "I like people with a little spark in 'em. Too many people walk around here like they're already dead, and I'm not talking about the Infected and Sick."

Questions sat on the tip of Skye's tongue. If Jack insisted on a conversation, she would at least get some answers.

"Are there a lot of Infected and Sick now the virus has made its way through the population?"

"Roaming around? Some, but it seems better."

"So, you don't see many new ones? They said some Infected would take months to show symptoms."

"I don't know. Maybe some Infected have taken to hiding before they totally lose their senses. We used to see their nasty, rotting corpses all over the place. Now, most of those are bones."

Jack turned to the driver and said, "You agree, Mark?"

"Yep, I'd agree with that," Mark said and nodded.

Jack resumed his conversation with Skye. "Of course, they still have quite a population in the Containment Centers."

Containment Centers. Skye shivered. Early news reports had shown footage of these places. Not a good place then—she couldn't imagine them now.

Her cousin Tom knew more about them than she did. From time to time—having no other recourse—he would take an Infected or Sick to the remnant of Army personnel who operated the Centers.

THE RESCUE: SANCTUARY'S AGGRESSION 5

Once, when she'd asked him about the place, he'd only shaken his head, refusing to answer. She had never asked again.

"Have you seen one?" Jack asked her.

"No."

"Well, you're going to see one today."

Kelsey's trembling began again. The girl had a morbid fear of the Centers. While living in the city of Fenton, she'd often hid from the military who swept the area looking for the Sick.

More than once, Kelsey had seen healthy people pushed into overcrowded trucks, then savagely attacked by the grotesque mob on it.

The sights and sounds continued to haunt her dreams.

"We would rather not see the place," Skye replied to Jack.

"Me either. It gives me the creeps—to say the least. But it's unavoidable. We're meeting some people there—the ones we're handing you over to."

Skye's stomach lurched. She had assumed Jack was taking her and Kelsey directly to these White Coats.

"What people?" she barked.

"I wish I could tell you I knew them well, but they aren't all that neighborly. It's pretty much a business arrangement. I hand over the merchandise, and they give me my payment."

"Not merchandise. People. You hand over people."

"I prefer to think of it as merchandise. Makes the transfer easier for me that way."

"Not it. Me. Kelsey and Skye. It is two women you are handing over to unknown people. Do you even know what they will do with us?"

"I don't ask. But when they recruited me, they said it was for a cure. Don't worry. I'm sure you'll be fine," Jack said, a sick look coming over his face before turning toward the front of the car.

Skye clasped her shaking hands. "Tell me what you know about these go-between people."

"I said you'd be fine."

"Is that what you would tell your wife? Your daughters?"

He ran a hand through his hair. "I can't think of that."

"It seems, Jack, that there is a lot you can't think about. Maybe that is something you should consider."

When Jack didn't answer, Skye continued, "You can either be the problem or the solution. We have a society to rebuild, a new way of living. Things can go well, or they can go the way you'd like it to go. People can help one another, or they can hurt each other."

Skye gripped the edge of her seat. Was she making any impression at all?

"Take us back," she begged. "Be the kind of person who helps others."

Mark shot a look at Jack.

Jack narrowed his eyes. "Shut up."

But Skye would not give up. She seemed to have struck a nerve.

"Do you have a little girl, Jack? What would you do if someone were carrying her away to unknown places for unknown reasons? Kelsey is trembling so hard her teeth chatter. Do you hear them, Jack? Do you hear her trembling?"

"Shut up! I said, shut up!" Jack's face reddened, and his hands clenched.

Skye scooted forward on her seat and pressed him harder. This may be the only chance she'd get.

"She needs your help, Jack. Yours and Mark's. Please help her."

Jack's fist flew.

Pain exploded across Skye's jaw and cheekbone. Blood ran from her bottom lip. She fell back into her seat, head down and gasping.

Kelsey screamed.

"I said, shut up! Only I talk now!" Jack twisted in his seat to face Skye. "Do you understand?"

Shaking, Skye held her tied hands to her face. There was no doubt that she'd pushed him, but his mood change had been sudden.

She worked her jaw, hoping there was no permanent damage.

Mark slowed the vehicle and asked, "Should I stop the car, Boss?"

"I don't know. Let's ask her."

Jack reached back, wrapped his hand around Skye's neck, and yanked her against the back of his seat. "Do I need to have him stop the car?"

Her eyes darted from one man to the other. Whatever stopping the car meant to them—it couldn't be good.

Jack's fingers sunk deeper into the tendons of her neck as he shook her.

He smacked the side of her face again. "Do I need to have him stop the car?"

"No! No," Skye blubbered.

"Those are the last words you will utter in my presence. Our pleasant conversation is over. Do you understand?"

Skye nodded, watching his every move.

Jack's beady eyes stared at her as he wrapped his hand in her hair until she winced. Tears stung her eyes.

"You cause any more trouble," he said, "and I will beat you senseless."

Jack pushed her back into her seat.

Skye slumped, her face on fire. She raised a hand to her

lower cheek, where his massive gold ring had caught her. A lump was already forming.

She swallowed hard.

Her neck throbbed, and blood dripped from her lips.

The next time Jack moved, Skye flinched. But he only opened the glove box and pulled out a towel, throwing it over the back seat at her.

Old blood stained it. Were the blotches from other "volunteers" he'd gotten rough with?

After cleaning up as best she could, Skye pulled a sobbing Kelsey into her arms again.

She started to whisper that everything would be okay, that somehow they'd get out of this, but was afraid it would send Jack's fist toward her again if he overheard.

And if Skye were honest with herself, she sincerely doubted anything would be okay again.

Not as long as Jack's web entangled them.

2

LOST

The ice that had started in the pit of Skye's stomach expanded, filling her entire body. She straightened and curled her almost-numb fingers.

Fear locked her in its hard grip. Skye understood the emotion behind it, but that didn't make it any better.

Besides her worry over their uncertain future, the threat of a further beating hung over her head.

Skye thought of and rejected numerous escape attempts as Mark drove through country lanes and black-topped roads.

Reaching the bottom of her brief list of ideas, she would have given up all hope—except for the fact that Mark turned onto an interstate—one she recognized.

She knew where they were!

Yes, they were driving South—away from the mountain.

They were still locked in this car. But it was something —a very big something.

This road had a direct exit to Colton. She knew the way home.

The way home to Dylan.

Skye squeezed Kelsey, and the girl looked up at her and returned Skye's smile with a small, watery one of her own.

Skye wished she could tell Kelsey, but one wrong whisper could set Jack off again. She glanced at his rigid posture. He was still agitated.

Jack wasn't as comfortable with his post-Agflu job as he would like others to think.

Skye smoothed Kelsey's hair, hoping that would suffice for now.

Skye had been on this highway before. The last time, streams of cars zipped up and down it, taking passengers to their daily destinations—work, home, shopping.

It was different now.

A strange mix of scenes went by. For long stretches, the road would be free of debris or vehicles, allowing them to travel without hindrance.

However, in other areas, Mark needed to wind the car through littered roads with care.

Once, clothing and other small items covered the street, looking as if an over-packed suitcase had exploded. Toys rolled across the pavement, and nightwear fluttered in the wind.

Had a family run from the Sick and Infected? And in their search for safety left these sad little bits of their lives behind?

She winced as Mark crunched over a toy robot lying sideways on the road.

But the hardest to view was the massive group of abandoned cars.

Skye had once been to a ghost town out west. This had the same feel.

She studied the cars as Mark struggled through a narrow path someone made through the clogged area.

Most of the vehicle doors remained open. As if everyone had walked away from their vehicles.

But where did they go? This was the middle of nowhere.

Skye's gaze lingered on the things left behind. A water bottle on the seat of one car. An open children's book on the floor of a truck, its pages fluttering in the slight wind.

Hunched rotting bodies sat in a few vehicles.

Exposure to the elements had given their skin a leathery quality. Mouths hung open as if they screamed in terror as their lives ended.

Perhaps they had.

Skye averted her eyes, staring at her feet.

So much death. So much horror.

She glanced at Kelsey. The girl stared at the back of Jack's head. She seemed less afraid of these husks than she was of the men in the front seat.

That was as it should be.

The living could hurt others in ways the dead never would.

When the car screeched to a halt, Skye sailed forward until her seatbelt caught her shoulder and yanked her back.

Out of the front windshield, a large horde of Sick milled on the road in front of them. There may be fewer of them, but there were still enough to cause trouble.

Most in the horde looked as if they had been in the elements for weeks, if not longer. Their ragged clothes covered little more than skin and bones. Many, in the end stages of the disease, seemed ready to fall over any minute.

Mark cursed and looked at Jack. "So, now what?"

"You're going to have to go through them," Jack replied with a wave of his hand.

Mark scoffed. "What? There's at least forty of them. If we get stuck in the middle, we don't have many options."

"Much as I'd hate to do it, we'll throw the women out to distract them and make a break for it, if necessary."

Skye sat back in her seat, trying to make herself as inconspicuous as possible as she bit her lips closed.

The man became more evil with every passing minute.

Mark's eyes widened as he stared at Jack as if trying to gauge his seriousness. When Jack just glared back, Mark let up on the break. "All right, then."

Skye swallowed and grabbed Kelsey's shaking hand as Mark nosed the car into the crowd of Sick.

The sound of the engine disturbed the horde, and they began groaning and growling.

Mark alternated between the brake and the gas as he tried to push through them. The front of the car gently bumped against a few of the Sick.

This horde had fallen into their walking pattern long ago and was reluctant to change it.

Skye had often wondered about this aspect of the disease. Was the walking pattern because this was the last actual decision they made? Or was fear something still living in them, and it somehow convinced their beleaguered minds that this route was safe?

Mark continued to push through the horde.

Gas, brake, gas, brake

Skye's head bobbed forward each time.

Most of the Sick lumbered to the vehicle's side except for two men and a small bunch further ahead. The men let the car push at them until it seemed as if they leaned on it.

The two Sick men turned their dull eyes to the windshield. Sweat dripped from their brow even on this chilly day. Their mouths worked, encouraging the ribbons of bloody saliva dripping from their mouths to thicken as it ran onto their chests.

Mark tapped the gas again but made no headway. The tallest of the two Sick pushed back with his hip and growled.

"Just run him over!" Jack said.

"Splendid idea," Mark replied with a sarcastic tone. "And what about the ones ahead of him, and the ones after them? We can't run over all of them. That's not how a car works."

"Well, you gotta do something. We can't sit here all day. We have a schedule to maintain." Jack crossed his arms and stared out the window with a worried expression.

"I know. Just give him a minute—maybe he'll move."

Skye stared at the Sick and bit the inside of her cheek as she willed them to move along.

How long did they have before Jack threw her and Kelsey out of the car as he'd threatened?

3

HORDE

The tall Sick man gave the car a final shove and lurched away, following a tattered woman who passed by.

After a moment, the second man trailed after them.

Skye let out a sigh of relief, only to suck her breath back in as Mark moved the car toward what had seemed like a small horde.

As the car drove deeper into the middle of the group, it was clear there were more here than Mark thought.

Skye's stomach tightened as she scanned the car's side windows. Every one framed with pale, sickly faces and slack blue lips with foamy drool.

She put a hand to her nose. The smell of their dirty bodies seeped into the car.

Stirred by the intrusion, the Sick banged against the car, using discolored fingers to swipe at the window as they tried to reach the passengers inside. Dirt, blood, and who knew what else now smeared the glass.

The tattered, broken people groaned as they shuffled along. The sound swirled around the car, echoing against the metal so loudly Skye wouldn't have been surprised to find one sitting beside her.

She scooted toward the middle of the seat when one bright-eyed woman bent to peer through the window, working her tongue against her mouth.

The woman wasn't as far gone as some others, but she still looked wild. A long, tangled mess of curls sprang from her scalp and fell well past her shoulders. Sticks, and small debris lodged in her once blond strands.

Dirt emphasized every line on her face and neck. Scratches and bruising covered her skin.

The woman widened her eyes as she pressed her nose against the glass.

A chill ran up Skye's spine at the bizarre scene. She drew further back against the sleeping Kelsey, waking her.

The startled girl's eyes opened wide at the sight of the nightmarish woman at the car window.

Kelsey screamed.

The shrill cry swirled through the car, piercing Skye's ears.

Everyone, inside the car and out, stilled.

Kelsey locked eyes with the woman and pulled in another huge breath.

Jack whirled around to face the back seat. "Shut her up!"

Skye put her hand to Kelsey's mouth and tried to rouse her from the waking terror.

"It's okay, Kelsey. It's okay. We'll make our way through them, but we have to be quiet. We have to be quiet now."

Despite Skye's attempt to comfort her, Kelsey hauled in another breath.

Jack pushed Skye away and slapped Kelsey. The sharp sound resounded through the car.

Kelsey fell back in her seat—her eyes squeezed shut and a hand over her reddening cheek.

The car was instantly quiet.

Skye narrowed her eyes at Jack and hissed, "Don't touch her!"

"She screams again, and I'll push her out that door. Doesn't matter how valuable she is—nothing is worth dying here with these things."

Kelsey bit her lip and scowled at Jack.

Outside the car, the grumbling and groaning became louder, and the Sick resumed banging on the vehicle as they wished the car and its disruptions gone.

Mark pushed on the gas, but his start stop method was less effective now. The mob crowded against the vehicle.

Skye scanned the way ahead, searching for a way through the horde. Her nerves stretched to their limits.

Something tapped Skye's foot.

She ignored it at first, but it bumped her each time Mark slapped on the gas.

Skye looked down at the car's carpeted floor to find a small cylinder about a foot and a half long.

A fountain firework display.

Skye snatched it up and shoved it toward Jack. "Look!"

Jack grabbed it from her. "Mark! There's one left!"

He pulled a lighter from his pocket and rolled down his window.

An arm pushed into the car and tried to get a hand on him.

Jack yelped and hurried to push it away. He handed the firework and lighter to Skye. "Here, you do it!"

Skye grabbed the items from him.

So he was only a big, strong man when he was abusing women. If only there were some way to use this on him. But getting out of this horde was the more immediate problem.

When the Sick beat on the windows, Skye said to Mark, "Blare the horn. Perhaps the distraction will startle them enough to move away from the windows for a moment, and I'll be able to throw this further."

Skye positioned herself in the middle of the back seat, hoping it was far enough away from any grasping hands that made it into the car.

Kelsey sat behind her, ready to push arms out of the way.

Mark laid on the horn, giving one long, loud honk.

The mob stirred and moved away from the car, giving Skye the gap she needed.

She held the end of the Roman candle out of the window, lighting it as quick as possible, then threw it up and over the crowd with all her might.

It went wide, but not as far as she hoped, falling on its side and skittering along the road.

After a moment, it began popping and snapping. Sparks spit as it bounced along the street and spun into the air.

Skye felt a stir beside the car and yanked her hands back through the window.

An arm covered in a dirty once-white long-sleeved business shirt snaked through her window, searching.

She pushed the button for the automatic window, hoping to close it on the Sick's arm. "Come on, come on!" she murmured as the whir of the window seemed to mock her with the way it crept toward the top.

The grasping fingers brushed Skye's hair.

She gasped and jerked back before his hand could wind itself in it.

Thankful that her hands were tied in front of her and not behind, Skye pushed at the arm.

It moved away from her and toward the driver.

"Get it out of here!" Mark yelled as he jumped forward in his seat.

Skye pushed at it again, and Kelsey gave it a few whacks.

The owner of the arm bent to stare into the car. His bloodshot eyes seemed to stare without seeing.

The Sick managed to run a hand down Skye's arm, catching on the rope at her wrist. He pulled, jerking her hands up against the window.

Skye pulled back, and a tug of war started until she made a sharp downward move, which bent the Sick's arm beyond its normal range of motion.

He wailed and let go.

Kelsey pushed his arm out of the vehicle, holding it as Skye raised the window and letting it go at the last moment.

Huffing, the two women flopped against the back of the seat, catching their breath.

Outside, the ear-piercing whistles of the Roman candle stirred up the horde. The firework's light drew some Sick but repelled those deep into the disease with oversensitive sight and hearing, and many moved off the road.

As soon as Mark had a sliver of empty road, he floored the gas and took off through it.

Skye and Kelsey fumbled with their seatbelts and turned to the rear window to watch the horde disappear.

4

THE CONTAINMENT CENTER

Skye smelled the place long before she saw it. The Containment Center sat on a hillside. Everything about it screamed that it was a quick build.

Two by fours shored up the massive fence where it sagged. Behind the enclosure sat a large white building.

A forest surrounded the area. Dozens of trees inside the pen had been sheared to stumps and served as rough chairs for the imprisoned Infected and Sick. On each stump sat some beleaguered human bent in misery.

A cheap roof covered the fenced area. Over time, the inferior materials had given way and opened large gaps now covered with large blue tarps that lazily flapped in the wind.

There was no mistaking what this was.

It's where the Infected and Sick went to die.

Skye's heart sank. She pitied these poor people.

Mark made a noise low in his throat. "I hate this place."

"Yeah," Jack said, "but it's a necessary evil."

"I don't know why these guys like to meet here."

"They drop off Sick before picking up these." Jack jabbed a thumb to the back seat.

Mark pulled up alongside the fence and turned off the car.

Jack glanced at Skye." Now we wait."

About ten minutes later, a large box truck lumbered down the pot-holed dirt driveway. A dark sedan followed it.

Skye's stomach clenched, and she felt sick. As bad as these guys were, the new ones could be worse. She watched the white truck pull up to their car and stop. Two men jumped out. Four exited the car behind it.

"No!" The word escaped Skye's lips before she could stop it.

From the look of these men, they had been rough long before the outbreak started. Everything about them spoke of danger—from their tattooed skin to their short, stubbled hair and dark, ripped clothing—not to mention the weapons crisscrossing their bodies.

Skye reminded herself that her own fiancé caused fear in others, but it didn't calm her.

She knew Dylan's heart. These men were strangers.

One of the men came to Mark's window and tapped it with his gun.

"Welp, here we go," Jack said, reaching for his door handle.

Skye had to try one last time. "Please, Jack, please don't hand us over to them—at least not Kelsey. I'm begging you!"

"Don't make me hit you again when we were getting along so well." He stared at Skye. "And I wouldn't try any of this on them if I were you. I don't think it would go over well." He eyed the men before glancing back at her.

Jack and Mark got out of the car and pulled a resistant Skye and Kelsey out of the backseat.

The new group looked them over. One tall man stepped forward, a hard look in his dark eyes. "This all you got?"

"Yeah," Jack said. "It's been a slow month."

"I'd say. Better pick up the pace. Unless you think this area is picked over already."

Jack scraped the ground with his foot and grunted.

The man strode over to Skye and grabbed her chin to inspect her bruised cheek.

She pushed his hand away.

He slapped her arms down and grabbed her face tighter.

"How have they been?" he asked as he eyed her.

"Not too bad. Had a bit of trouble with that one." Jack pointed at first Skye, then Kelsey.

"But this one's been quiet. But you know how it is. Once I got tough with the troublemaker, she settled down all right."

The man's gaze scraped over Skye. "You give him trouble?"

Skye trembled. "Sir. We have been kidnapped—taken away from our family."

"Shut up." The man's eyes narrowed. "Of course, you gave him trouble."

Skye looked at the ground.

"Do you know what happens if you cause me trouble?"

Skye shook her head.

"Let me show you."

Skye yelped when the tall man grabbed her arm and dragged her along to the fence. He jabbed a finger at the Sick inside it.

"See them?"

Skye glanced and nodded.

"I come round here every week. I'll bring you back and shove you in. I know what you're thinking. You don't get sick. But have you ever seen them go after a person when they're all—Well, let's just see, why don't we?"

His hand became iron as it tightened on Skye's arm, forcing her closer and closer to the wire.

The man shoved her cheek against the fence with a hand that boasted a tattoo of a screaming woman.

Skye fought back, frantically pushing at him and the fence. Anything to get her away from it.

The tall man snapped at her. "Stop, or I'll put you in there right now."

Skye stared up at his face. His eyes were bright with excitement.

She stopped fighting. He was in control now, and there was nothing she could do about it.

A few of the Sick moved nearer to them, showing aggression.

She shuddered.

"Here we go." The man shoved her cheek harder against the wire fence.

Skye groaned, and without thinking, put her hands to his. He gave her a hard look, and she put them down.

It took everything she had not to fight him.

If she obeyed, he wouldn't hurt her. She was valuable to him, wasn't she?

A sick woman lumbered closer, picking at the fence as she came.

The tall man yelled, and the Sick woman snapped her teeth at him.

He continued to antagonize the ill woman until she was almost upon them.

Skye's heart thundered as her hand curled tight around the fence's cool metal. "I won't cause trouble."

"I know you won't. I'm gonna let this woman take a chunk of out of your cheek so you have a daily reminder."

His eyes glinted as he spoke. "Have you ever seen them rip a piece of someone away?"

Skye's knees weakened. "Sir, I will not cause trouble. You don't have to do this."

The tall man banged on the fence beside Skye's head. It drew the sick woman.

"Don't tell me what I need to do," he growled at Skye.

The woman came closer. Her deep congested rattle became louder with each step. She snapped her teeth as she worked her jaw.

Sweat ran down Skye's back. Her voice broke as she begged. "Please, Sir!"

He brought his face closer to hers and laughed. "I like to watch it happen."

Again, he slapped the fence.

The metal bounced back and hit Skye's already battered face.

The sick woman wrapped her fingers around the fence, grabbing a chunk of Skye's hair as she did so.

She jerked her mouth toward Skye.

Skye groaned, eyes darting between the tall man and the sick woman.

If she didn't move, she would lose part of her face. If she did move, the tall man had said he would put her in with them.

The Sick woman's putrid breath steamed against Skye's cheek.

She couldn't stand here—she just couldn't.

She tensed, ready to jerk away.

The tall man tightened his iron hold.

Skye's arm numbed.

He brought his face to hers and growled, "I will feed you to that thing."

5

THE STANDOFF

P anicked, Skye scanned the watching men.
Most of them were as eager for action and blood
as a hockey game fanatic. A few looked away but offered no
help.

Kelsey was bowed low on the ground, her body heaving
with sobs. The poor girl had gone through so much. She
had finally broken.

Skye ached for her, wishing she was free to comfort her.

Kelsey lifted her head and locked eyes with Skye. She
nodded from Skye to the ground.

Smart girl. Smart, smart girl. Give the man what he
wants.

Skye let tears fall over her cheeks. "Please, please, don't
do this." She jerked against the fence when the Sick woman
snapped her teeth. "Please!"

She allowed her wobbly knees to weaken further until
the man's hands on her arm and head were almost her only
support.

The sick woman snapped again.

Skye squeezed her eyes shut. Maybe it was too late.

"No. No, no, no," she muttered to herself.

The woman's stink washed over her.

Skye shuddered.

A good portion of her cheek sunk through the metal chain of the fence—the woman would take it all.

The Sick's teeth scraped against the exposed skin. Skye instinctively jerked and screamed.

Kelsey's shriek echoed hers.

The tall man laughed as Skye's eyes grew wide with fear, and her frantic hands clenched at his shirt.

His eyes danced in amusement. "Will you be good?"

His game burned Skye, but not so much that she wouldn't play it.

"I will, sir," she rushed to answer him. "I will be good. I will be very, very good."

She sobbed.

As much as Skye would've liked to convince herself that this was all for show, it wasn't true. It had been a relief to show her fear—especially if it meant the end of this torture.

The tall man let her go.

Without his support, Skye dropped to the ground. She stayed there and put a hand to her cheek, letting the tears stream down her face.

He towered over her and folded his arms. "Now we have that all straight."

Skye nodded.

He pulled her from the ground. Skye's weak legs worked against her, and she stumbled.

The tall man hauled her up by her bruised arms. "Yeah, I know," he said. "That was scary."

Skye walked on legs that felt like noodles as she stared North.

If only she could break free and run up that highway to

Colton—all the way to Cole's Mountain and into the safety of Dylan's arms.

Home.

A pang of misery stabbed through her chest. She shook her head. Thoughts like that wouldn't change a thing.

Keep your eye on the game—that's what Dylan would say.

She searched for Kelsey and found a large, barrel-chested man holding the girl face-forward, his arm around her waist as her feet dangled just above the ground. His other beefy hand was over her mouth.

Skye bit back the scolding she would like to give him.

The big man was gentle as he lowered Kelsey back to the ground and guided her to the back of the box truck alongside Skye and her captor.

At the back of the vehicle, Skye stared at its interior. Stains smeared the walls and floor, and it reeked of dirty bodies and urine. This vehicle had been used to haul the Sick.

Skye glanced at the tall man.

He eyed her for any sign of resistance.

Skye strengthened her resolve, then stepped onto the truck's flat bumper.

The tall man pushed Skye face-down into whatever vile goo ran through the floor's ribbing.

Skye lay there, frozen. The foul smell filled her nostrils.

She jumped up, hoping the mess hadn't soaked her clothes. Without a glance at the tall man, Skye reached back and helped Kelsey into the truck.

The two women clung to each other as the rolling door slammed down and the tall man laughed.

Skye had expected total darkness, but light came from the front of the truck. Turning, she spotted a decent-sized pass-thru window between the cab and the back of the vehicle. It reminded her of the one in Dylan's pickup truck.

The women used the faint light to find the cleanest part of the floor to hunker down on.

Kelsey put a hand to Skye's bruised face. "Are you all right?"

"Yes, terrified but not hurt."

"Your face is purple already."

Skye pushed at her cheek and winced. "It could have been worse—much, much worse. You were smarter than I was."

"I've been in that situation before. Men like that—they always want to be the most important person in the room. It's easier and safer to just let them think they are—until you don't have to anymore."

The pass-thru window opened. The barrel-chested man threw two bottles of water and two protein bars through and slammed it shut.

At the sight of the food, Skye and Kelsey's stomachs growled. It had been hours since they had ate. They rushed to grab them.

The barrel-chested man settled himself in the passenger's seat, as another man hopped into the driver's seat and started the truck.

The tall man wasn't in this vehicle. Skye assumed he was in one of the cars that zipped past them onto the road.

It would be a relief not to have those evil eyes on her for the entire ride.

Skye examined the box truck, but they had locked it tight with no way of escape.

And after what the tattooed man had done, she knew that there would be no botched attempts for freedom. She and Kelsey needed to be sure that any plan they came up with would work. It meant their lives.

The barrel-chested man looked back through the window, his eyes softening as he looked at Kelsey. Sadness pulled at his face as he opened the pass-thru and said, "I'm sorry. I don't want to do this, but if they don't find a cure, my own daughter could die."

He gave them one last look of pity and guilt as the truck lumbered onto the road, then turned away.

Skye and Kelsey slid down the truck walls to sit on the hard metal floor.

Pity and sadness would only go so far to help them.

What they needed was outrage.

6

OUTRAGE

W ade, Jesse, and Joe piled into one of the community's shared pickup trucks, a granite-colored Ram 1500.

Joe stuck his arm out the open window and banged on the side of the truck. "Only thing tougher'n this would be a tank."

Wade threw him a savage grin and spun out of the driveway. "Yeah, well, that might be an idea."

"Okay then, we see one—we take it."

Jesse shot a glance from Joe to Wade. He'd learned to read people early in his life, and it had saved his hide on more than once. There was a dangerous glint in Joe's eye—the same one he'd seen on occasion in Wade's and Dylan's.

The thing was, Dylan kept his own untamed side in check, as well as Wade's. Who was keeping who in check now?

Jesse picked at the seam on his jeans.

Maybe he didn't care. All he wanted was Skye and Kelsey back. Maybe whoever took them would get what they deserved.

As if Joe could read Jesse's thoughts, he said, "So what are we gonna do to the boys that took our women? Teach 'em a lesson?"

Wade glanced at Joe and said, "Not now."

Joe scoffed. "Boy has gotta learn sometime—if he hasn't already. Ya think Dylan would just grab his girl up and waltz out of there with a thank you? Nah, that famous temper of his would do some damage."

Wade nodded. "I know that too. But he said to keep the boy safe, and that's what we're doin'. Get the women. Keep the boy safe. Then we'll see."

The men exchanged a knowing glance.

Joe smiled and rapidly banged on the pickup's door again. He let out a long howl and a yip as he raised his hand to brush against the tree leaves lining the long drive.

"Quit piddlin' around here then, Wade, and step on it."

Wade stomped the gas, and gravel flew, pinging off the vehicle behind them.

Once the five-vehicle caravan made it to the site of the kidnapping, Jesse jumped from the truck.

"Here! This is it!" he said, pointing to the blood on the paved road.

He shuddered as he recalled the beating they had given Spencer and Reed.

The boy ran up the hill to the intersection Jack and his thugs had taken and studied the pavement.

He didn't have to look too hard.

A large, blue arrow was spray-painted on the road. The sign Spencer and Reed had promised to leave.

Jesse waved at the rest of the group still milling around on the road below. "They left sign up here. Plain as day."

Wade waved back.

Once everyone loaded back into the vehicles, Wade

picked up Jesse at the top of the hill. "Good job, Jess! Now let's go get 'em."

They followed one blue arrow after another. Two times they worried they had passed a vital clue, only to find a new sign to ease their concern.

At last, they came across Spencer's gold car sitting on the side of the road.

Wade frowned as he studied the area.

Jesse, Joe, and Wade stepped from the car and rushed over to Reed and Spencer. The white bandage wound around Spencer's head was seeping blood.

"You all aright?" Jesse asked.

"Got a pretty nasty headache, but okay other than that."

"Doc should take a look at that."

Spencer nodded. "Soon as I get back to the mountain."

Joe looked around. "What is that god-awful smell?"

"I thought we were gettin' close to this place," Wade said as he grimaced. "It's the Containment Center for the Sick. But I can't reckon on why they would be bringin' the women here."

Reed shook his head. "Me either, but we figured we'd hang back and talk to the authorities once Jack and his guys left. It'll be clear Skye and Kelsey don't have the AgFlu, so the people in charge should let them go without a problem."

"Who *is* in charge?" Joe asked.

"Military, or what's left of it," Wade said. "Official or not, I don't know. If Tom were here, he might."

Spencer threw Wade a puzzled glance. "Tom didn't come?"

"It was his turn to stay in Colton. He didn't make it back before we skedaddled outta there."

Spencer glanced from Wade to Joe. "That's too bad,

coulda used him to talk to the men in charge here. You know—sheriff to military."

Wade shrugged. "I been here before with him—maybe that'll be good enough."

"Hope so."

"Car." Wade perked up and pointed. "That theirs?"

Reed squinted toward the moving vehicle. "Yep."

"You two stay here. Let me'n Joe handle this."

Reed disagreed. "They need to see we have a force here."

"Fine but keep everyone back."

Jesse took his place beside Wade and Joe as he wrapped his hand around the hilt of his blade.

Reed waved the others from their vehicles to stand behind them.

As if Wade had just noticed him, he said, "Sorry, Jess. You get in the back."

"No."

"Yep. Don't give me no guff now. Dylan wants you safe."

"I ain't goin' in back."

"I'll tie you up if I gotta. I brought rope."

The fire that had started in Jesse's belly at the beginning of this thing rose higher. He shot Wade a mutinous glance.

Someone laid their hand on Jesse's arm. He tried to shake it off until he saw it was the injured Spencer.

"Could you help me out, Jesse? I can't take another bash on the head. If things get rough, I'll need someone I trust to have my back."

One side of Jesse's mouth turned down. He wasn't stupid. He was aware of what was going on. But it would be worse if Wade threw him over his shoulder and hogtied him. At least helping Spencer gave him some dignity.

Still, his frustration grew as he stared at the oncoming car before following Spencer.

As they moved to the back of the group, several patted Jesse, offering praise.

"You did great, Jesse."

"You got us here."

"Woulda never found her if it weren't for you, boy."

One older man named Bert said, "You got some good makings. Give yourself some time to learn the rest. Ya did your job. Let us do ours."

Each word of praise helped cool the fire raging through Jesse's body.

Even if he did feel useless here at the back of the group, it was nice to be recognized for getting them this far.

Besides, there would be plenty of time to make Jack and his goons pay once Kelsey and Skye were safe.

7

ANSWERS

W ade narrowed his eyes at the slow-moving white car driving down the back road. The light-color flickered through the trees as it came their way. He rubbed his wrist across his nose. The smell from the containment center was putrid. Filth, muck, death, and if one paid attention, the sweaty scent of fear.

Rage built in him. If they left Skye and Kelsey in there to rot in that mess—Wade's anger just about choked him.

Jack had told Jesse they were working on a cure with the White Coats. Wade didn't remember seeing any of doctor-types here. What was the man up to?

Wade's hand tightened around the rifle in his hand. He grunted his understanding when Reed whispered two cars had gone in.

There was only one now.

Wade's pickup blocked the road out. They could be patient and wait for Jack.

The car rounded a curve and slowed. They were close enough to see Wade and his group now fanned along the side of the road.

Wade saw the passenger's puzzled expression as he said something to the driver.

"Joe!" Wade said as he sprinted for the car before the driver put it in reverse.

Fury fueled Wade, and for a fleeting moment, he wondered if this was how Dylan felt during one of his rages. It was freeing but also frightening—even to himself.

Wade and Joe reached Jack's car and yanked the door handles. They were locked.

Joe raised his gun and used the butt end to break the window.

The driver cringed against the back of the seat.

When Joe punched the button to unlock the doors, Wade rounded the front of the car and threw the passenger's door open. He dragged the man he assumed was Jack out of the vehicle.

One glance at Jesse told him he had the right man.

"Where is she?" Wade roared at Jack.

Jack shook his head and put his hands up.

Wade shouted again.

When the man still didn't answer, Wade's fist flew.

Jack dropped to the ground.

Wade bent over him as he lay in the dirt. His voice was quieter, but every bit as hard. "Where is she?"

"Who?" Jack asked, his eyes wide. "Who are you talking about?"

Wade gathered Jack's shirt in his hand and pulled him toward his group.

The man fought for release.

Wade bashed him until he stopped.

He turned Jack toward Jesse. "Recognize the boy?"

Jesse stepped forward.

Jack's face fell. He dropped to his knees.

The boy's face turned red. He was fuming.

Jesse's jaw hardened. He kicked Jack in the gut and spit on him. "You took my mom. You took Kelsey."

When Wade hauled Jack to the front of the crowd, Jesse put a hand up.

He drew back his foot back again and again.

Jack gasped with each blow.

Spencer laid a hand on the boy's shoulder. "Jesse," he said in a mild tone.

Joe, still holding the driver at gunpoint, turned to stare at Spencer. "Leave the boy be. He's got a right."

Spencer ignored Joe and instead asked Jesse, "Is this what Dylan would want?"

Jesse spit on Jack one last time and rubbed his shirt-sleeve across his mouth before walking back to the group.

Wade now stood over Jack, pushing his rifle into the man's neck. "You answer me now, or I'm gonna let the boy back at ya. Then I'll take my turn."

Jack glared at Wade, and the mountain man pushed his gun a little deeper into his skin. "I already gave them away." Jack dropped his gaze to the ground.

The anger that burned Wade's chest spread to his entire body. It was all he could do to keep his finger from tightening on the trigger.

He stared at Jack. "What does that mean? To who?" He pointed to the Containment Center. "Them?"

"No, not them. We only meet here."

"You better say more, or I'm gonna start blowin' parts off ya."

Wade moved his rifle to the man's knee.

Jack's eyes widened. "We have an arrangement with these scientist-types. I've only seen them once, and I'm not sure where they come from. They have some go-betweens come to pick up the merchan—people."

Jack looked from Wade to the group. "But we already made the trade, and they're gone."

Wade stilled for a moment, then said to Joe. "Ask him."

Joe hauled the driver, Mark, up and bent him back over the car. He flipped the safety off the gun and put it to Mark's head.

Mark was quick to agree with Jack. "Jack's right. They're gone. They never stay long."

Joe gave him a cold look. "Where are they from?"

"We don't know. We really don't."

Joe looked to the sky and sighed. "I need to let you know somethin' about me. I don't like to get my hands all roughed up like Wade over there. They hurt for days when I go bashin' someone. I'm not gonna hit ya, I'll just shoot ya. It's a lot easier on me."

Mark's voice rose as he rushed to give Joe an answer that would appease him. "We already told you. We told you everything."

Joe shook his head. "Nah, you haven't. There's always somethin' else."

Mark moved his head side to side as Joe pulled him higher on the car. "There's nothing—there isn't. I --"

Joe shoved his gun into the meat of Mark's thigh and pulled the trigger.

Mark screamed.

Joe shook him. "Stop that yellin'. You ain't even feeling it yet. It's just a flesh wound—ain't like you're dying. I should know, I've had enough."

Joe lifted his shirt to prove it, then dropped it and leaned toward Mark with his eyes narrowed. "That was a warning shot. You'll get more if you or your buddy don't start talking."

The driver's face paled, and he started to talk. "There's

three to five of the go-betweens at any given time. They look kinda rough. They go south on the Interstate. That's all I know, I swear." He looked at his partner. "Tell them, Jack!"

Joe moved the gun to Mark's other thigh. "Names?"

"We don't ask names, and they don't trust us with any information!"

Joe leaned closer to Mark, almost nose-to-nose. "Did you hurt either of those women?"

"No! No, I didn't, but he did. Jack hit the one that told us her name was Skye. Hit her till she bled."

Joe dropped Mark, letting him fall to the ground where he stayed holding his leg and groaning.

Joe's jaw hardened, and he stiffened, his chin high.

He strode over to Jack and crouched, putting his gun to the man's head. He glanced up at Wade. "Get the info you want, then we'll put a bullet in his head."

"You picked the wrong women," Joe told Jack. "Skye is my friend—and his brother's—girl. We ain't people to mess with. You'll pay for what you did."

Wade tightened his hand on Jack. "You beat her? Put your hands on her? I could kill you for just that. So if you've got anything else to add, now's the time."

Jack shook his head. "Why should I? One of you is gonna kill me, anyway."

"Tell us," Wade said, even though it made him sick to deal with the man, "and I'll make sure you get a fightin' chance."

Jack looked from Wade to Joe. When Joe agreed, he said, "They take them way South into the Carolina's. I heard them talking one time. South Carolina along the coast."

"To these White Coats?" Wade asked.

"Like I said, I only met them once when we set up terms. But most had on lab coats. You know, like a doctor wears. The leader wore a suit—a real suit—can you believe that? And he was real clean—right down to the smoothed hair and perfect nails. People like that stand out nowadays. Don't see a lot of them anymore."

"That it?" Wade asked.

"That's all we have, and that's the honest truth."

Wade nodded and told Reed to get the rope out of his car.

Jack protested. "You said you'd let us go!"

"Nah, I said I'd give you a fightin' chance—meaning I won't shoot you in the head like Joe here wants me to—like I'm aching to do. Instead, I'm gonna tie you to those trees over there."

Jack's voice shook. "How am I supposed to untie myself?"

"That's your problem." Wade hauled Jack up and pushed him to the nearest tree while Joe dragged Mark over.

They shoved the men's backs to the trees and pulled their hands behind them, tying them tight.

"I'm wounded. I'll bleed to death!" Mark cried.

"What a baby! I ain't cried like this since I crawled." Joe rolled his eyes. "It's only a bit of fat I shot off you. Shut up, or I'll give ya another one."

Jack tried to make a case for himself as Wade tied him to the tree. "This is as bad as killing us. You're just leaving us here to die. Think about it."

Wade turned his furious gaze on Jack. "I have thought about it. I've thought about how much you deserve to die, and still, I'm leavin' you here with only a few bruises. You steal people away from their families after we've already gone through all this." Wade waved his arm at the Containment Center.

"You hurt Skye, you scum. You could be sending them

to some kind of nightmare. There ain't no law to take care of you, so we have to do it, or you'll be out there doin' this again to some other family."

Wade pointed a stiff finger at his own chest. "We are your judge, jury, and executioner. You better be happy I've got an audience, or this woulda went down a lot harder."

Wade turned and walked away.

Jack yelled after him. "Where's my fighting chance?"

Pointing to the road, Wade said, "Maybe one of the trucks passing by will see ya."

"This far back?"

With a shrug, Wade said, "There's a chance."

"That's it?" Jack sounded desperate.

Wade pulled his extra knife from his boot, looked at it, then threw it out of the reach of either kidnapper.

He turned and walked away.

Jack stared at the hilt sticking out of the grass and broke down. "I was only trying to take care of my family!"

Wade kept walking. "Ain't we all."

8

A BULLET IN THE BRAIN

As the group walked away from a stone-faced Jack and bawling Mark, Wade stared at Spencer as the man threw an arm around Jesse. It was clear Spencer hadn't liked the day's events, but he was the only one who had objected.

Joe glanced from Wade to Spencer. "I'll take care of this," he murmured to his friend.

Joe jogged the few steps to Spencer, separating Jesse from him as he did so.

"Hey, I apologize if I came on strong back there," Joe told Spencer as Jesse and Wade listened in. "But the boy's got a right to beat on that man for a while if he wants. They took his mom and friend."

Spencer grimaced at Jesse's set face. "With his background, violence is not something we should encourage."

"With his background?" Joe stuttered. "Ain't any worse'n me and the Cole's." He shook his head. "Look, you gotta remember when it comes to parents, the four of us drew the short straw. That had no advantages the way things used to be, but it does now. You want the boy to survive?"

"Of course."

"We can show him how to do it. Keep an eye open—seems you could learn a thing or two."

"Yeah," Jesse added. "I want to learn. If Wade and Dylan hadn't taught me stuff, I probably wouldn't have made it home with the medicine. And wouldn't have been able to find these guys at all!"

Wade put his hand on Jesse's shoulder. "You've done great, son. Why don't you head over to the truck and fire it up for me?" He pulled his keys out of his jean pocket and handed them to the boy.

"Sure!" Jesse grabbed them and ran for the pickup.

Spencer watched him go. "Dylan is trying to show him a better way."

"He is. Hopes to anyway. But with men like that," Joe pointed behind them, "there ain't but one. Dylan would be the first to agree with that."

Spencer shook his head. "I don't think so. We could have taken them to the authorities."

"Ain't much authority around," Wade said. "I coulda killed 'em. It's what I would've done if you all weren't here."

"They're as good as dead. No one is going to see them back there in those trees." Spencer pursed his lips.

"Good. A bullet in the brain is what I should've done. But if they suffer a little, like others have suffered under their hands, that's okay with me too."

Wade stopped and put a hand on Spencer's arm, stopping him. He was sick of this conversation—there were more important things to do.

"First off, the boy's our kin now. We'll raise him the way we see fit—which means how to survive in this world. When you got a kid, let's see how you raise him. But for now, don't be trying to cause problems. Especially right in front of the boy."

46

Spencer nodded and glanced at the rest of the group, who listened in. "You're right. Not the right time or place."

"Second," Wade continued. "You gotta better way to deal with those two back there, do it as long as they are punished or dead. You take whoever agrees with you. I'm here to get Skye and Kelsey, not babysit the people who took her."

"Oh, I don't—I—" Spencer backtracked. "It's just you know nothing about them."

"I know enough. Those men take people against their will to a place no one knows for what sounds like medical experiments. If they have to kidnap people, what kinda things do you think they do, uh? Think they'd be fun?"

Spencer didn't respond, so Wade went on, "Skye and Kelsey have been healthy. What if what they do gives them the AgFlu, or does something worse?

Jack kills people—murders them—even if he doesn't pull the trigger himself. Only one way to deal with people like that—destroy them. Destroy them before they destroy you."

Wade scoffed and continued, "But hey, if you think he needs some coddlin'—that we treated him too rough, you get yourself a couple of friends and go sing him some lullabies. But I ain't waitin' for you. We're moving on."

Spencer looked from Jack, who now bellowed in anger and desperation, to the people from Cole's Mountain.

For a moment no one moved, then one woman walked back to the trees where the two men were tied.

She stared at Wade's knife stuck in the ground and pulled it out of the dirt.

"I don't truck with evil men. None of us do."

She walked to the vehicles, returning Wade's knife as she passed him.

Wade gave her a quick nod. "I guess you got your answer," he told Spencer.

Wade waved the group together. "Well, I'd hoped we'd find Skye here. So, now we need to split up. Me'n Joe will take half of you on ahead to scout the way—if we're fortunate—maybe even rescue our girls. The other half will go on home and tell Dylan what is goin' on. He's gonna want to come out as soon as he can, and he'll need people with him. How's that sound?"

Everyone agreed, so Wade split the group. He put Spencer into the group going home. Not only was he not on board with what was going on, he needed to see the doctor for his injuries.

Wade walked where Jesse sat in the pickup, pushing a CD into the player, and explained the plan.

Jesse stared at Wade. "What about me?"

"What are you thinkin'?"

"You want me to go home."

"I want you to help Dylan. I can't be both places, and he's all alone. The people he cares the most about are out here, and it's gotta be driving him crazy. There's only a handful of people he'll be honest with about how he's doin' and you're one of them."

"Okay. I want to help Mom, but I want Dylan to be okay too."

Jesse slid down from the truck seat and threw himself against Wade, mumbling into his shirt. "Take care of yourself."

Wade thumped Jesse on the back then put his hand on either side of the boy's head, giving him a long look. "You too."

When Jesse turned to leave Wade stopped him. "Jess, I get where Spencer is coming from, but things aren't that way anymore. They just aren't."

"I know. I get it. It just takes longer for some people."

Wade laughed and ruffled the boy's hair. "Okay. You go on now."

As Wade watched Jesse go, his heart sank like a stone. It wasn't good for the family to be broken up like this. He didn't like this—not one bit.

He ran a hand over his face.

Joe walked up and pounded him on the back. "Everything will be okay, man."

Wade hoped so. He really did.

But he'd be a fool if he didn't question whether they would ever be together again.

PURE OPTIMISM

Skye shifted yet again against the wall of the box truck, her sore body finding no comfort in the truck's hard metal bed.

She moved closer to Kelsey, and they leaned against each other for physical—and emotional—support.

The truck bounced over another of the million potholes, jarring them against each other and the hard wall behind them, causing Kelsey to groan.

Skye patted the girl's arm, and Kelsey laid her head on the woman's shoulder.

They had grown close during the girl's counseling sessions. It took a while to work through everything that happened to her in Fenton.

"We certainly are going to have some interesting sessions once we get out of this one," Kelsey said as she hugged Skye closer.

Skye smiled. "That's what I love about you, Kelsey, your eternal optimism. It's a wonderful thing at a time like this."

"I wasn't always that way. When I was alone in Fenton, I wished death would get it over with." Kelsey shuddered.

"But then Doc and Bre found me. If I got out of that—we can get out of this. It's just a matter of time."

"We have to keep our eyes open for the best opportunity—one we're sure will work."

Kelsey agreed.

Skye looked at her with approval. Kelsey may still be a young teen, but her experiences made her far wiser than her years. She would need that wisdom to survive in this strange world.

"I knew things were bad out here, I really did," Skye said. "I believed everything you and others have told me. But I realize now, more than ever, that Dylan and Wade sheltered me from the worst of it—from as many of these ruthless, uncaring men as possible. I didn't see the world for what it is—the individual troubles but not what it meant as a whole."

"Well, that's your optimism. It's not always a bad thing."

"No, but it could get me killed, and now, you too." Skye hung her head. "Dylan told me that once, and he was right. I can't go into situations with pure optimism—as if the people will react like they used to. There's no veil of civilization now. People can be as evil as they want to be."

"Strangers." Kelsey shook her head, disagreeing. "We have to be careful of strangers. Look at all the good people living on Cole's Mountain. There are good ones—lots of them. The world went all topsy-turvy, and everyone's all mixed up. But pretty soon people will divide—the good and the bad. It'll be easier to tell." She shrugged. "That's how it was in Fenton, anyhow."

"I believe you're right, Kelsey. As time goes by, it will be easier to tell who people are. Until then, we need to treat new people like enemies until they prove otherwise. Some optimism is good, but it needs to be tempered with caution." Skye stared through the window at the big man who had seemed sympathetic to their plight. "I'm not sure how that helps us now, but I am aware I need to think like you. My instinct is to fight, but that's not possible yet. As you said, let them be top dog for now. Don't fight until we're sure we can do damage. We may not be able to beat these men physically, but perhaps we can out-think them."

Kelsey giggled. "Did you get a good look at them? That shouldn't be hard to do."

"I hope you're right."

Skye laid her head back against the wall as she pondered the Containment Center. How long had it existed? Had it always been so horrible? People penned like animals, not even sheltered from the elements. Were they fed?

She shuddered. Would she and Kelsey end up in a place like that?

The disease was tragic enough, but to be treated that way—what a nightmare.

But maybe those Sick were the lucky ones. Soon, they would be out of their misery.

But what would happen to the people who survived this disease? If the evil people of this world won, what would happen to the people of Cole's Mountain?

There were no answers to those questions.

Skye pushed her worries away as she straightened her legs, bouncing them up and down to get the blood moving in them. This drive seemed to last forever—every mile taking her further and further away from Jesse and Dylan.

Skye's nerves were stretched so thin even time was wonky. It could have been thirty minutes or three hours that since they entered this truck. She wasn't sure.

The sun still shone through the pass-through window to the cab, but they'd driven long enough she needed a restroom.

THE RESCUE: SANCTUARY'S AGGRESSION 5

Skye sighed. Now that would be all she would think about.

As if someone read her mind, the truck slowed and stopped.

Skye's heart almost came to a standstill.

Kelsey clenched her hand, and Skye murmured it would be all right, even though she had no idea if it would be.

"Don't cause trouble," Kelsey reminded her.

Only Skye's anxiety stopped her from laughing.

How many times had she told Wade that? Yet, what she wouldn't do for a little of *his* trouble now.

The back door of the truck rolled up, and the tall leader stood there. "You want to take care of any business?"

When the women nodded, he waved them down.

Skye and Kelsey jumped out of the truck's back to the pavement of the road and looked around.

No vehicles moved on the desolate interstate. Long grass waved in the gentle wind as far as Skye could see. In the far distance, a few sparse tree groves stood. Three tall trees grew near the road, and an old gray-weathered house was about a half a mile away. It looked deserted.

Skye startled when the tall man grabbed her by the arm and pulled her toward him. "You gonna cause me any problems?"

Skye lowered her head and avoided eye contact. "No, sir. I will not."

He seemed satisfied with that, pushing her on her way.

It was the truth. Where could they go with five men just waiting for them to try? Now was not the time.

A short, stubby man pushed through the grass to a tree.

"I'll watch them," he said as he waved his gun. "I could use a little target practice."

He waited for the women to find their spot and turned to relieve himself against the bark of a tree.

Skye and Kelsey crouched in the tall grass, hoping the men would only see the tops of their heads.

On the way back to the truck, Skye looked for anything that would tell her where they were, but found no signs on this empty stretch of road.

But the air was warmer and more humid than when they had entered the vehicle at the Containment Center.

They were going South.

Her stomach dropped.

Just how far away from home were they?

LIFE LESSONS

Sue Ellen sat in a straight chair at Dylan's bedside, staring at him as he lay in bed, recuperating.

He was a tough guy—she had to give him that. The bullet and the infection might have killed a lesser man, but he hung on.

Doing better than hanging on really—he was healing.

Still, Dylan was off his game. Usually, when someone looked at him for very long, his eyes popped open like he had some kind of sixth sense.

Finally, after several minutes of Sue Ellen's intense gaze, Dylan stirred in his sleep.

Satisfied with the sign of his returning health, Sue Ellen went back to tossing a tiny red ball from one hand to the other.

She snickered. Was that kid still bawling over losing this?

She rolled her eyes. Kids were such easy marks.

She'd been sitting on Doc's front porch, dangling her feet, when the mom and little boy walked by.

The ball slipped from the boy's hand and sped over the bumpy ground, stopping right in front of her.

She'd plopped the toe of her tennis shoe over it.

The little boy wailed.

The mom looked around with a frown on her face as the boy cried, "Ball," over and over.

She'd even asked Sue Ellen if she'd seen it.

But the girl had made big eyes, shrugged, and shook her head.

Then she'd stared the kid down.

"You should've hung onto it," the mom said as she dragged the little boy through the clearing.

The boy cried louder.

"I'll find you another one!" The mother said in desperation.

Sue Ellen snorted. That might have worked before the AgFlu, but really, was the mom going to try and promise that now? It was the apocalypse, lady. Not so easy to get toys like little red balls. Even the kid realized that.

Sue Ellen tossed the ball again and giggled. Her blonde curls and big blue eyes always did the trick. And the fact that parents always blamed their own kids for stuff helped, too.

"What's so funny?"

Sue Ellen startled and grabbed the ball from mid-air. Her gaze flew to Dylan. "Nothing. I was just thinkin' is all."

Dylan's eyes narrowed, and she looked away.

Sometimes she swore he had the ability to read her mind. But it was probably just that he didn't like her. He never had.

From the minute he'd seen her, he'd been suspicious of her. She could tell. She'd tried to get him to trust her, but it hadn't worked yet.

56

Wade, though, he'd been on her side more often than not, always wanting to help her do better.

As if she wanted to—being herself is what kept her alive.

"What are you doin' here, girl?"

"I'm just checking on you since no one else is around. I thought you'd like that."

Dylan grunted and ran a hand over his face. "Anyone hear anything yet?"

"Geez, Dylan, they just left."

"Watch your mouth. Don't be sassin' me."

Dylan never yelled at her. He just got real still and quiet and gave her that intense stare.

It disturbed her.

She enjoyed being the only one in the room able to read people, but he did it better than her.

Sue Ellen shivered. She didn't want anyone to guess her secrets.

Dylan pointed to the ball. "And give that back to the kid."

Sue Ellen's chin dropped, leaving her mouth open. "I-I found it."

"Right. Give it back to him."

"All right," she mumbled as she shoved it into her pocket.

"I'll be checkin'."

"Whatever!" Sue Ellen stood up so fast her straight chair almost tipped over.

"Then, get your butt back here."

Sue Ellen ground her teeth. "Why?"

"Cause I want to get outta this bed, and you're going to help me do it."

"I ain't your babysitter."

Dylan laughed. "You are now."

Sue Ellen put her hands on her hips. "Why me?"

Dylan's blue eyes turned icy. "You know why."

Her gaze darted away. She ran out of the room.

Sue Ellen hurried down the hall, ignoring Bre's greeting as she passed her in the kitchen, and slammed the door as she left the house so that everyone would be aware of how upset she was.

Grandma would say that Sue Ellen couldn't trust a man like that. A man like Dylan knew too much for Sue Ellen's own good.

But, who was he to tell her what to do? It was her ball now, and she was going to keep it. Wasn't much Dylan could actually do about it anyway—laying there weak as a newborn kitten.

Sue Ellen laughed and threw the little red ball into the air, watching it sail up into the sky and back down toward her again.

Ain't nobody gonna tell her what to do.

She had plans for today, and those plans didn't include being someone's nursemaid.

Sue Ellen waved to the man keeping watch and skipped away.

After wandering down by the creek for a while, she found herself at the quiet little clearing where Annette and Mrs. Gilmore lived. She stopped at the edge of the tree line, hiding behind some scrub brush, and spying on Annette as she sat on the porch crying.

Everyone felt bad for the woman. No one really knew her or the guy that died—they'd kept to themselves so much.

But after he died, everyone brought Annette lots of food —the good stuff.

Sue Ellen swatted at a gnat circling her head.

She'd visited Annette, too. She would not miss out on

scoring some of that food. Besides, she needed to keep an eye on that woman.

Sue Ellen considered another visit.

Annette might still have treats left.

As Sue Ellen set her foot in the clearing, the dark, delicious aroma of chocolate chip cookies wafted to her.

Mrs. Gilmore first then. Nothing beat fresh treats. Sue Ellen's stomach rumbled at the thought.

On top of that, Mrs. Gilmore loved her. The old woman's eyes always sparkled the instant she saw her.

The fact was, Sue Ellen couldn't remember anyone who looked at her the way Mrs. Gilmore did—not even her own grandma and definitely not her parents.

Her parent's eyes had always been dull with drink or hot with anger. Even though her father saved the beatings for Jesse, their mother hadn't been above giving Sue Ellen a smack or two.

And then there was Grandma.

Someone had once told her she was lucky to live with her grandmother as if all of them were soft, loving, and smelled like cookies.

They obviously didn't know her grandmother.

Her grandma was into what she called Life Lessons.

Every day held a lesson—and if Sue Ellen didn't learn quick enough—anything from a long lecture to a few smacks and an afternoon in the dark, cobwebbed cupboards awaited her.

She shivered as if those creepy crawlers still covered her skin.

The most consistent theme of her grandmother's lessons was all the many reasons a person couldn't trust—well, anyone.

"Stop cryin' over your dead mama!" Grandma would say. "I can't stand your caterwauling. She never wanted you while she was alive, anyway. She's pry up in heaven happy she ain't putting up with you no more."

"You only have yourself to rely on, girl. You need to practice that, so go find your own dinner tonight."

"Why d'you bring that little girl from school home? Friends don't do you no good—they leave you. That's a lesson you need to remember, and I'm going to make sure you do."

Grandma did real good teaching all those Life Lessons.

Sue Ellen remembered each one of them as if they'd happened yesterday.

11

CHOCOLATE CHIP COOKIES

Sue Ellen kept her head down as she passed Annette on her way to Mrs. Gilmore's house.

Annette sniffled and tried to hide her tears, offering Sue Ellen a thin smile and a wave.

"Nice to see you, Sue Ellen."

Sue Ellen waved back—a quick little tip of her hand. She didn't want to seem too friendly and feel forced to talk to her. Not until after she'd had her cookies, anyway.

After running up the porch stairs of Mrs. Gilmore's house, Annette tapped on the door. If the old lady was baking, it was likely she was right on the other side. There was no sense in banging on it too loud.

Just as Sue Ellen suspected, the door popped open in less than a second. She pretended to be startled and laughed. The old lady liked that.

Mrs. Gilmore pulled her into a hug. "Oh, Sue Ellen, it is so nice to have you visit! I wasn't sure you'd be able to with everything going on with your family and all."

She quickly cleared cookie trays off the table to make room for Sue Ellen. "There you go. Have a seat."

Mrs. Gilmore poured a glass of milk and put a plate of cookies in the middle of the table.

Sue Ellen grinned and flashed her blue eyes at the older woman. "Oh, my, Mrs. Gilmore. These look amazing!"

Mrs. Gilmore put a gentle hand on either side of Sue Ellen's face.

"You are so adorable. You remind me so much of my grandchildren, the poor dears. Well, no sense in dwelling on that. It won't do anyone any good."

She patted Sue Ellen's puffy curls.

Sue Ellen frowned as Mrs. Gilmore turned to remove another batch of cookies from the oven. She'd rather Mrs. Gilmore like her for herself and not some dead grandchildren.

She shrugged as she bit into a chip-laden cookie. A girl like her wasn't able to be picky. She had to take what she could get.

When Mrs. Gilmore turned back around, Sue Ellen smiled at her.

Several cookies later, as Sue Ellen patted her taunt belly, someone knocked on the door.

Mrs. Gilmore brightened. "Oh, my! This is a busy day."

She leaned toward Sue Ellen and half-whispered, "How much do you want to bet they smelled my cookies baking?"

Sue Ellen giggled. "Of course, they did. What do you think brought me here?"

"Oh, you!" Mrs. Gilmore lightly poked Sue Ellen's cheek on her way to the door. Sue Ellen rolled her eyes behind Mrs. Gilmore's back. But if that was the price one had to pay . . .

"Oh, look who it is, Sue Ellen!"

The girl turned to see Travis, Mrs. Gilmore's one remaining grandchild lingering in the door, frowning at her. What was up with him?

"Should we give him a cookie?" Mrs. Gilmore asked. Without waiting for an answer, she shoved one into his hand.

Sue Ellen quickly counted up how many of the sweet treats were left and said, "Sure. He works hard."

"Here, Travis, sit down and have a treat."

Travis hesitated. "Well, I can't stay, Grandma. I just --"

Mrs. Gilmore fussed at him. "You haven't visited for a while. Just stay for a moment—just long enough for one cookie."

Travis gave up and sat in the chair. Once her second guest was seated, Mrs. Gilmore also sat and crossed her arms. "So, if the cookies didn't bring you, what did?"

Travis tipped his head toward Sue Ellen. "She did."

Sue Ellen gave Travis a double-take without giving away the fact she found him super-hot. Why in the world would he come here for her?

"You came here for Sue Ellen?" Mrs. Gilmore asked, echoing Sue Ellen's thoughts.

"Yep. I was sent to fetch her. Seems she was supposed to be back at Doc's a while ago."

"What are you talking about?" Sue Ellen fired back. "Doc doesn't want me."

"Dylan does. Said you were supposed to be there hours ago."

Sue Ellen put her hand on her hip. "Are you kidding me?"

Mrs. Gilmore put her hands to her mouth. "Oh, Sue Ellen, you must have forgotten! And here I've been filling your ear with nonsense."

The woman stood and packed up all the cookies. "Please tell poor Dylan that I am so sorry! And give him the rest of these cookies. That poor man. Everything he's gone through!"

Sue Ellen watched the treats disappear into a paper bag that Mrs. Gilmore handed to her grandson.

Sue Ellen steamed. She'd never lay eyes on a single one of them again.

Bag in hand, Travis rose and waved Sue Ellen up.

She ignored him. What could he really do? Drag her out of here?

But Mrs. Gilmore watched her, and the last thing Sue Ellen wanted to do was jeopardize future treats. She jumped out of her seat and rushed to the woman, hugging her. "I wish I could stay longer!"

That was certainly true. The last thing she wanted to do was to see Dylan.

As Travis hurried Sue Ellen out of the house, she glanced over at Annette's home. The woman still sat on the front porch but was no longer crying.

Sue Ellen gave the woman a greeting as they passed by. At least Annette was staying put and not causing any trouble.

The sweet aroma of the chocolate chip cookies wafted to her, and she side-eyed the bag Mrs. Gilmore had packed for Dylan. Another one of those would help her get through the day.

"So, Travis, how about we have a couple of cookies?"

"Grandma said these were for Dylan."

"I'm sure she wouldn't mind, and besides, she wouldn't need to know."

Travis shot her an uncertain glance. "We'll see what Dylan says."

"He doesn't need to know either."

He stopped short, staring at her. "You're a sneaky one, aren't you?"

Sue Ellen gave him a bold stare. "For heaven's sake, they're only cookies. Get a grip."

Travis took a few steps. "They are for Dylan. You want one, take it up with him."

Sue Ellen stayed where she was, hands on hips.

He turned and looked at her. "Come on now."

"I ain't going."

With a frown, Travis asked, "Because of the cookies?"

"Because I don't want to, you nitwit."

"Well, you have to." Travis walked back to her.

"Why?"

"Cause it's where Dylan wants you to be."

"Well, I ain't going!" Sue Ellen turned to stomp back the way they had come.

Before she got too far, Travis wrapped his hand around her upper arm. "You're coming with me if I have to drag you all the way there."

"You wouldn't."

Travis moved, forcing Sue Ellen to walk or fall on her face.

She resisted at first, then fell in line after giving Travis' shin a hard kick.

He gritted his teeth and tightened his hand.

She wiggled as far away as she could get. "Travis, let me go! You're hurting me!"

Travis snorted. "I doubt that."

"I'll kick you again!"

He looked her over. "I was wrong. Not so much sneaky as downright mean."

"Why are you going to all this trouble for Dylan?"

"Because he asked me. I'd do whatever he needed me to do cause he'd do the same for me. Besides, Dylan is not someone a person wants to cross. I guess that's a lesson you ain't learned yet."

Not another person with lessons. "Shut up!"

"You're not as smart as you think you are."

"At least I'm not as dumb as you."

Travis laughed. "Well, we'll see, won't we? We are here." He let go of her arm and gave her a little push toward the stairs.

Sue Ellen scowled at him and made a big show of rubbing her arm, though it didn't hurt at all. She shot a glance at the woods. Could she make a run for it?

No, he stood there waiting for her to make a move. He was so devoted to Dylan that he'd probably tackle her.

"And just so you know," Travis said, his voice stern, "I'm on watch out here, so if I see you escaping, I'll march you right back in."

Sue Ellen huffed and stomped up the porch stairs just as Bre opened the front door.

"Hi, Sue Ellen!"

Sue Ellen crossed her arms and continued without comment. In the hallway, she turned and watched Travis pass the bag of cookies to Bre.

"These are for Dylan only. No one else," he said.

Bre eyed him, a twinkle in her eye. "Of course, Travis. No problem."

Sue Ellen let out an impatient groan.

Travis looked from Sue Ellen to Bre and leaned against the door frame as if he had all the time in the world to talk with the giggling girl.

Idiot boy!

Sue Ellen pulled a face before walking to Dylan's room.

A MEAN STREAK

S ue Ellen inched her way around the doorway of Dylan's room. The man was sitting up, but his eyes were closed, and his face still pale.

Her gaze drifted around the room. Bare white walls, a couple of chairs, the bed, and a nightstand with a magazine on it.

No wonder Dylan wanted out of here.

Sue Ellen looked from the magazine to Dylan and back again.

He didn't look like a magazine type of guy.

Maybe—if it had a truck or a picture of a big buck with a thousand-point antlers—or whatever. But the one sitting beside him had a grinning woman holding up a decorated cake against a pink backdrop.

Sue Ellen almost snorted. No, she didn't think so.

When her gaze made it back to him, Dylan stared back at her.

She startled but quickly recovered. Sue Ellen frowned at him. "That's creepy, you know. You're not going to make any friends like that."

"I got plenty of friends. You, on the other hand . . ."

Sue Ellen crossed her arms. "I've got friends!"

She didn't really, but she hadn't tried making any. It's how she wanted it.

Dylan's expression softened. "Things have been hard for you, before and after this outbreak. You should talk to Skye more. She's helped Kelsey."

Sue Ellen scoffed. "I don't need shrinked. That's for idiots that don't know nothing."

"Is that what your opinion of your brother is, girl?"

"No. Jesse's different," Sue Ellen backtracked. "Dad—Dad was real hard on him. Hurt him. Grandma never hurt me like that, and Dad never laid a hand on me."

"There's lots of ways to hurt someone."

Sue Ellen thought of all those lessons, the mean things grandma called her, and the cupboard. She shrugged. "I ain't talking about that."

She turned away but couldn't shake Dylan's gaze.

"Sue Ellen." Dylan waited for her to turn back toward him. "I've had it all. And sometimes there are things worse than being hit. Words can hurt more."

Tears sprang to her eyes. She quickly brushed them away.

What was this about? Tears? Like she was a soft little girl again? What would Dylan think of that? He sure wouldn't want some wimp around. "I ain't weak!"

"That's the last thing I'd call you."

Relieved, she nodded.

"I'm just sayin' sometimes the way we were brought up gets to us. It's good to talk things out."

"Okay. Whatever."

Dylan sighed. "Well, get over here and help me up."

"Are you sure we should be doing this?"

"Come on, girl."

"What if you hurt yourself more?"

Dylan chuckled. "Don't pretend you care now."

Sue Ellen looked at the floor. "I do care. You're the strongest one in this community. If you go down, we all go down."

"Figures my getting better somehow comes around to you," Dylan said with a twinkle in his eye. "Can't really blame you, though."

He waved her over. "But it's fine. I gotta get up sometime. And it's killin' me to be here when Skye's somewhere out there. Taken." His voice broke. "I can't—I can't—I need to get better fast."

Sue Ellen was taken aback by how openly this strong, tough guy showed his feelings for Skye.

So this was what it looked like when someone deeply cared for another person.

"Okay, fine," she said with a frown. "But if you hurt yourself more, it ain't gonna be my fault. And then you won't be able to go after her. That'll teach you a lesson."

"Shut up and stand right here." Dylan pointed to a spot on the floor beside the bed.

Sue Ellen moved closer.

It was clear that every move Dylan made was agony. But that didn't stop him.

After he made it to the edge of the bed, he used her shoulder and the back of the straight chair to stand.

Well, at least tried to stand.

Sue Ellen critically eyed him. He was still kind of bent. As she watched him, a seldom-used emotion came over her.

Sympathy.

She put her arm around his waist and took more of his weight.

Dylan gave her a quick grin of approval.

The warm sensation of satisfaction spread through her. She was stunned. She'd never felt that over *helping* someone before. She was getting soft.

That wasn't allowed—not with the world the way it was.

Dylan swayed, and his fingers dug into her shoulder.

Sure, the guy was in pain and had lost a lot. He may never get Skye back. But she couldn't let that get to her.

Sue Ellen sighed and said in a cranky voice, "Are we done yet?"

"No."

She rolled her eyes. "I'm sorry I stepped foot into this room."

Dylan ignored her as he slid one foot forward. "I want to go out there."

Sue Ellen looked skyward. "Fine."

This was going to be more trouble than it was worth.

Once they made it to the bedroom doorway, Dylan stopped and leaned against the frame. The sweat poured off him.

"You should stop now," she said. "You look like you're gonna throw up."

"No."

"I'm just sayin'."

"I said no."

Dylan laid an arm over her shoulder instead of merely clutching her.

She rubbed it after he let go. Without a doubt, she'd have a bruise there tomorrow.

"Talk about something," he demanded.

"Uh?" Sue Ellen sent Dylan a surprised glance. When did he ever want to chit-chat? She searched her mind for something he'd be interested in but came up blank.

"You talk, or I'm gonna." With his voice gruff from pain, it sounded like a threat.

"Whatever."

"Why d'you take that ball from the kid?"

Sue Ellen's head whipped toward him. "How did you know how I got that ball?"

"I have my ways."

"What? Like you're a secret agent now?"

Dylan snorted. "Somethin' like that. Don't sidetrack. Why?"

Sue Ellen looked at the floor. It was a question she'd asked herself about a number of things she did, but she didn't have a real answer for why she was so mean. "I don't know. It's funny to see people's shocked faces, I guess."

"So, this is a regular thing?"

Sue Ellen shrugged.

Dylan took a couple of steps down the hallway. Then smacked the back of Sue Ellen's head. Not hard, but enough to get her attention.

Sue Ellen frowned and jerked away. "Hey!"

"You're right. It's funny."

Sue Ellen's scowl deepened.

Dylan continued, "Now every time you do something mean to someone else, you remember how you feel right now."

Sue Ellen rolled her eyes, but he ignored her and continued with his warning.

"Every time you do something mean to someone else, I'm going to do something mean to you."

"Like making me give you a walk?"

"I ain't kidding."

Sue Ellen stilled. "Like what?"

"Like putting you in your room and telling you that you can't leave."

"Grounding me? That's what you're going to do?"

Dylan shrugged. "If that's what it takes."

Sue Ellen huffed and tried to turn away.

Dylan may have been weak, but he was still stronger than her. He pulled her back. "If that doesn't work, I'm going to start taking things away from you."

"Well, jokes on you because I don't have anything."

"You have that music thing."

Sue Ellen's mouth dropped. "My iPod? You can't do that. That's so—so—"

"Mean? I think we just saw I can be mean too. You don't be mean—I won't be mean. Got it?"

Sue Ellen ground her teeth. Well, he couldn't take her iPod now anyway—she didn't know where it was. "Why are you doing this?"

"Because I'm your parent now."

"No, you ain't."

"I don't see anyone else around here claiming you. I'm your family now. Get used to it."

"And that's what you think dads do? They ground their children, like, all the time?"

"The good ones do it—if necessary."

Sue Ellen crossed her arms. "Wade wouldn't do this."

"Wade's too soft on you. He sees your curls and big eyes and forgets what's inside."

"I want him to be my dad."

Dylan burst out laughing, then held his side. "Yeah, I bet you do. It ain't happening. He can be the fun uncle. I'm the mean dad."

Sue Ellen stomped her foot. "No."

He looked at her foot as if it offended him. "You want the grounding to start right now, girl?"

"Are you kidding me?"

Dylan raised his gaze and stared at her until her defiant one turned to the floor.

"You already sound like a dad," Sue Ellen complained.

"Good. Must be doing somethin' right then. Now help me back to bed and get me a glass of water."

It was a mystery to Sue Ellen why she didn't just run out the door as soon as he was seated.

Sure, he protected all of them, including her, but she could find someone else for that. She shot him a glance out of the side of her eye. He was tough, for sure, tough as they come. Why was he taking time to worry about what she was doing in the middle of everything going on?

Why did he care?

Wait. Did he care?

No. Her grandma hadn't ever said she'd cared in all her life. Her dad certainly hadn't. She did remember her mom holding her and rocking her, especially after she'd been drinking.

So if none of them cared all that much, how could this guy after a few months?

Quietly, Sue Ellen walked to the kitchen and filled a couple of glasses of water for him. It was Dylan's habit to drink two cups of water at a time.

When he drank those, she went and filled another and sat it on the bedside table for later.

"Well, if we're done here, I'm going to head home."

"Okay, come back in the morning. Directly after breakfast, which you need to eat at daybreak. Understand?"

Sue Ellen's mouth dropped open, and she sputtered. "I ain't getting up that early!"

"Yes, you are, or I'll send Travis after you with orders to drag you back here. We got a lot of work to do."

Sue Ellen stomped out of the room, wondering why she'd ever agreed to come to this mountain in the first place.

∾

DYLAN CHUCKLED as he watched Sue Ellen leave, hissing and spitting like a mad kitten. The girl had issues, no doubt about that. She needed firm direction.

Sue Ellen had been left to her own devices for too long. Skye had thought Sue Ellen only needed time to settle in. But Dylan had known from the beginning that the girl had a mean streak a mile wide.

She reminded him of himself when he was a teenager.

Yes, she tried to play him, but he played her better.

Dylan laughed as the front door banged shut.

The girl was going to be doing a lot more door slamming in the days to come.

13

WHATEVER

The next morning, Dylan groaned as he lowered himself into the straight chair across from his bed. He eyed the short trail he'd taken to get there and shook his head.

What a sorry state he was in!

He heard the ruckus before he saw Sue Ellen and chuckled.

She entered the room madder than a wet hen. Travis just about dragged her through the door.

Her angry scowl was the worst face Dylan had ever seen, and he'd seen plenty of her sour looks.

Travis pulled Sue Ellen until she stood in front of Dylan. "Here you go, Boss."

Unused to the title—and not sure how he felt about it—Dylan winced.

Sue Ellen turned and kicked Travis above his ankle.

The young man dropped her arm and took a few steps backward, then leaned over and rubbed his shin.

Dylan nodded his appreciation to Travis. It couldn't have been easy getting Sue Ellen here.

Then he turned to the steaming girl, "Why don't you sit down?"

She let out an exaggerated sigh and plopped into a matching straight chair across from Dylan.

Travis straightened and stood over her with crossed arms.

Sue Ellen let out a muted scream, crossed her own arms, and slammed herself back into the chair. Her blond curls had gone wild, and her blue eyes blazed like lightning.

Dylan leaned forward, elbows on knees. "I'd feel sorry for ya, but I warned you. I don't have days to waste. Every day I'm stuck in that bed is a day without Skye—not knowing — "He shook his head, trying to get rid of the constant uncertainty circling his thoughts.

What was happening to her? Had Wade found her? Or was she miles away and getting further away by the minute?

Dylan pushed his concern away—first things first. He needed to get stronger. And if he was able to teach the girl something while he was doing so, that'd be a good thing.

Dylan pressed his lips into a thin line and sat back in his chair, staring at Sue Ellen. Stares were effective weapons. If one stared at another person long enough, they often became uncomfortable and started talking.

A person could learn a lot that way.

Sue Ellen may think she was immune to mind games, but she wasn't. Within a minute, she was spitting venom. "I don't have to be here. You can't make me!"

Dylan didn't say a word—just kept staring.

Sue Ellen huffed. "It's not my job to take care of you. I have other things to do!"

Dylan raised an eyebrow at her. Sue Ellen shifted her gaze to the floorboards.

He cleared his throat. "Everything you just said is wrong."

"It ain't. I've got things to do!"

Dylan barked out a laugh. "What? Steal from kids, sass your elders, and kick people?"

Sue Ellen bristled, but before she blurted anything out, Dylan put up a hand to stop her.

"She kick you before now?" he asked the young man.

Travis's face reddened. "Yeah, a few times."

If the girl had known what was best for her, she would have apologized, at least looked contrite.

Instead, Sue Ellen smirked.

Dylan leaned forward. "Sue Ellen, I'm disappointed in you."

The girl looked surprised, and her smile faded. For a moment, she gave Dylan a blank stare then shifted in her seat. "Whatever. I don't care what you think."

"Too bad, cause if you did, you'd know I was thinking that you'll be staying here with me all day."

"I ain't!"

"You are. Travis will be here to make sure you don't slither your way out."

Sue Ellen shot a glance of pure hatred to both Dylan and Travis.

Dylan's jaw tightened. No one could do that quite as well as a teenage girl.

Dylan studied the sullen Sue Ellen. He would not get anywhere goading her like this. It was time to change tactics. "Sue Ellen, I'm troubled about Skye and Kelsey—Jesse—all of them. I want to get on my feet as fast as I can, and I need your help to do that."

Sue Ellen slumped in her seat. "Why me?"

"Cause, girl, you're family now. All we got in this huge, empty world is this community—this family. You need us, and we need you. I need you to help me get better so I can get to Skye."

Sue Ellen's face lost some of its frown, but she still refused to look at Dylan.

"'Sides, the faster I get myself together, the faster I'll be out of here. If you don't look forward to nothin' else, look forward to that."

She shot Dylan a wry glance. "Now you're talking."

"Yeah. Thought you'd like that."

"Okay." Sue Ellen stood, shooting Travis daggers when he moved closer to her. "What do you want me to do?"

"I want to get out of here. Walk around outside."

"That's it? You couldn't have had this bully of yours do that."

"I told you. It's your job to help me. Travis has other things to do."

"Like harass innocent citizens?"

"What?" Travis sputtered.

Sue Ellen walked over to Dylan, waiting for him to stand. "Fine. Whatever. I'll help you."

"Not whatever. It means a lot."

She nodded.

If her upbringing were anything like his, she'd rarely heard words like that. Dylan understood. The sudden sheen in her eyes told him his praise affected her.

Dylan kept Sue Ellen with him throughout the day. He hoped this forced time together would help him gain her trust. The girl needed to know she had a support system. He doubted she'd ever had much of that.

Besides, something was eating at her. Dylan would have noticed it behind every guarded glance and every careful moment of hers, even if he hadn't seen the evidence out in the field with his own eyes.

Dylan let out a long groan at the end of their walk as he

dropped onto the bed, a hand covering his wound. He kicked off his shoes, letting them fall to the side of the bed. "So, you gonna be here tomorrow?"

He waited for her snarky answer, and she didn't disappoint.

"You plan on sendin' that goon after me if I don't?"

"If I need to."

"You won't. Need to, I mean." She uttered a long-suffering sigh. "I'll be here."

"Goodnight, girl."

Sue Ellen didn't answer until she reached the door when she turned back toward him and grinned. "Whatever."

14

CONFESSIONS

Dylan and Sue Ellen developed an uneasy alliance. Dylan made progress, getting stronger throughout the next day. He was sure being out in the fresh air—in his beloved forest—had something to do with it.

Sue Ellen slapped her arms, unhappy with their surroundings. "What are we doin' out here with all these bugs? Can't we at least stay closer to the houses?"

"Sure. When we're done with this round."

Dylan gripped his walking stick tighter and picked up the pace, happy he no longer needed to lean on Sue Ellen as much. It couldn't be easy for her to haul around a guy his size.

Dylan led them through the woods and into the glen where the shooting happened.

Sue Ellen scanned the area, her eyes round.

Though he noticed, Dylan said nothing. Instead, he crouched near the spot he'd fallen after being wounded.

The memory hit him hard.

His pounding heart as he'd waited to see if the shooter would rush over to finish him off.

The white-hot pain driving through his middle like a poker.

His worry the shooter would go after Skye next as he lay there almost defenseless.

He studied the ground but saw little he didn't already know. He stood and stared across the glen--at the spot he reckoned the shooter had stood. Dylan walked over to it.

Sue Ellen gasped and trailed him.

Dylan scanned the ground for a few minutes before finding evidence of what he suspected—where the shooter lay in wait.

Time had gone by, but there could be no mistaking the bullet casings and cigarette butts.

Dylan turned and stared at Sue Ellen. "Anything you want to tell me?"

Sue Ellen kept her eyes to the ground and shook her head.

Dylan's eyes narrowed. "You take up smoking?"

"No—no, sir. I ain't."

Dylan crouched and ran his fingers along the grass. He found what had caught his eye. A thin gold money clip, minus any money. He frowned.

"What happened here, Sue Ellen?"

"I don't—I didn't—" Sue Ellen turned to run. Dylan reached out just in time to catch her, almost losing his balance.

He squeezed her shoulder. "You can tell me, girl. Whatever it is, you can tell me."

Tears sprang to Sue Ellen's eyes as she looked at Dylan. She opened her mouth, trembled and shook her head. "I can't," she sobbed, "I don't know nothin'."

Dylan stared at her for a moment. She couldn't trust him any more than he'd trusted anyone at her age.

Sue Ellen's sobs intensified, and she folded in on herself, becoming smaller and smaller.

"You ashamed of yourself, Sue Ellen?"

Her face flooded with color. She gulped and trembled. Her nod took over her entire body, shaking it from head to toe. She sank to the ground.

Dylan looked from the girl to the money clip and back again. This sure wasn't hers. He slipped the clip into his jean pocket, then leaned down and pulled Sue Ellen up. Dylan put an arm around her and kept his voice soft and comforting. "It's okay now. It's done. Nothin' anyone can do about it now."

~

SUE ELLEN SWALLOWED hard and opened her mouth, but only nodded.

"You can tell me. You can tell me anything. I've made a lot of mistakes myself, so it ain't like I'd judge you harshly. I know you were out here that day."

"I wasn't here. I wasn't!"

Sue Ellen wrapped her arms around herself. She had to stick to her story—she had to.

She'd thought little of this place—this community—until she realized she could lose it. If they were aware she'd known about the rat among the bunch and didn't tell them, they'd throw her out. Then where would she go? She wouldn't survive all by herself.

At her denial, Dylan nodded and walked back to where he laid bleeding that day. He took a few steps to the left, picked something off the ground, and handed it to her. The iPod.

"It was there that day, Sue Ellen."

She gasped and stepped back, numb with shock. How did she get out of this?

She wanted to run, but even if Dylan was slower than normal, there was nowhere to go.

"I didn't—I swear, I didn't shoot you." Her voice shook.

"But you know something."

Sue Ellen closed her eyes. Tears trailed down her cheeks, and she wondered how she could be such a baby. Her grandma would have whacked her for sure and left her alone for hours under the stairs in the dark with the spiders.

"Please—please don't hate me! Don't throw me out. I wouldn't make it, and I'd become one of those—those things! I can't—I can't—"

Her legs weakened as she imagined them tearing at her —turning her into a useless husk of a person.

"I'm sorry—I'm so sorry," she mumbled between sobs.

Dylan put a hand on her shoulder. "Sue Ellen. No one is going to throw you out of here."

"They will."

"This is my mountain and I'm tellin' ya—I won't allow anyone to throw you out." He patted her shoulder. "Whatever mistake you've made--I can guarantee I've done worse."

Worse? Sue Ellen doubted it. She wasn't sure the shooting had anything to do with Skye and Kelsey's abduction, but she strongly suspected it. And if that was the case, he would definitely hate her.

"Skye being gone." She hiccuped. "It might be—I'm not sure—but something I knew—"

"We ain't gonna know until you tell."

She eyed him. He was eager to hear what she had to say, but not furious. "I was here, but I was so scared I ran at the first shot. I didn't know you and Skye were here until later."

83

It was true. There was no way she would've left knowing Dylan lay bleeding.

Dylan took the news well. It gave Sue Ellen the courage to continue on. Once she started, the story poured out of her.

"You know that guy that died?"

"Ethan?"

"Yeah. Him and Annette fought one day, and I over-heard. He talked about someone he worked for—someone who expected some kind of shipment. I thought that was weird because of how things are, you know."

Dylan gave her a quick nod.

"Annette didn't want him to go through with it, but he said they had his family. It was the only way to get them back. It was his family or this community, and he'd give us up in a heartbeat to save them."

Sue Ellen glanced at Dylan to see if he hated her yet, but he seemed okay. But the next part would be the hardest part.

Sue Ellen's stomach jumped with nerves. "I kept an eye on them. I really did. Nothing seemed to happen. Then he died. So I thought—I thought it was all over. But when Skye—I just don't know—should I have told you?"

"You should have." Dylan's voice turned rough, and his jaw was hard. He hadn't moved a muscle. He was mad.

Sue Ellen eyed him as she wiped the tears from her face. "If you need to hit me, it's okay."

She squeezed her eyes shut and waited.

"Sue Ellen, I ain't gonna hit you! I thought you knew me better."

"Yeah, but this is really bad, so ... "

"I ain't gonna hit you. Okay?" He grasped her arm to steady himself as he walked. "Let's go see Annette. See what she knows."

As they made their way back to the community, relief flooded through Sue Ellen. She hadn't noticed its weight until it was gone.

Now she seemed lighter—walked taller.

She wiped the last of the tears from her face, unable to believe that Dylan could forgive her like that.

Somehow he had, and somehow all this emotion had cleansed her, made her feel different—better. Safer, even.

She frowned as she navigated a narrow part of the trail, pushing some thorny bushes out of the way.

Safer? Maybe this light emotion wasn't only relief.

Sue Ellen glanced at Dylan. Could this unfamiliar emotion possibly be—

Was this what trust felt like?

15

PIECES

Dylan wearied as they walked up the back way to Annette's house, but he pulled in another deep breath and continued. There was work to do.

A quick word to the watchman on duty sent him scurrying to find Tom. The sheriff should be here for this.

Dylan put a hand to his aching side as he climbed the stairs to Annette's porch. The house was dark, but there were few places the woman would be.

Behind the door, something stirred. Dylan put a hand on the hilt of his large knife.

The door opened a quarter of the way. Annette's face peeked around. "Yes?"

"Annette," Dylan said. "I was sorry to hear about Ethan. I reckon we haven't gotten acquainted real well. But I think it's time we talked."

"I'm sorry about your injury and appreciate you stopping by, but I want to be alone."

She started to push the door closed.

Dylan slapped his hand against the wood. "Nope. Ain't gonna happen. Seems like Ethan's death and the shooting are connected. Maybe even the kidnapping of Skye and Kelsey. Is that right?"

The woman's face paled and her eyes widened. "How am I supposed to know anything about that?"

Sue Ellen glanced over her shoulder and murmured, "Tom's here."

Dylan appreciated the information, though he'd been aware of that a few minutes ago. The man tromped through the forest like an elephant trodding on bubble wrap.

"Thing is, Annette," Dylan said. "We know you do. And there ain't no way I'm leaving here without every scrap of information I can get. Somethin' you know may help me find my Skye."

Determination and desperation had stirred his emotions, and he almost broke down.

Annette stared at him for a moment—then she opened the door and waved him in—whether from guilt or pity, Dylan wasn't sure.

Tom and his deputy, Aaron, piled in behind him.

Annette plopped into an upright recliner, her hands covering her face as if afraid to look at them.

"I told him," she began, "I told him none of this would work. I told him to ask for help—that was the only way to go about this. I finally had him talked into it. He was going to come to see you the next morning, Sheriff. But then— And honestly, I don't think it was a natural death."

Tom nodded. "It certainly was nothing we'd ever seen before, that's why the Doc was taking so much care."

"No. What I mean is—someone did that to him. Poisoned him."

Tom quickly sat back in his seat.

Dylan understood his surprise. He felt gut-punched himself—if Ethan had been poisoned, who had done it?

Aaron ran a hand over his tight curls. "Annette, perhaps you should start at the beginning."

Annette squeezed her eyes shut as if praying for strength before she began. "Ethan's family and mine were on the road together—runnin' to somewhere safe. A gang of men came along and tried to take some of our people. A fight broke out. I lost my entire family on that road."

She let out a shaky sob. "But Ethan didn't. They were taken. The leader said he'd bring his family back if he helped find more people to replace them. When Ethan said he didn't know where any people were, the guy pointed at this mountain. "Head up there," he told us. "Get me them, and I'll give yours back.""

Annette held up her hands and shook her head. "I wasn't for it—told Ethan not to do it, and he was starting to change his mind. We thought you all could help with his family. I think someone realized that and killed him before he talked to you, Sheriff."

"Why are these people going around takin' others?" Dylan asked.

"They said there was a group called White Coats offering food, jewels, and gold for healthy people. They are experimenting for a cure." Annette scanned their faces. "That's good, right?"

Dylan scoffed. "Then why do they have to kidnap people? If it was a good thing, people would be linin' up at their door."

Annette's hair covered her face as she looked at the ground. "I'm sorry. I'm so, so sorry this led to your family being hurt."

"What do you know that will help find Skye and Kelsey?"

"The White Coats are located along the ocean. I'm not sure where, but you take the highway South."

The group left Annette and convened outside.

"I hate to say it but what if there's more like Ethan—traitors here on this mountain? What if someone in the community is working against us and poisoned him?" Tom said.

"It's possible, but it could've been a stranger," Dylan answered. "Look around. This little glen is the farthest from the center of the community. A stranger could've come up the back way like we did today. No one would see them if they were careful to creep in."

Aaron nodded. "And anyone could have shot at you in that field."

"I found this." Dylan pulled the gold money clip out of his pocket. "Look familiar?"

Aaron, Tom, and Sue Ellen shook their heads.

"I think," Tom said as he stroked his chin, "that we should still be on the lookout for anyone acting suspicious, just in case. We don't want to be caught unaware again."

Sue Ellen's brow wrinkled. "I can help with that."

When Tom shot her a dubious glance, Dylan defended her. "Take her up on it. The girl's got a sixth sense when it comes to readin' people—like I do." He ruffled her curly hair until she protested. Dylan smiled down at her. "It runs in the family."

Sue Ellen suppressed a smile, but Dylan could tell she was pleased.

The little group started down their different paths for home. As Dylan and Sue Ellen got closer to the doctor's cabin, a shadow separated itself from the building.

Dylan's heart jumped.

Jesse!

Dylan quickly glanced around, but there was no one else. He squeezed the girl's shoulder and mumbled, "Maybe it's okay."

He rushed over to the boy and gave him a bearhug.

Over Jesse's head, Dylan's eyes darted around the camp, hoping to see Skye.

But when his eyes landed on Spencer, the man looked at the ground.

No. Not here then.

Dylan looked at Jesse. "What happened? Where's Skye and Kelsey?"

"We trailed them to a Containment Center. But the men who had them traded them to someone else."

"What?" Dylan's stomach hardened.

"They met the White Coats there and gave Skye and Kelsey to them."

Dylan let go of Jesse and ran a hand through his hair. "Where's Wade?"

"He talked to the guys who took them. Now he's following the new bad guys. We came to get you."

Dylan nodded. "Let me get packed up."

Sue Ellen came up behind them. "Dylan?"

Dylan turned, a question in his eyes.

"Are you sure you're ready for this?"

"I gotta be, girl." At her instant frown, Dylan put a hand to Sue Ellen's shoulder. "I'd do the same for you. It'll be okay. Talk to your brother while I get my stuff together."

Dylan rushed through his packing and stepped back outside, going directly over to the teenagers. He shoved his pack at Jesse. "Take this to the truck. I want to talk to your sister."

As Jesse walked off, Dylan turned to Sue Ellen. "Where have you been stayin'?"

She shrugged. "At the cabin."

Dylan didn't like it. She needed someone to watch her back. "You doin' okay there?"

Sue Ellen shrugged. "Gets a little lonely sometimes."

"Why don't you stay with this girl here, Bre?"

"Cause she doesn't like me."

Dylan huffed out a sigh. "You been mean to her too?"

Sue Ellen scuffed the toe of her shoe in the dirt.

Dylan shook his head and bent to peer into her face. "See what that gets ya? No one around when you need help."

Sue Ellen bit her lip.

"If you get lonely, go to Tricia's. She'll take you in whether she likes you or not. She's family."

Sue Ellen scoffed.

"Sue Ellen, you're sixteen. How about you not shove everyone out of your life just yet? You got an entire lifetime to do that."

She turned red. "Yeah, well--"

"Don't say whatever. This is important." Dylan drew the girl to him and gave her a quick, hard hug. "And that ball you still carry in your pocket? Give it back to the little kid. Got it?"

"Okay, sure," she said and shrugged. "Why not?"

"And one more thing, Sue Ellen—try to be good. Try to do better."

Dylan turned to walk away.

"Dylan?"

He stopped and looked back at her. "Yeah?"

"You're right."

"About what?"

"About, well, everything."

Sue Ellen gave him a quick hard hug. "This is a good place. You all are a good family. I'll try harder."

She waved him off. "Now go get our girls. I have some apologies to make."

16

SEASIDE

Despite Skye's best efforts to keep her eyes open, the sway of the truck lulled her to sleep.

A few times Skye startled awake, and once more determined to stay alert. Once the driver had wound his way through a snarl of abandoned vehicles. Another time as they bumped over what felt like the meridian and back again.

But then the familiar hum of the road would begin, and she would fall back into an exhausted sleep.

The rapid staccato of raindrops pounding the metal roof of the vehicle jerked her awake.

Beside her, Kelsey sat upright, eyes open wide. "I'd forgotten," she said.

Skye squeezed her hand, then inched her way toward the front of the truck. If she could get close enough, she would be able to peer through the pass-thru window to the outside.

The trick was not being seen.

Skye gave a quick glance at the men in front to assure her their attention was on the road before peeking out.

Flat grasslands rippled from the stiff breeze into the horizon. The few tall, slim trees grew in clumps and swayed, bumping against their close neighbors.

Skye sniffed. No ocean yet, but it wasn't far off. She could smell it.

She slid down to the floor and scooted back to her spot beside Kelsey.

"Where do you think we are?" the girl asked.

"East coast. Definitely, near the ocean. Do you agree?"

"Yes, I smell it too."

"Not many houses out there. The ground must be too marshy to build on."

Kelsey's shoulders sagged.

Skye understood. Their best chance was a place where they were able to lose themselves. If they could find a nearly abandoned neighborhood where someone still lived and was willing to help them that would be perfect.

These grasslands wouldn't cut it.

The driver and the big man began talking.

Skye scooted closer, trying to hear the conversation.

Tattered billboards came into view.

Welcome to Seaside.

Pet the dolphins at Seaside's Marine Center.

The driver turned at the next left and Skye perked up.

Small colorful houses, many missing siding or shutters, lined the street. As they weaved through the heart of the town, a brick building with battered blue awnings came into view. It was clear that a terrible storm had blown through the once pretty town.

A few minutes later, the driver pulled into the parking lot of a large domed building. The sign over the structure had lost a few of its letters, but enough remained to read it.

Seaside Marine Center.

Skye frowned. Why were they bringing them here?

The property's metal outbuilding lay in twisted ruins, but the primary structure seemed in good repair even if a few windows and doors were boarded up.

Beyond the major building lay the ocean—surging and churning as if the storm hadn't done enough damage and it wanted to try again.

The driver slammed the truck to a stop.

Skye slapped her hands against the wall, trying to find something to grab. Her palms squeaked against the smooth panels, but she kept her footing.

The front doors squeaked open and slammed shut. The men's shoes slapped against the pavement as they walked to the back of the truck.

Skye held her breath as the vehicle's back door rolled up.

Skye and Kelsey squinted and shielded their faces with bent arms.

The driver growled his impatience, but the large man waved them toward the back of the truck with a gentle hand and seemed considerate as he helped Kelsey from the tall vehicle.

As Skye got closer to the edge, the driver yanked her to the ground. She stumbled, then pushed off the pavement, scanning the lot as she did so.

Other than a few deserted vehicles, it was empty.

Now was the time to run.

17

MAKE IT THROUGH

Before Skye could make her move, the tall man with the bad attitude and iron grip came around the vehicle.

He gave Skye a long scathing stare. "Just wanna make you aware that this place uses tasers—strong ones. So I wouldn't go getting uppity for them. Got it?"

Skye deflated and nodded, unsure if he wanted a verbal answer or not.

Another truck rattled into the parking lot and came to a jarring halt.

Three men jumped out, dragging a blindfolded and tied man and woman. The woman's shrill screams shattered the relative quietness of the place.

The men were rough with the couple. The woman's bare legs bleeding after scraping the uneven concrete.

As captive man struggled, the men punched and kicked him. Even when the captive man stopped and curled into a ball, they continued to beat him.

The tall man pulled Skye close—a hand wound tight

around her upper arm. "And you think I'm mean," he said as he hauled her to the front door.

As they passed the other group, the tall man sneered, "None to gentle there, uh, Max?"

"Hey, they don't pay me to be nice, just to get them here. I don't remember hearing any other condition but alive. So if we have a little fun on the way . . . "

His associates sniggered.

The tattooed man scoffed. "Pervert," he muttered.

Skye gave the beaten couple a sympathetic glance. Wishing there was something she could do.

The tall man pushed her through the front doors of the Marine Center. A woman and boy swept the floor along the far wall in the dim, but spotless, lobby.

Old demonstration kiosks were shoved into a corner, replaced by a couple of long plastic tables.

Skye's gaze darted from one side of the massive, echoing room to the other. How many captives had come through here on a regular basis?

Kelsey seemed calm as she examined the interior of the building—much better than Skye's thumping heart allowed her to be. She was so on edge—her skin hurt.

The tall man pushed them toward a table. The woman behind it refused to look at Skye or Kelsey—instead, she focused on the tall man. "Name?"

"You know my name. Don't act like I'm a stranger."

"But then you kinda are, aren't you, Zane?"

"I'm here when I'm here. I'm not when I'm not. Take it or leave it."

Skye's gaze darted between Zane and the woman behind the table. A lover's quarrel? It would have been funny in any other circumstances.

"Whatever, Zane." The woman's gaze wavered toward

Skye but never quite made it. She talked aloud as she wrote. "Two women."

Skye pulled in a breath to protest that Kelsey was a child. Before the words formed on her lips, Zane slapped the back of her head so hard she stumbled against the table. He grabbed the back of her neck, pulling her upright. "Manners!"

The woman taking his information flinched and took a step backward.

Zane punched his finger at the paper she'd slid toward him. "Two women today. Sam brought in a bunch yesterday."

"Yes. Well, you may want to talk to Kevin about that."

Zane's eyes narrowed. "You guys better not be trying to jack me up."

The woman's voice wavered. "Kevin knows more about it than I do." She picked up the paper and handed it to him. The white sheet shook.

Wow, lots of trouble in this little paradise.

Zane's gaze scraped over the woman as he grabbed the paper from her hand. "I'll be around tonight."

She nodded but said nothing.

Zane re-wrapped a hand around Skye's upper arm and jerked her across the lobby toward a hallway.

On their left stood a massive water tank filled with dirty water with undulating ribbons of algae. For a moment, Skye looked for other sea life.

Scowling, Zane came to a halt and began a terse conversation with a large, round man in a white coat. "What's going on, Kevin?"

"Well, I hate to tell you, but half of yesterday's isn't going to make it."

"Run the tests again."

"We already did."

"Fine," Zane growled. "Here's two more, maybe they'll make up for the others—and I want my bonus if they hit the jackpot."

He shoved Skye at Kevin. She had no choice but to grab him or fall.

Kevin wrinkled his nose. Skye would've loved to be offended, but she could smell herself. Some was her—some was the goo from the floor of the truck.

Zane laughed. "They already spent the night with the Sick, and they're just fine."

"You know the rules. That doesn't count. We do that here."

"I know, I know. If they don't make it through the night, I don't get paid."

"If you want a room for yourself—see the woman up front."

"Yeah, I'll do that," Zane threw over his shoulder as he swaggered off.

Skye looked through the lobby windows to the parking lot outside. If they got any further into this building, they may not get a chance to get away. It was now or never.

She threw a glance at Kelsey and readied herself to bolt.

"I wouldn't do that if I were you," Kevin warned her.

Two large men with guns slung over their shoulders and tasers pointed at her seemed to appear out of nowhere.

Skye eyed them, then sagged.

She looked at Kelsey, who nodded toward Kevin.

The girl was right. What choice did they have?

Kevin took the lead with Skye and Kelsey following. The sharp-eyed men with guns trailed after them.

Skye glanced up at Kevin. "Please tell me what is going on!"

Kevin sighed. "I hate this part, but I've found it is easier to answer the questions as they're asked. I'm not sure what you've been told so far, so I'll start at the beginning."

He gave her a sharp glance. "We are looking for a cure to the AgFlu. To do that, we need immune people. You have volunteered to help us with the research."

"First off, I disagree," Skye bristled. "We did not volunteer. They kidnapped us. And the AgFlu has swept through the world. It has done its damage. Why are you worried about it now?"

"I'm explaining the facility—not conversing with you. This is the only explanation you will get, so keep your mouth shut and listen."

Skye frowned and looked away.

Kevin continued. "If you make it through the night with no signs of AgFlu, the testing will begin in earnest. If you do not, I will make other arrangements for you."

It sounded morbid. Skye glanced at Kelsey. The teenager's suspicious expression mirrored her own.

"Make it through the night? What does that mean?"

Kevin stopped in front of a large barred room similar to a jail cell—or an animal cage.

The room was divided again with steel bars. One side was small, no wider than a twin bed. The other side was much larger and filled with filthy, disgusting Sick.

Skye's heart dropped. She tensed, fighting the guards as they shoved her and a struggling Kelsey toward the cell. When Skye and Kelsey seemed to gain ground, the guards picked them up and threw them in.

Skye landed hard against the concrete floor. Quickly, she and Kelsey stood and plastered themselves against the gray block wall.

The Sick leaned into the bars on their side, hands grasping as they extended their arms as far as they could go.

The metal barred door clanked shut, sealing their doom.

Kelsey jerked and moaned as a Sick woman grabbed a handful of her shirt and pulled her closer. She and Skye hammered the woman's filthy hand until she yelped and let go.

Skye pulled Kelsey to her. They cowered together in the tiny corner between the door and block wall.

Skye threw a frightened, pleading look at Kevin.

Kevin repeated her former question. "What do you have to do to make it through the night?" He put a hand around one of the bars separating him from their prison. "You survive this."

Skye put her hand on his. "Please, Kevin. Have some pity."

He stared at her.

If he saw them as fellow humans perhaps, he would change his mind. "Some food or water?"

His gaze turned flinty. "Nope. We don't waste that on the dying."

Skye dropped her hand from his as she barely missed the grasping fingers of another Sick. She swallowed hard. "And when we make it through this?"

"We inject you with it."

Horrified, Skye shuddered.

She tightened her hold on Kelsey as Kevin walked away. Icy dread filled her, but she fought it. She and Kelsey would make it through the night—she knew they would—they had both been this close to the Sick before.

But injected with the disease? Had anyone ever made it through that?

"Oh, Kelsey. I'm so sorry."

Kelsey hung onto Skye. "Don't give up yet, Skye. I never

thought I'd get out of Fenton, and I did. We'll get out of this."

Skye laid her head over Kelsey's as her eyes filled with tears.

She wouldn't tell the girl, but she'd given up the moment she heard the barred door clang shut behind them.

18

THE LONG NIGHT

Skye and Kelsey stood until exhaustion set in. The adrenaline surging through Skye from the beginning of this fight until now had sapped her energy.

Here, in the dim light, minutes seemed like hours and despite the threat, her body ached for rest.

Kelsey stumbled and grabbed Skye, saying, "I'm falling asleep on my feet. Literally. I didn't know that was really possible."

"I'm almost there too."

Kelsey pointed out a thin strip of concrete against the block wall. "I think, if we lay lengthwise along this wall, we would be out of their reach. I can scoot to the top. You could have this area."

Skye nodded. It looked like two women of average height could fit. "Let's try it but be careful."

"I will—believe me."

Kelsey inched her way forward, staying as close to the wall as possible. She jerked to her side and sucked her stomach in when one Sick man's long arm almost grabbed her.

On reaching the back wall, the girl settled in as best she could against hard concrete and bars.

Despite the harsh conditions, Kelsey gave Skye a thumbs up and closed her eyes.

Skye ran a hand through her grimy hair. She couldn't imagine sleeping right now but needed to move to the floor too. Any kind of rest would be helpful.

Who knew what tomorrow would hold?

Skye stretched onto her side with her back against the wall. She kept one eye on Kelsey to make sure she was truly out of harm's way and the other on the Sick.

The horde lumbered around their cell. Now that the women were still, they didn't attract as much attention, but even a small move from them brought the Sick closer to them.

These people were deep into the disease and almost senseless. Because of that, they didn't crouch to the floor, but stayed standing when they thrust their hands through the bars.

Skye uttered a deep sigh of relief. Other than breathing the same air as the horde, they were safe. And she wasn't afraid of the germs, she'd already had the disease and been one of the fortunate few to live through it. No, what scared her the most was the Sick's long, blue grasping fingers finding her.

Despite Skye's fears, her eyes grew heavy, and she slept.

SKYE JERKED AWAKE. Nothing seemed to have changed. Without moving, she scanned the room.

Something had nudged her from sleep.

A light tune carried down the hallway. Whistling.

She pushed herself to her feet, avoiding the newly stirred horde.

Kelsey sat up and pushed her long, dark hair back over her shoulder.

The tromp of boots announced several men and one brawny woman.

Kevin led the group. He rattled some keys and opened the prison door, waving them out.

Two men in white coats approached them. One spoke. "We are going to take your temperature and some blood."

Skye shot a glance at the big men. If she caused any trouble, there was no doubt how this would go.

So she agreed and glanced at Kelsey.

This was the moment of truth. Well, this and whatever came after.

Everything Skye knew about the Agflu she could count on one hand, and even that was a bunch of guesses. If they passed this test—and the next one—they were truly immune.

Once the white coats took what they needed, they nodded to the guards.

Security marched Skye and Kelsey several yards down the hallway and shoved them into a couple of stadium chairs lining the wall.

They sat there for a few minutes, staring at nothing, before one of the white coats popped his head around a door and gave a thumbs up.

Skye shot a worried glance at Kevin.

Thumbs up, they passed? Or thumbs up, take them out and shoot them?

Kevin smiled. "Well, good news. You just earned yourself a shower and a meal."

Skye and Kelsey sagged with relief.

Kelsey grabbed Skye's hand and squeezed it.

"A shower sounds good, doesn't it?" Kelsey asked.

Skye agreed. The mere mention of the word made her

realize how grimy she was. And a toilet was becoming an urgent need too.

Kevin waved them further down the hallway and through a bathroom door.

Skye began a sprint toward a stall until an enormous hand grabbed her arm. She glanced from the massive guard who held her in place to Kevin. "Look, I have to go, I really, really have to."

Kevin waved the guard's hand away, but said, "I'm sending Sydney in." He pointed to a tall, muscular female dressed in a guard's uniform, then back at the male guard. "This one will be inside the door, but he will give you your privacy."

Skye quickly nodded, not sure she cared anymore as her need grew.

Kevin gave the go-ahead.

She ran to the first stall. Kelsey wasn't far behind.

As Skye exited the stall, she eyed Sydney, who watched Skye washing her hands.

The male guard remained in the room but faced the hallway.

Once the women washed their hands, Sydney pointed at a blue sign that said, "Showers" at the end of the row of sinks. A matching arrow pointed through a door with a small square window.

They pushed through the door and found three showers with thin, clear shower curtains.

Skye winced. Well, it was better than nothing.

Sydney had trailed them into the room and now pointed out two small piles of green medical scrubs and two pairs of white boat shoes sitting on a bench. "There's one for each of you. Shampoo and soap in the showers. Good kinds too. We treat our Immune well—there are so few of you. In fact, if you pass the next test, you'll get a shower every day."

Surprised, Skye stared at Sydney. "Aren't all of you immune?"

The woman shook her head. "No. Most have just stayed away from any Infected or Sick."

When Skye asked another question, the male guard appeared and said, "Get in there. You have limited time."

Once the male guard turned his back, Skye and Kelsey showered.

Skye threw her smelly clothes on the floor outside, happy to be rid of them, and sighed as the warm water smoothed over her, taking the filth away.

What? Warm? They had enough energy for that?

Skye picked up a shampoo bottle and raised an eyebrow. They certainly did use the best. Though there probably wasn't a run on this at the local salon anymore.

She hurried but shampooed her hair twice before it seemed clean. Just as she reached for the knob to turn the shower off, the water stopped.

The male guard had told the truth. There was a time limit. Good to know.

Skye wrapped a towel around herself and moved toward the bench.

The male guard still faced the opposite way.

Sydney averted her eyes.

Skye was grateful for what privacy they allowed. She scanned the room and sent a pointed look to Kelsey as she exited the shower.

The girl shrugged.

Neither had found a single solid unattached item they could use as a weapon.

Skye glanced back at the only two items she'd found in the stall—her washcloth and a mini-shampoo bottle.

MacGyver might be able to do something with those—she sure couldn't.

Skye and Kelsey turned toward the guards and followed them out into the hallway.

Kevin continued to lead them down the same corridor.

This hallway seemed like an assembly line, and they were the product. The further down the line she and Kelsey moved, the safer they were—at least, she hoped that was the case.

The guards ushered them into a normal exam room—though it was larger than she was used to. Besides the regular equipment, there were small medical machines lined up on a long countertop that stretched along one wall.

A man with messy brown hair wearing a white lab coat walked toward them. He held two vials in his hand.

She didn't have to imagine what they were. Kevin had already told her. Skye shuddered.

Her gaze darted to the door. Two guards stood there, closing off the exit. Two other men and Kevin stood near the exam table, and Sydney waited in the hallway.

Skye turned back to the man in the white lab coat. "Is this—"

Kevin stepped forward. "Don't talk to him. This is hard enough for him as it is."

"Hard enough for him! We're the ones who—"

Kevin gestured, and one guard thrust a taser toward Skye.

She jumped away, and it narrowly missed her.

"One more word," Kevin said curtly, "and he will use that."

Skye took another small step away from them and said nothing.

The White Coat waved her to the table.

She climbed up, her jaw clenched.

As he prepped Skye's arm for the injection, she trembled so hard she wondered how he would find a vein.

But then, maybe he didn't need a vein.

Kelsey moved to her side and grabbed her hand. "Hey, at least we'll die clean."

Skye couldn't help the small chuckle even as her heart fell. She threw a pleading glance at Kevin, but he stood as if made of stone.

She turned to Kelsey, "If I don't make it, tell everyone I—I—"

"It's okay, Skye. I will. But you'll be fine." The girl gave her a wobbly smile. "I know it."

The White Coat laid the hard needle against Skye's skin.

She instinctively jerked back.

One of the muscular guards moved to stand close behind her.

Skye leaned away as his hot breath washed over her only to have him wrap a beefy arm around her shoulders and yank her back tighter against him.

Another guard took her arm, holding it from the shoulder to wrist and pulling until Skye groaned in protest.

The needle was back. Cool against her skin.

Skye glanced up at the White Coat.

Uncomfortable with his job, he gritted his teeth as he plunged the needle into her. Skye gasped in pain.

It sunk deep—slamming against her—coming to a stop only when the hub hit her arm.

The fluid burned as if a river of fire entered her body. Skye tried to hold back a sob but failed.

The injection felt like the deadly contagion it was.

The white coat jerked the needle from Skye's arm and

THE RESCUE: SANCTUARY'S AGGRESSION 5

sped away to get the second injection ready. Blood trailed down her arm.

Who put someone so bad at injections in this job?

Kevin stepped closer, wiped the blood away, and bandaged her.

Skye hugged her arm to herself when he finished.

"You need to stop fighting, Skye," he said. "It's just a waste of energy, and we don't put up with trouble."

Skye scrubbed some wayward tears off her face and hopped off the table.

Kelsey's face paled, but she obediently climbed onto the table when instructed.

Kevin put on latex gloves and took the syringe from the technician. He pulled Kelsey's unresisting arm forward and gave the girl a look of approval. "Good girl," he told her.

Kelsey closed her eyes and took the hand Skye offered, squeezing it tight.

Like an expert, Kevin slid the needle into Kelsey's arm and pushed the plunger. "This will burn for a bit, but it will be over soon."

Kelsey grunted as tears ran down her cheeks. She hissed as the burn moved through her.

Kevin stood back. "Okay, the worst is over. Now we wait twenty-four to forty-eight hours. I'll show you to your new room."

They went out to the hallway and turned left, continuing down the same hallway.

Another few yards, another few rooms.

19

FIGHTERS

Kevin stopped at a door, opened it, and threw out his arm. "Big upgrade from last night, uh?"

Skye barely controlled her eye roll. Did he want a thank you? Better think again, buddy.

Still, she scanned the room with relief. Two twin beds, a bedside table with a light, a few old magazines, and what seemed to be their own bathroom through a half-closed door.

And no Sick for next-door neighbors.

It was Kelsey who was the polite one. "Thank you, Kevin. It's so nice and clean."

Kevin nodded his head, soaking in the praise like it was due him. When he glanced at Skye, she hurried to give him half a smile.

She was labeled a troublemaker, and it only made them more suspicious of her. She needed to become a better actor.

Skye pushed on one of the mattresses. "Seems comfy."

Satisfied, Kevin turned to the door. "I'm going to bring you ladies something to eat."

110

Skye put a hand to her growling stomach. Now that was something she could look forward to.

Kevin and his gang turned and left, shutting the door behind them. It was not a surprise when Skye heard the lock engage.

Skye and Kelsey exchanged a glance as they listened to the guard's shoes slap against the hallway floor.

When they were gone, Skye spoke but kept her voice quiet in case a guard was still stood near.

"Oh Kelsey, we keep getting deeper into this complex."

"Yes, well. I'm sure that's on purpose."

"If we can get out of this room, I know the way out of this building. But with all the guards, their weapons ... "

Kelsey shook her head. "There isn't a way—not yet. We just have to do what they want until they trust us and give us a chance to bolt."

"I agree." Skye rubbed a hand over her face. "But I'm not sure how much time we have or what they will do to us next."

Kelsey grabbed Skye's other hand. "We have to do what they say. It's the only way out, Skye. It's what worked in Fenton."

Skye gave the girl a sharp glance. "What do you mean?"

Kelsey sat on the twin bed across from Skye. "That group in Fenton—they caught me once, you know that." The girl's gaze stayed glued to the floor. This was a subject that the girl always avoided in therapy.

Skye listened as Kelsey continued.

"I fought them at first, but I learned real quick. You take it until they trust you enough that you can get away."

The girl shuddered. She glanced at Skye from under her lashes, her face red. "At least, they want something different from us here."

"Oh, Kelsey," Skye said around the lump in her throat.

She moved closer and gently put her arms around her. "I'm so sorry that happened to you."

Skye ached to take away all of Kelsey's trauma—as if it never happened.

Kelsey's voice was a low murmur. "Me too."

Skye comforted the girl as well as she could.

Kelsey was brave—a fighter. There was no doubt about that.

A rapid knock on the door startled them.

Kevin threw the door open.

"Here you go, girls. We don't get fancy anymore, but it is food."

Skye grit her teeth. She rarely minded being called a girl. Her mother had often referred to her dad and his friends as boys. So it was all the same to her. But the way Kevin drew out the word, he used it to demean them—put them in their place.

She didn't like that.

Skye's stomach rumbled, taking her mind off Kevin. She glanced at the tray a guard sat on the bed in front of her. Peanut butter and jelly, a few potato chips, and a little can of juice.

It looked delicious.

Kevin returned to the door. "You have a good night. And don't worry, overmuch. I have a good feeling about you girls. You're gonna make it."

He gave them a wide smile that faded away.

Kelsey tentatively raised her hand. "Can I ask about the man and woman who came in at the same time as us?"

"Oh, yeah. Sadly, they didn't make it through the night —got sick. We added them to the pit."

Kelsey ducked her head.

Skye wasn't sure what the pit was. Perhaps the other side of that jail cell—the side with the Sick?

She put a hand over her mouth.

Kevin shrugged. "Here there is a place for everything and everyone. It's very ship-shape. If you don't fit in one area—well, you'll fit in another."

Once Kevin left, the food didn't look as appealing anymore.

THE NEXT TWO days were little more than sleeping and eating—always in that small room. Their recreation comprised taking and retaking magazine quizzes. Their favorite was Which Celebrity are You? They made up pandemic stories for the celebs.

On the third morning—as usual—the morning alarm sounded. A blare, similar to an air horn. It startled Skye and Kelsey from their deep sleep.

Skye rolled over in bed, wishing to leave this room and yet afraid of what would happen when Kevin finally came for them.

She stood and rushed over to Kelsey, feeling her forehead. "Any headaches, sniffles, anything?"

"No. You?"

"No. Only a few hours more to go, according to Kevin. I think we've made it, but I still don't like to think of the Sick's goo oozing around my system."

Kelsey shuddered. "Ew, Skye, don't say that."

"Sorry, kiddo." She patted Kelsey on the shoulder. "Well, maybe we'll get out of here now."

Kevin trooped in with their breakfast—pancakes, scrambled eggs that looked like they were from a powder, and juice.

Each day they survived, they received better meals, and yesterday, they had even asked Skye and Kelsey what sizes they wore.

Kevin smiled as he laid a tray on the bed in front of Skye. "I have a surprise for you both. I brought some jeans and t-shirts for you. And some socks and shoes! I thought it might be nice for you to dress normally again."

"Yes, thank you, Kevin, that is considerate of you," Skye said.

Kevin beamed.

She congratulated herself. Her acting skills were coming along well. To thank him without choking on it was a vast improvement. But it wasn't easy. She'd spent her career seeking the truth behind her clients' troubles. Now she had to ignore Kevin's blatant personality problems just to live through the day.

Kevin waved in Sydney.

"It will be Sydney's honor to assist you. Anything else you need—you ask her. She will be with you the most from here on out."

Sydney smiled, laid two piles of clothing on the bed and smoothed the tops of them. "I helped pick them out," she said, pride in her voice. "I tried to get something comfortable for you both."

"Thank you. We appreciate it," Kelsey said.

Skye ran her hand over the clothes. A t-shirt, the super-soft kind, and blue jeans. "Thank you."

Sydney nodded and stepped back.

Kevin cleared his throat. "So, girls, this is a great day! One more blood test, just to be absolutely sure, and then you can go to your permanent rooms. And you will have the honor of meeting the founder of this place. He doesn't do this for just anyone—he is busy—working to help all humankind. Well, remaining humankind, that is."

Skye glanced from Kevin to Sydney.

They were fawning over her and Kelsey, literally fawning. Just how few people made it through these tests?

20

THE MEETING

·

After Skye and Kelsey changed into their new clothing, Kevin ushered them out of their bedroom and down the hallway once again.

This time they marched all the way to the dead end.

Skye gulped, looked left, then right, and shot a glance at Kevin.

He chose left and moved toward a door on the right, opening it with a flourish.

Kelsey sent Skye a fear-filled glance but held her head high.

Skye returned what she hoped was a comforting smile as she ignored her own misgivings. When Kevin urged her to enter the room, she hurried to step in. After giving it a quick scan, she sighed in relief.

Similar to one in a hotel and twice as big as the one assigned them the last two nights, this room held a queen-sized bed with a blue bedspread on one side of the room. A large desk and chair sat on the opposite side near the footboard. A big, over-stuffed lounger was in the far corner.

Bolted to the wall was a large-screen TV. DVDs and books lined the shelving unit below it.

Nothing scary, so far, other than this meant they would be here a while.

Kevin walked to the other side of the room and pulled back long, cream-colored vertical blinds to reveal an entire wall of floor to ceiling windows.

The vast, rolling ocean filled the glass. A decent-sized piece of blond beach was on the right side of the picture window with a parking lot on the other side of the sand.

Fascinated by the amazing view, Skye took a few steps forward and watched a new wave surge toward the beach. When no one stopped her, she waved Kelsey over as she moved to stand closer to the glass.

It seemed like it was just them and the limitless blue water.

The two women watched as the powerful wave slowly built up, only to tumble onto land and thin out as it rode the sand as far as possible. It was the most gorgeous thing Skye had seen since leaving the mountains.

Three stories up, only the glass kept Skye from tasting the salty air from the moody, blue-grey water.

In the distance, a massive red rock wall towered over the blond beach, easily withstanding the waves crashing against its side.

The two side by side seemed out of place—as if someone had picked up the rock formation from Bryce Canyon and dropped it on the Carolina beach.

The oddness rang a bell. She'd heard of this place. Spire Cliff.

She knew exactly where they were.

Skye pulled Kelsey close, hugging her.

"Yes, it is beautiful, isn't it?" Kevin said.

Skye beamed, letting Kevin think her joy was simply over the view. "It is."

She reached for the slider door, but it didn't budge.

Kevin shook his head. "They're locked for now. We'll see how you do." He turned back to the hallway door. "One of you gets this room and one the next room. Don't worry. It is just as nice."

Skye's smile faded. "We'd rather stay together."

"I understand that. But for this phase, it's important that you have no contact. We need to know what is working and what is not."

Skye and Kelsey clenched each other tighter.

"Don't worry, Mommy," Kevin said as he took Kelsey's arm. "She'll be fine."

The girl gave Skye a long, sad look but released her.

Skye closed her eyes and sighed.

There was nothing to do about it right now. Their choices were to cooperate or fight—and there was no way to take on the muscle who had trailed them to this room.

Skye stared at the four goons. Kevin expected trouble.

Skye put a hand on each of Kelsey's shoulders and gave her a long look.

"It'll be okay," she whispered and hoped it was true.

Her heart tugged as she leaned in to kiss the top of the girl's head.

Kelsey's eyes flooded with tears, but she nodded. "I know." Her chin wobbled.

As Kevin led Skye out of the room, she said, "I want to see her every day. Even if it is from a distance."

Kevin scratched his chin. "I'll have to get permission for that, but he might allow it."

"Thank you." It went against Skye's every grain to show any appreciation to her captor, but she would do anything to stay in touch with Kelsey.

Her eyes settled on a tablet of paper sitting on the desk. "And please ask if we can write to each other."

"Sure."

Skye's stomach dropped as she walked away, brushing tears away.

Her gaze swept the group, landing on Sydney. She sent her a pleading glance.

The woman's hard face softened. "I'll make sure she has the best care possible. I promise."

Skye would need to be satisfied with that.

She glanced back, giving Kelsey one last look.

The girl looked small in the enormous room. She wrapped her arms around herself as she stared back at Skye—her eyes round and too large for her face.

The door between them shut, blocking Skye's view.

Kevin took Skye to the next room—a copy of Kelsey's. After opening the blinds in this room, Kevin lingered at the door. "Our founder would like to meet you."

"And Kelsey?"

"Of course—but you first."

"Okay."

Skye ran a hand over her hair, wanting to make as good an impression as possible. It was vital for this founder to see her and Kelsey as fellow human beings and not just test subjects. She looked in the mirror and squared her shoulders before following Kevin back across the hall they had come down and to a door further down on the right.

Without a word, he motioned her in.

The room seemed dark against the daylight cascading in from the floor to ceiling windows that were a copy of those she had in her room, especially since the lights were off.

Against the panorama of the ocean stood a silhouetted figure.

A man—lost in thought.

Skye and Kevin stood for a moment waiting for recognition until Kevin uttered an awkward cough.

The shadowed man dropped his hands and sighed. He clicked on the lights.

Skye blinked against their brilliance and scanned the room.

The office was pristine, orderly to the point of perfection. Skye was almost afraid to breathe for fear of messing something up.

Every item was so precisely laid out, she wondered if he used a tape measure. From the pictures on the wall to the pens, stapler, and office accessories lining the desk like little soldiers.

Everything was either black or white and so starkly done, it set one's teeth on edge.

This was the room of a troubled person. A person who looking for order in life and not finding it there demanded it here where he could control it. That did not bode well for the rest of this facility or for her and Kelsey.

Since it is impossible for the world to exist at the high level of perfection a person like this demanded, this room was most likely the only place this man found rest—relief.

No wonder he had sighed. Their presence broke his respite.

Skye studied the man as he walked toward them. Not a wrinkle marred his dress shirt and tie, or the blindingly white coat he wore over it.

He smoothed a hand over his dark hair.

Of course, he did.

He would refuse to have a single strand out of place.

Did he insist on the same high level of perfection in others?

Silly question.

Undoubtedly.

Skye imagined the rage this man had over what he perceived as other's shortcomings. He would release those dark emotions in some way.

She shuddered to think what it might be.

His dark eyes seemed haunted and sad—but there was also a hard edge to them.

He moved with a confidence that said his way was the only right way, and it would be impossible to convince him of anything else.

The founder stopped and clapped his hand behind his back, tilting his head at her rather than give Skye a handshake.

"Hello. My name is Devon. Doctor Devon Shade."

2 1

THE STORY OF MY LIFE

Although Skye believed most people were good, despite any personality flaws they needed to work through, she instantly disliked this man.

Some perfectly healthy people were quite neat and enjoyed stark decorating. But that along with Devon's insane need to find a cure for a disease that had already run rampant through the world as well as his willingness to hurt people while he was doing it, told her much about him. Her last few days under his roof had shown her the extent he would go.

This man was not healthy. He was not even remotely normal.

Still, she needed to treat him as though he *was* healthy —as though there were no any evil intentions toward her or anyone else.

It would be her biggest acting job yet.

"Skye Jackson," she introduced herself. "But I suppose you already know that."

"I do. I have read the reports about you and your

companion—interesting cases. I look forward to working with you."

Skye tried to tame the shudder attempting to overtake her as Devon looked her over. "You two are special. Few patients make it to this phase of the testing. Things . . . happen."

Skye pulled in a slow breath, keeping its raggedy edges at bay. He made evil sound like an everyday occurrence.

And in this place, it just might be.

"What exactly are you doing here?" she asked.

"Why, trying to find a cure." Devon gave her an incredulous stare. "No one explained that?"

"Yes. But why are you so sure you'll be able to accomplish what no one else has done? What are your credentials?"

"Oh, I see." He gave a little chuckle. "Don't worry, I have all the schooling and, more important than that, the hands-on experience with this virus. I am intimately familiar with its every twist and turn. If I could only tell you . . . perhaps one day I will."

Skye's stomach tightened. She wouldn't be here long enough for an explanation. Hopefully.

She stared at him, trying for a little intimidation of her own. "I'm a doctor myself, so if you would explain, I would appreciate it."

"A doctor of?" Devon arched an eyebrow. "Anything that can be of use to me here?"

Skye barked out a sharp laugh. Definitely something that could be of use.

"I'm a psychologist."

"Interesting." Devon looked at the floor. "I would like someone to talk to. I haven't been the same since the death of my wife."

He turned his back to her and faced the wall of ocean. "It was all their fault."

"Who's fault?"

Devon turned back toward Skye. "You won't understand if I only tell you. Seeing it though, then you must believe."

What was he talking about? Perhaps the man was more irrational than he'd already let on.

"So, Dr. Skye, can we set up some sessions?"

Skye almost cringed. The last thing she wanted to do was spend more time with her captor—the man behind the torture of countless people. But if this helped their situation, she'd do it.

Skye glanced at Devon. Her hesitation had already put a sharper edge to his stare.

Did she have a choice then? Maybe this would help gain his trust—or someone's. Trust could lead to fewer restrictions—and eventually—escape.

"Of course, whenever you like." Skye forced a tight smile.

Devon ran his hands over the lapels of his white coat. "I have some work I need to get to right now. Perhaps you would like to rest awhile, and we will meet again later."

"Sounds fine." Skye tightened her icy fingers into fists.

She waited for her dismissal. When the scientist remained quiet, she took control and tipped her head, then headed for the door.

She'd take what little power was given her.

Skye spent the next two hours picking through, and discarding, the pile of mostly bodice-ripper novels before moving on to the more interesting movies. But this was too dire of a situation for such mundane entertainment to hold her interest.

Eventually, Kevin knocked on her door and again led her down the hallway to Devon's lair. When he tapped on the boss' door, Devon's muffled voice called for them to enter.

Surprised, Skye found Devon's gloomy attitude from this morning had changed into a downright cheerful one. She hoped it had nothing to do with the droplets of blood staining the front of his white coat.

"Hello!" he said to Skye as he passed the dirty jacket to Kevin and ordered him to take it to the laundry.

Devon's henchman bunched the jacket up, covering the large red spot, but Skye couldn't pull her eyes away from the cloth.

Would her blood, or Kelsey's, soak this crazy man's clothing one day?

As Kevin handed the garment off to a guard, Devon clapped his hands as if to get her attention. "Okay then, how should we do this? Do I lay on the couch or sit?"

Skye turned her attention to him and reminded herself that this needed to go well. Whatever the man needed to discuss or confess, she needed to handle it.

"Whatever makes you more comfortable is fine," she said as she pasted on a pleasant expression.

Devon looked from the chair to the couch. "I feel as if I need to do this the proper way. The couch it is."

He motioned for most of the guards to go to the hallway but told Kevin and Sydney to stand on the other side of the room.

Devon dragged a chair closer to the couch while darting looks at Kevin and Sydney. When he was satisfied, he invited Skye to sit.

He laid on the couch, changing positions a few times until he seemed comfortable.

"So, Doc," he said, "does talking about people's darker moments help them?"

"Most people have told me it helps them learn more about themselves and work through problems. I will warn you—it can be work, hard work. Some were not happy with what they found and made the needed changes, and in the end considered it well worth the effort."

"Of course, of course. So where should I start?"

"Wherever you would like. This is your time. What do you want to talk about?"

"A story. The story—the story of my life." Devon glanced at Skye. "I believe the best place to start is the day I became a different person. The day of my parent's murder. An Atlantian attacked them, crushed them, as I watched."

Skye froze. She had tried to prepare herself for anything, but mostly for gruesome details of his work.

But Atlantians? No, she had not prepared herself for that.

So, okay, more than a little crazy then.

She forced her pleasant expression to hold. It would do no good to lose his trust at the very beginning.

Devon stared at her, waiting for a reaction.

Skye raised an eyebrow.

Certainly, he didn't expect her to accept such an outrageous claim. He was sane enough to know the statement was strange.

Devon laughed but seemed satisfied with her response.

As he continued, Skye glanced at Kevin and Sydney. Both seemed unfazed. Clearly, this wasn't the first time they'd heard these crazed memories.

Skye turned her attention back to Devon and the tale he told. To some extent, they made sense.

An attacker may seem superhuman to a child watching his parent's murder, but Devon should have grown out of that idea. To maintain these underwater people exist at this stage in his life was far beyond the norm.

Devon's twisted story continued. He claimed he was groomed by fellow humans to hunt the Atlantians, trained to conduct gruesome medical experiments on them, and gleefully murdered the underwater people all in the name of helping humankind.

Skye had trouble holding her nausea.

No doubt these "Atlantians" were human victims. If what he said was true—and from what she'd seen—Devon was more than a serial killer. He was a mass murderer.

Skye paled and sat a little straighter, willing her stomach to settle.

Eventually, Devon sat up and ran his hands over his face. He looked at Skye as he gave his final confession. "It was my fault. I created this disease to destroy those abominations. And it turned against us. Instead, I infected—I killed—all of my beloved humankind."

Devon broke down, sobbing. "Now I'm determined to find the cure, no matter the cost."

Skye gripped the armrests of the chair. This man—this monster—created the disease that killed almost everyone on earth?

Her mind flew from the loved ones she had lost—her mother, father, the rest of her family—to every gruesome death she had seen, and the poor restless souls who still wandered through deserted towns and wasted lands, sick and confused.

This man had done that. Unable to hold it in any longer, Skye raced to a garbage can sitting beside a desk and vomited.

As Skye wiped her mouth with a tissue she took from Devon's desk, she realized how silent the room had become.

THE RESCUE: SANCTUARY'S AGGRESSION 5

Of course, this man would find this reaction to his confession a personal affront. On some level, he thought he was a hero fighting to save all humankind.

Skye glanced at Devon. His expression hardened.

Her mind swirled with excuses he might accept until she latched onto one.. "I'm so sorry. How-how horrible this must be for you. What you have been through!"

Devon eyed Skye, then the garbage can she held. He motioned for Kevin to take it out of the room.

Everyone was silent as Kevin did as instructed.

Devon heaved a sigh. "It has been hard. I've had a difficult life, and I appreciate your intense appreciation over my hardships. I can tell you truly understand."

Skye nodded, hoping there would be no lingering after-effects causing her to need the trash can again.

Devon pointed to a door on his right. "There's a bathroom through there if you should need it."

"Thank you. But you've worked hard today. Perhaps we should take this up tomorrow."

Devon nodded. "I agree."

Skye said her goodbyes, trying not to appear too rushed. Her mind whirled as she walked back to her room, a hand on her still upset stomach.

When Skye and the guards reached her room, she reached for the door handle eager to get away from them so she could release her genuine feelings about the mad scientist.

Her hand grazed the handle when Sydney spoke.

"You're lucky. The Doc told you about the Atlantians already. He normally works up to that."

Skye glanced at her. Did Sydney also accept the super-human beings as real?

"I saw a newspaper article about the Atlantians early on but figured it was all fake news," Skye replied.

"Well, I expect now that Doc has told you, you'll get to see one."

Skye shot a glance at Sydney. "Have you seen one?"

"I'm still waiting, but Kevin has. He says they're just as huge as Doc says. Strong, too. They have to be sedated at all times to handle them."

Skye dropped her gaze to the floor. If Devon had true converts, the situation would be even more dangerous than she'd expected.

As for the so-called Atlantian, whoever was at the non-existent mercy of Dr. Devon Shade, her heart went out to them.

22

DAY ONE

That night as Skye fell asleep, her mind drifted away from the evil and to Dylan.

She imagined him tall and strong, even though the infection had still raged the last time she'd seen him. She had to believe that Jesse made it home with the medication and Dylan had healed. Because to think anything else would be unacceptable.

She snuggled further under the covers as she imagined his muscular arms wrapped around her, soothing her as he had so many times before. Skye hugged a pillow to herself, trying to ignore the tears that coursed down her cheeks.

She daydreamed of the future they were making—the mountain, their cabin, and the warm sunlight waking her and Dylan each morning in their hand-carved four-poster bed.

Each memory was bittersweet. To remember now, in this place, made any dream seem unattainable.

A sob escaped Skye. She needed Dylan. Her soul seemed empty. How she yearned to hold him to her—his solid body strong and sturdy again.

Would he find her?

He was an excellent tracker but tracking hundreds of miles away seemed beyond even his considerable skills.

But if anyone would be able to, it would be him.

Dylan, her love.

But she wouldn't just wait for him to appear. She and Kelsey would be on alert for any opportunity to escape. Then she would make her way back to his arms and stay there.

THE NEXT MORNING Skye stood in front of the large window, watching the lazy tide push onto the shore when a knock sounded.

Before she crossed the room to answer it, the door sprang open and Kevin strolled in. He gave her a tight nod. "Doctor Shade needs you in the lab."

Skye's heart stopped. "The lab?"

"Yes. They have moved your schedule up."

A million horrible scenes flashed through her mind.

Skye glanced at Kevin. The man knew what would happen. How many other victims had he led to that evil place?

Instinctively, Skye stepped away from him.

He grabbed her arm in an iron grip and pulled her toward the hallway.

Skye tried to yank her arm away, but Kevin tightened his grip.

"I want to see Kelsey before I go!" she said.

"Do you really want her to see you like this? You look all freaked out."

"I am freaked out."

"It'll be fine. Nothing big ever happens on the first day."

Was he just saying this to make his job easier?

THE RESCUE: SANCTUARY'S AGGRESSION 5

She pressed her lips together. Could she believe him?

Skye had little choice as Kevin pulled her along. He led her in a different direction this time—through a maze of corridors before they reached a different lab.

Once they arrived, he quickly left, almost turning on his heel to make his escape.

Skye stood where Kevin left her, watching as he waved two guards over and stationed them at the door. Then she let her gaze drift around the room as she shifted her feet against the tile floor.

This lab seemed exactly as the first one she visited in except for three things. To her left sat an enormous desk holding a small stack of papers. And across from her stretched another long white countertop with a larger array of small medical machines than the other room.

Beyond that were the cages.

Along the wall beside her, under the row of windows, stood barred enclosures. Small to large, plastic and metal barred, at least twenty of them.

Her gaze halted on the largest one—large enough to hold a man.

A finger of ice ran down Skye's spine. Evil slithered through the room.

She took a nervous step to one side and bumped into the most disturbing item of the room.

The deafening clatter of metal on metal startled her, and she jumped away.

The steel table looked more like something used in a morgue than in any regular doctor's office.

She prayed it wasn't still in use, but she knew better. The shackles attached to the table with a bulky chain left no doubt unwilling victims had laid here.

Skye whirled at the tap of leather-soled shoes.

That would be him. Her stomach lurched.

Her gaze lingered on the metal table even though she begged her eyes to move on. If this was the "nothing big" Kevin promised, what was in store for her later?

Devon entered the room and stopped. He gave Skye a tight smile and an odd look.

Skye put a hand to what she was sure was a pale face after the fear rushing through her.

Devon put the chart he held onto the desk and rushed over to her. "Oh my dear, you do seem to be in a fit. Here hop up on the table before you fall over."

"Please," Skye muttered, a wave of dizziness coming over her. "Please, don't make me get on that table."

Devon put an arm around her and hurried her to a chair behind the desk. He crouched down, looking her in the eye. "Here you go then. Better?" He chuckled. "You are a sensitive one, aren't you?"

Skye closed her eyes and put her hands to her face. "What are you going to do to me?"

"Oh, Skye," he said as he patted her arm. "This room isn't for you. I wanted to show you where I have done some of my best work. I'm sorry if it frightened you."

Skye continued to draw in several deep breaths until her head stopped swimming.

As soon as Skye felt herself return to something resembling normal, she straightened.

Devon started talking, and she let him rattle on, but tried to ignore most of what came out of his mouth. It wouldn't take much right now for her to end up on the floor in a faint.

Eventually though, she tuned in.

Devon ran on about DNA experiments and the similarity and differences between the two races, Human and Atlantian. But he definitely didn't consider Atlantians simply another race of people.

The man abhorred them on a level Skye had rarely seen. To the point where once he'd identified them as Atlantians, he then used the term abominations.

As much as Devon hated them, the Atlantians also fascinated him. He bragged about their build, their strength, and their mannerisms until Skye doubted her own certainty the people did not exist.

Devon pointed to the metal table. "I've had them strapped and chained to that very table and only kept them still by drugging them out of their mind. They are strong, so strong. Their organs are larger than ours and are more efficient. They breathe far less often than we do. That is how they survive underwater."

Devon pointed to the large cage at the end of the room. "I kept them there."

At the sorrowful drop of Skye's face, he said, "I know, but I had too. Drugged and confined in spaces too small for them was the only way to keep them docile. Don't underestimate them, Skye. Never do that. If you do, it will be the end of you. They will make sure of it."

Devon waited for a response.

All Skye could manage was a nod.

"I wish I could show you more, but the time is not right. However, I have this chart." He grabbed the papers off of the desk and shoved them into her hands.

Skye's stomach tightened. Listening to Devon's tirade had been enough—now he expected her to read it blow by blow?

She glanced up at him. His hard expression told her she wouldn't be able to talk her way out of this.

She flipped open the folder.

On top was a picture of a man lying on the table that stood in front of her. It was clear he was either unconscious or near to it.

The drugged man was in fantastic shape, muscular and toned to the point he almost appeared sculptured. His feet hung over the end of the table. So he was very tall—maybe as tall as some of the larger basketball players—but not tall enough for people to gasp in amazement and pronounce him nonhuman.

Devon punched the picture with his index finger. "That was the last one before this all started. He called himself Ian."

Devon fairly spit the word as if it was an insult the man had so human a name.

"This abomination wasn't as big as some others, but he was enlightening." Devon turned to the next image.

Ian sat, curled against the bars of the cage, and turned away from the camera.

Skye swallowed her sympathy. Devon would judge her harshly for it.

"See here?" Devon pointed to Ian's back. "They all have these tattoos. They embed the decoration into the skin at birth, and it grows along with them."

Skye examined the picture. The mark shimmered in the light and seemed a language, though not any she had ever seen. "What does it say?"

"It is the names of both his father's and his mother's house. It's his lineage."

"How do they get that shimmer to it? I've never seen anything like it."

"They have . . . ," Devon's mouth twisted, "different technology than we do. The abominations say it doesn't hurt the children when they are tattooed, and it doesn't warp as they grow."

"Interesting." If the situation would have been different, Skye would have chuckled over how hard it was for Devon to admit these people had more advanced technology than humans.

"That barely scratches the surface." Devon turned the page again.

Page after page, picture after picture, until Skye felt the bile again rise in her mouth. So much cutting, so much blood, so much invasion.

Despite her fear of this man, Skye slammed the file closed as Devon was in mid-sentence.

Skye put a hand to her forehead. "I'm sorry. I'm not that sort of doctor. It's too much for me."

"Oh yes, of course, dear. You are a doctor of the mind and spirit. Well, I'm sure you would have found something interesting there too. It might make you feel better to know he lived through all this. It was the virus that killed him."

Skye pushed the chart toward him, not believing his claim. "How could he live through this?"

"I told you, the abominations are resilient. But the virus killed them all, I'm sure of it. And that one took it home to the rest of his nest. Just like a poisoned ant."

He chuckled. "At least I know my work amounted to something. They are gone. All gone."

Devon's eyes lit. "Except one, I still have one here. But we've spent enough time on them today. We need to get to you."

Devon rose and turned to the door leading to the hallway. "Come along now."

Skye's heart thundered. Her hand tightened around the Atlantian's folder of horror.

What did he have planned for her?

She tried to stand, but her legs gave way. She swallowed a sob that tried to escape.

Devon glanced back at her and frowned. "Come along."

Skye put her hands to the desk and shoved herself up. "I ask again, what are you going to do with me?"

Devon's eyebrow rose. "Today? Just get a general idea of your health. Nothing more painful than a blood draw. I promise you."

Did she dare believe him? He could be lying through his teeth, and there was absolutely nothing she could do about it.

Skye followed, surprised the numbness spreading through her body allowed her to do so.

Once again, she was at this evil man's mercy.

23

SOMETHING MORE

Devon glanced back at Skye as they walked down the hallway.

She was a little unsteady but managed on her own.

She was a tough one, strong. Most of the women he tested became puddles of tears by this point, and they hadn't seen the chart of experiments Skye had.

Skye stumbled. A guard reached out and grabbed her arm to steady her. Once she got her feet under her, she pushed him away.

Devon smiled. Good—that was good.

She would need that determination. It would help her through the days ahead.

Devon liked these two women. They reminded him of his nieces, both of whom he believed dead.

His heart grew heavy. Even though his family had turned on him, he still mourned them.

They hadn't understood—that was all—weren't capable of it. How could they? Most people didn't have the intellect to understand the need for the experiments even before the AgFlu.

Had he used his family? Yes, but the years he'd watched them while feeding that information to his higher-ups had been hard on him. He didn't like using people who he cared about.

Devon shot Skye another glance. He also didn't like using people who interested him, and this woman was interesting.

But the testing was more necessary than ever now. It was only by finding those truly immune could he ever hope to create a real cure. Then everyone would realize he was right all along.

DEVON'S MIND drifted to his earlier meeting with Kelsey. She had seemed extraordinary in her own way.

It had been clear she was nervous. Her hands clenched the arms of her chair during their entire conversation.

He'd tried to put her at ease. "Kelsey dear, this is only a conversation. There is no need to be uneasy."

Kelsey quickly nodded. "Uh-ah."

When her hands only gripped the chair tighter, he decided a brief conversation might help her become more comfortable.

"Tell me about your family," Devon said.

Kelsey stared at the tile floor. "They are all gone now."

"From the AgFlu?"

"No. Not all. Someone shot my dad. My mom too, but she had the AgFlu so she would've—you know—anyway."

Devon picked up a pen and jotted down a few notes. It was rather common to find immunity ran through families. Kelsey's father may have been immune.

"I'm sorry for your loss. Any siblings?"

"They all died during the outbreak."

Devon scribbled in his notebook. Kelsey was the only one who inherited the immunity.

Devon put his pen back in his pocket and smiled. "We help people. Do you like to help people?"

Kelsey looked from Devon to the floor and back again. "Of course."

Devon smiled, his heart warming at her willingness. "I'm so happy to hear that. I have a good feeling about you."

The girl gave him a weak smile.

Devon's heart ached a bit. He missed his nieces so much, and this young girl had the same lovely spirit they did.

Sydney later reported Kelsey sobbed on the way back to her room, but Devon gave that little consideration. The girl seemed perfectly happy to him.

Ahead, a door banged closed, bringing Devon to the present.

HE TURNED to Skye and pointed out several rooms along their route. "These recovery rooms are used after procedures. Would you like to see one?"

"No, not really."

Her quick response amused him, and he laughed. "Of course, you would. Then you will see how well we'll take care of our Immune."

He stopped in front of one door and knocked. A nurse answered the door. Devon smiled. She was one of his favorites—always happy with a smile on her face.

Behind her, tucked into bed, a patient slept peacefully.

"How is she doing?" Devon asked the nurse in a low tone.

"Very well." The nurse smiled. "As soon as she wakes up, she'll be able to go back to her room."

Devon turned to Skye. "See. Everyone is happy. Everything is going to plan."

Skye gazed at the woman in the bed. The panic that had hovered in her expression eased as she returned the nurse's smile.

Devon's tension eased. It was critical to gain the trust of a test subject—at least, at first.

But as he eyed Skye, Devon wished for more than her trust. He wanted her respect too.

And maybe, he thought as he rubbed his chin, something more.

THE DARK ROOM

Skye had to admit her afternoon was going as smoothly as Devon had promised, she had to give him that.

Other than being tired from another massive blood draw, she had nothing to complain about. All other tests were non invasive.

There were questions, a lot of questions, but Devon seemed to be happy with the answers. Especially when she told him her father died of a heart attack and not the AgFlu. After that, he'd taken to whistling as he went about his work.

Skye sat on the padded exam table, staring at the recovery rooms across the hall.

How could she get into one?

She'd love to believe that each one held a happy, though drowsy, patient—but somehow, she doubted it. And if that was where she would end up, she wanted to know exactly what to expect.

Skye bided her time. Once Devon and his assistant were engrossed in their work and they had excused the guards for a break, she was ready to make a move.

With another glance at the restrooms lined up beside a set of recovery rooms, she said, "I'm sorry, Devon. I really am, but can I go to the restroom."

She held her breath. Hopefully, he didn't have one here in the lab.

Devon frowned as he looked at his glove-covered hands and the test tubes laid out in front of him. He glanced at the bathroom in the hallway, then at Skye.

She wiggled a little. "I'm sorry."

"Go ahead," he said.

Almost unable to believe Devon would allow it, Skye jumped off the table. "I'll try not to be too long."

She gave him a quick smile that he seemed to appreciate and turned for the door.

As she reached for the knob, he stopped her. "Skye, consider this an exercise in trust. You do not want it to go wrong. Untrustworthy patients don't stay in a nice room or come to this lab. They go to another one."

The assistant winced and added, "He means it."

Skye curled her suddenly icy fingers against her palms and nodded.

After one more glance at Devon's stony stare, she gulped and looked at the floor.

Her show of submission worked, Devon's hard face eased, and he nodded. "Go now."

Skye rushed out of the room, walking directly to the bathroom.

Once in the bathroom, she leaned back against the wall and tapped the block with a fingernail. She had to wait at least a few seconds before venturing out in case they watched her.

After about thirty-seconds, Skye peeked around the door and at the lab. Through the large windows, she could see both Devon and his nameless assistant bent over the countertop.

She glanced to the closest patient's room and back at the lab. She could make it. Maybe.

If they kept their eyes on their work.

After hauling in a large breath, Skye ran to the room. It was only a few footsteps, but it seemed like a football field.

She rapped on the door and ran back to the restroom. If there was a nurse in that room, they'd open the door and see no one.

Heart pounding, she waited, trying to watch both the recovery room door and the lab.

She waited. No one peeked their head into the hallway.

Another glance at the lab assured her that Devon and his assistant were hard at work.

Skye raced back to the patient's room and turned the knob. For a moment, it resisted. Then it opened.

She slipped inside the dim interior and closed the door behind her.

Skye blinked her eyes, waiting for them to adjust to the low.

A click and a rush of air broke the silence.

A groan of pain.

Skye pushed back against the wall, every sound amplified, wishing she could see better.

Once her vision adjusted, she saw a larger room than the one Devon had shown her.

Four patients—two women and two man—lay on metal tables similar to the ones in the Atlantian's lab.

Straps held three in place. The fourth man had no restraints but was intubated.

Another groan.

Skye stepped closer.

One man raised his shaky hand, motioning for her to stop.

A sheet covered him to the waist. Tubes crisscrossed from his arms to the pouches hanging from an IV hook above his head.

His eyes rolled back into his head even as he tried to warn her. His arm dropped back onto the table.

The slow rattle of a chain against steel sent a shudder through Skye.

The woman lying on a table to her right dragged the sheet around her down, exposing red, angry skin. Massive boil-like sores covered the woman. Some of them appeared lanced, but not well. The ooze rolled down her side onto the table.

Skye's stomach turned.

Her gaze darted back to the man and landed on the large red bumps trailing along his side. Soon he would look just like the woman.

The sick woman cleared her throat, and their eyes locked. Skye stepped toward her.

The woman slowly shook her head and rasped out, "Go back. Don't make him angry."

Skye's hand flew to her mouth.

The woman raised her hand, pointing at the door. As she did, the chain circling her wrist dragged link by scraping link across her metal bed. "Go."

Another voice echoed hers. "Go."

A third voice resounded, and it shook Skye into action.

Quaking, tears blinding her vision, Skye blindly yanked open the door and raced down the hall to the bathroom. She threw a blurred glance at the lab window.

The assistant was there. Devon was not.

Skye gasped.

She ran into a stall and pushed her fist against her mouth to help stop the scream building in her.

Was that room *her* fate? *Kelsey's?*

And where was Devon? Did he realize she'd strayed from the restroom? Was he out there looking for her right now?

Skye tore a piece of toilet paper off the roll and mopped her forehead.

Leather shoes tapped across the floor right outside the bathroom door.

She froze.

After gulping in a breath of air, Skye flushed the toilet. Somehow, she needed to make this look good.

After rushing to the sink, she splashed cold water on her face and scrubbed it off with a hand towel. Perhaps now her eyes wouldn't seem blotchier than the rest of her face.

Devon strode in.

Skye's gaze met his in the mirror.

His expression gave nothing away.

Afraid to breathe, Skye willed herself to remain calm. If she wanted to survive, she needed to keep up the act.

She gave a nervous laugh and put a hand to her middle. "So sorry. I'm afraid my stomach is giving me a little trouble."

Devon's narrowed gaze swept the room. "You shouldn't let your nerves upset you like that."

"Yes, of course. I'm sorry. You said I'd be okay, and I was. I'll work on that."

"Make sure you do. Now come along."

Devon scanned the room again, then turned on his heel, expecting Skye to follow him.

She did, dragging her reluctant feet.

What other choice did she have?

145

YOU'LL LOVE IT

Devon led Skye back into the lab. After pulling a wooden straight chair away from the wall, he indicated she should sit in it.

Skye dropped into it with no more emotion than a limp doll. But while her body obeyed, her mind rebelled, looking for any chance of escape.

Devon stood over her for a moment, staring at her, before saying, "Your tests came back within normal ranges. There is no reason we can't begin today."

Numbness washed over her. "Begin?"

"Just something small."

Skye's fingers curled around the edge of her chair.

"Small?" She couldn't keep the tremble from her voice as she thought about the dark room across the hall. She realized she was little more than an echo, but it was all she could manage.

Devon put a hand to her chin and tipped her head back. With a clinical gaze, he looked from one of her eyes to the other. When satisfied, he moved his hand to her hair and stroked it as if she were some sort of pet. "Don't worry, dear. It is only a small contagion—something you would pick up from the grocery store."

Devon's patronizing manner angered her out of her stupor, and she barked at him. "You're injecting me with a disease?"

Devon gave her a dark look, but no answer.

Skye eyed a pile of straps that had appeared on top of the counter during her restroom break. If she wasn't careful, he'd use those on her.

She was trying to earn trust, not lose more of it.

Devon moved around the room, opening and shutting drawers as he got an injection ready.

At one point, his back was turned, and she frantically scanned the lab.

The assistant had left, but the guards were back and standing outside the door. There was no chance she'd get past them.

Skye bit the inside of her lip as Devon walked toward her, needle in hand. She scooted as far back in the chair as it would allow.

"Tell me why you do this?" she quickly asked.

"Test subjects' reactions to various diseases tell me a lot. I'm hoping to find the—well, I'll keep it simple for you— the reason some are resistant to the AgFlu. And if there are common markers between it and other communicable illnesses."

"I see. How does this help your initial goal of finding a cure for the AgFlu? Shouldn't you be focusing on that?"

Devon's face reddened. He stopped and folded his arms. "How dare you question me. A doctor of the mind knows nothing about my area of research." He leaned over her. "Skye. Am I going to have a problem with you?"

She gave a quick shake of her head. "Of course not. I would do anything to help sick people get better. I'm just confused over the reasoning behind this type of experimentation."

Devon took a step back. "It isn't for you to understand."

"How can we continue our sessions if I'm sick?"

Devon rapped on the window and waved the guards in.

Skye closed her eyes. She either allowed this and kept Devon's trust or fought it and lost it.

"Can you at least tell me what this disease is?"

"A variant of the common cold. That is all."

Skye trembled as she pushed the sleeve of her shirt up. "Fine. Go ahead."

Devon laid the needle on her arm, and she instinctively jerked away. One of the guards stepped forward, and Skye forced her body to relax. Anything to avoid being held down again. "Just do it already," she said through clenched teeth.

Devon flashed her an excited look. He enjoyed her discomfort even though he claimed otherwise. "I promise this will only hurt a bit."

"Do you do this with everyone? Keep the hurt to a little bit?"

Devon heaved a regretful sigh. "I try. Some don't cooperate, and they—well, let's just say they have a rougher time of it."

"But if I cooperate?"

"The hurts are minimal, and the conditions good. Just like the patient I showed you."

Skye nodded. The woman in chains had said not to make him angry.

Devon slid the needle into her arm. There was hardly a pinch.

Once done, Devon cooed over her as he bandaged her arm. It reminded her of some of her client's parents. More than one abused their child, then tenderly cared for the very wounds they inflicted.

Even if Devon's abuse was medical, the man was sick—so very sick.

The moment he loosened his grip on her, Skye pulled her arm from his clinging fingers.

Devon turned and threw the needle away in a small garbage can. "Okay, then, dear. We are done for the day."

The words were barely out of his mouth before Skye shot out of her chair and rushed to the door. After pushing through it, she turned left—back to her room.

She couldn't stop a sneaking glance at the recovery room doors.

Perhaps it would have been better not to know what was in store for her and Kelsey.

But now she did, and it was clear they needed to get out of here fast. Who knew what the next injection would be?

Somehow, Skye needed to talk to Kelsey today, but how? She couldn't think of a way until she and the guards stopped at her bedroom door.

Sydney walked into Skye's room and stepped toward the back of the room and everything changed.

The female guard pulled a key out of her pocket and unlocked the large sliding glass door leading to the balcony. "The boss said you did well today and is rewarding you with balcony access for the rest of the day." She pulled in a deep breath. "It's nice out here—you'll love it."

Skye beamed. "I sure will."

Skye waited until they brought dinner. After that—if this night was like the others—there would be no more visitors.

She pushed the recliner chair against the front of her door. If someone tried to come in, it might buy her a moment or two.

She stood there and listened, making sure she hadn't alarmed anyone who may be guarding the hallway.

After making sure she was safe, Skye sprinted through her room, grabbing a few DVDs as she went.

After opening the slider door, she stepped out and surveyed the ground below. No guards.

She studied the balcony next to hers.

Kind of far, but doable—just—maybe.

Skye eyed Kelsey's glass door and raised her arm, letting a DVD fly.

It sailed across the drop between the balconies, tapped against the door, and fell to the tile floor with a small, plastic splat.

When Kelsey didn't appear, Skye tossed another one.

The girl's curtains were thrust to one side and Kelsey's frowning face appeared. Her palms slapped against the glass, and her expression brightened.

Kelsey slid her glass door open wide and stepped out onto her balcony.

2 6

THE PLAN

Kelsey rushed across the patio, eyeing Skye's pale face. "Skye! Are you all right?"

"Are you? Were you injected?"

"No," Kelsey said, wishing she could reach out and hug her troubled friend. "I had an interview—of sorts. Then they stuck me back in my room."

"But how did you get access to the balcony?"

"Oh, that!" Kelsey chuckled. "I had that lock picked five minutes after they locked me in. I've just been trying to figure out how to get to you."

Skye's shoulders sagged in relief. "So, no shots?"

"No shots."

"What about you, Skye?"

The woman looked out to sea and nodded her head. "He injected me with something. He says only the common cold. But how can I know for sure?" She wiped a finger over the corner of her eye. "Crying won't help anything."

"I think you were the one who said we have to allow ourselves to feel." Kelsey frowned. Something else was wrong. The tension seemed to radiate from Skye. "Skye? What happened?"

"I snuck around a little today. I walked into one of their recovery rooms. It was—it was bad." Skye shuddered and wrapped her arms around herself. "So very bad. They were —Well, I'll just say dying will be a blessing for them."

Kelsey's gaze sunk to the tiled floor. "When they take me, I'll try to look around too."

"No." Skye put out a hand. "We need to leave tonight. Now."

"How?"

Skye looked over the railing to the ground below.

Kelsey did the same. The soil was sandy, but rocks were scattered throughout it. And the way down seemed endless. Kelsey felt dizzy and pulled back.

"We have to," Skye explained. "Anything—anything is better than what I saw. I have a plan. We may have to drop the last few feet, but we can make it."

Kelsey set her shoulders. "You know I hate heights, but if it means getting out of here, I'll try."

Skye's fingers whitened as she gripped the rail, studying the lower levels of the building. Windows lined the bottom floor.

"Hopefully, those rooms with windows are empty. If not, we'll be caught right away."

Kelsey nodded. "We must be careful. But the sooner we get out of here, the better. This place resonates evil." The girl tried to shake off some of her tension. When was the last time she'd felt safe?

Cole's Mountain.

Kelsey let the memory envelop her—allowed safety's warm comfort to wrap around her like a thick blanket. Remembering would give her the strength to get from here to the ground far below.

They would make it home. She had made it out of Fenton, and she'd make it out of this place.

"Okay, what's the plan?" Kelsey asked.

"We are going old school," Skye replied. "Strip the sheets off of your bed. Then drag your mattress out here and push it off the balcony."

"Okay." It wasn't an original plan, but it just might work. Especially if she could maneuver the mattress to fall so it would protect her from that large rock below.

The girl ran inside and pulled the covers off her bed. She tipped the mattress onto its side and wrestled it over to the sliding door.

After getting it there, she tipped it up against the wall and took a moment to pull her hair off her sweaty neck. She also threw a change of clothes, some leftover dinner, and a bottle of water into a pillowcase. She threw that out onto the patio and took up the battle with the mattress again.

Once she reached the railing, she closed her eyes and prayed no one on the lower floors would see the thing go sailing by, and that it would land where she needed it.

A sudden rush of wind off the ocean almost blew the mattress out of her grip and back toward the room, but Kelsey managed to hold on to it.

She pushed at the top half, trying to tip it over the railing. The bed fought her, but in the end, its own weight worked against it.

The mattress landed against the rocky sand with a dull smack. Dirt bounced up around the sides and settled back to earth again.

Kelsey sent Skye a triumphant look. It had landed in the perfect spot.

"Okay. Good!" Skye said, "Now let's tie all our sheets together."

Kelsey rushed back into her room.

Skye held out a hand and said, "Wait!"

The girl spun around.

"Kelsey." Skye ran a hand over her face, then looked up, drilling Kelsey with her gaze. "If something happens . . . if we get separated . . . you must go on without me."

Kelsey shook her head.

"Listen," Skye continued, "you have to. You can't fight these people alone, but if you can get back to Dylan—back to the mountain—you can get help. But whatever you do, never, ever come back here. Do you hear me? Even dying out there is better than anything here. Promise me, you will run and never come back."

An icy chill ran up Kelsey's spine. Whatever was going on here had Skye petrified.

But leaving her?

Skye must have seen the doubt on her face because she continued.

"There is nothing but a slow, painful death here. You have to go and get help. Promise."

As much as Kelsey would like to take on the whole place, Skye was right. "I will. I promise."

"Okay." Skye gave a sharp nod. "Go get your escape sheets ready."

Kelsey grabbed the sheets and pulled them, trailing a long tail behind her. It reminded her of the one and only time she'd snuck out of her room before the AgFlu had gotten bad. That had been one floor, and she'd panicked and fallen most of the way—this was three.

At the balcony, she looked down and bit her lip.

She had to do it. She had to.

Kelsey wound one end of the sheet around the railing, tying it in a secure knot. She braced her legs and pulled, testing it. It held without slipping.

As Kelsey waited for Skye to return, she tested the makeshift rope one more time, then threw it over the railing. It unfurled, ending sooner than Kelsey would've liked. It would be a long drop to the mattress. But at least it was something soft to land on.

Kelsey glanced up as Skye rushed through her sliding door, dragging her bedding behind her. She saw Kelsey's packed pillowcase and turned back for her room. "Start down while I get a couple of things."

Kelsey glanced at Skye, the sheet, and the ground. Her stomach seemed as knotted as the bedding. She'd rather wait until Skye came back.

But every minute would count. And there was nothing Skye could do to help her climb.

Kelsey heaved a breath and grabbed the railing, throwing a leg over.

Then froze.

After a few panicked gasps, she hardened her jaw and squared her shoulders. She wiped her sweaty hands on her jeans, grabbed the railing, and swung her other leg over before she could think too much about it.

After a bit of fumbling, she had her arms and legs around the dangling sheets, her hand clenching the material with everything she had.

A sharp burst of wind off the open ocean caused her to sway. She gasped and looked down.

Bad idea.

Skye's gentle voice came from the balcony. "You can do it, Kelsey. Loosen one hand a little, let it slide down, then do the same with the next. You'll be off this in no time."

It took Kelsey a minute to work up the courage to move anything, but once she did she set a pace.

Skye's continual cheering helped. "You're doing great,

Kelsey! This is nothing. You've done harder things, survived worse."

Skye was right. This was nothing.

Kelsey was more than halfway down when she heard a distant knocking.

Her gaze darted to the windows before looking up at a pale Skye leaning over the railing. "Go, Kelsey. Run far!"

"Skye!"

"Do you hear me?"

Kelsey gave a quick nod, tears springing to her eyes.

Skye glanced at her room. "I may be able to get rid of them. Leave a note at—at that pawn shop we saw on our way here, if you can. Saving yourself will save me. Remember that!"

The knock sounded again, louder this time. Skye ran a hand over her hair. "I love you, girl, but you need to go." She gave Kelsey a wobbly smile and disappeared from view.

Kelsey clung to the twisting sheets. She allowed one sob before pushing the fear away.

At the end of the material, she hung for only a second or two before working up the courage to drop to the mattress below.

Her landing was softer than she'd imagined, except for one large stone that pushed its way through the bedding and into her hip.

She rubbed it as she stood and grabbed her pillowcase, then rushed toward the building. As she crouched below the windows, she looked up. Her sheets seemed like flags announcing her escape, but there was no way to get rid of them.

Kelsey stared, willing Skye to swing a leg over the railing and join her, but she didn't.

With an angry hand, she scrubbed at the tears trailing down her cheek.

She had no time for this. She needed to save Skye. And to do that, she had to move. Now.

Kelsey scanned the length of the building. Did they patrol here?

She picked her way across the rocky soil to the corner of the building and peeked around the side.

It was the same parking lot they'd used when Zane had brought them here—the one that led straight up the hill to town.

This time of day, the sun was low, setting over the storm-ravaged town. Soon, she'd have all the cover she needed.

Kelsey studied this end of the domed building. No windows.

They must have kept those for the walls facing the ocean. That was good for her.

Giving the dome one more glance, she raced across the empty parking lot and up the street, heading into town.

Once again, alone.

2 7

THE WAY OUT

K elsey stayed to the side of the parking lot, out of the eye-line of anyone peeking out the lobby's glass doors.

At the top of the small hill, the first town building to Kelsey's left sat a surfboard rental shack. She rushed to it and hunkered down beside its shadowy, weathered wall.

She gasped, her heart tapping faster than the spotted bunny she'd had as a pet when she was younger.

Kelsey put a hand to her chest, willing her heartbeat to quiet. She needed to calm down. No one made good decisions when panicked.

The night was still—quiet and clear. And the ocean waves lapped against the sandy beach behind her. The dark had deepened and without the town's light pollution the stars thrown across the sky shone with extra brilliance, and the moon seemed overly bright. Not the best when one was on the run.

She scanned the street but found nothing alarming.

Could it be this easy? Slide down a rope and walk away.

She squinted back at the massive building, hoping to see Skye behind her.

Kelsey wanted to stay put and wait, her eyes glued to the building until Skye came out. But that was exactly what she'd told Skye she wouldn't do. She needed to go.

Kelsey sighed and pushed a few stray strands of her long, dark hair back into her ponytail.

She needed to go now.

They could be knocking on her door right now if they hadn't already. Every minute counted.

Kelsey scurried to the shadow of the next building and the next until she came to the center of town. Ahead, the moon lit the pawnshop sign.

At the next crossroads, she stopped.

Better to find the escape route first, then leave a note for Skye.

Kelsey peered down the street to the right, looking for a vehicle but finding few that seemed acceptable.

The two cars directly in front of her had dead bodies in them. She would only use those if she had no other choice. Even the thought of touching those things gave her the chills.

Further ahead, three other vehicles were smashed together.

Kelsey turned left, staying in the shadows and racing to the first crossroad. On the corner was a parking lot with a few acceptable vehicles. A large black truck in the middle caught her eye.

Not black. Kelsey took a step closer. Midnight blue.

Jesse had told her trucks were the best, so that's the one she'd try.

She didn't know a lot about pickups, but this one was huge. And big seemed safer right now.

Kelsey moved into the open, staying alert. Step by cautious step, she moved toward the vehicle.

After reaching the driver's side, she pulled on the handle. When it refused to budge, she pulled a face and crouched, running to the passenger's side. It was also locked.

Perhaps the owner was like Wade and never completely closed the rear cab window.

Kelsey grabbed the tailgate and dragged herself up and over into the truck's metal bed as quietly as possible.

From there, she could see the back cab window was open an inch or so.

She swallowed her excitement and pushed it open. Then wiggled herself over the toolbox spanning the width of the truck and made her way into the cab.

Kelsey plopped into the seat. The cab was massive—especially for one smallish teenage girl.

She pulled down both visors, checked the glove box, and felt under the seat, but there were no keys. Hot wiring a truck this new wasn't an option.

Kelsey pushed the door open and hopped to the ground. She slid under the truck and ran her hands along every bump, nook, and cranny of the bottom. When she found nothing, she wiggled her way out.

There had to be a key somewhere. There just had to be.

Kelsey hauled herself back into the bed of the truck and studied everything. A tool pouch sat in the back corner.

No, probably not. There were too many holes.

She eyed the big metal toolbox attached to the vehicle and smiled.

After running her hands along the bottom outside edge with no success, she reached further—until her arm and shoulder disappeared under the thing.

Kelsey practically exploded with relief when she found what she was looking for—a little magnetic case.

The key was inside.

She jumped over the side of the truck, her tennis shoes tapping against the pavement.

Key in hand, Kelsey turned to the driver's door.

A rattle echoed from mid-town.

Kelsey froze.

She scanned the shadowy buildings across from where she stood.

If only she could see better.

Her excitement had gotten the better of her. There were evil people on her tail. And there were still Sick and Infected out here.

She gripped the key, then slid it deep into her jean's pocket.

Now she had a good vehicle and a plan.

But maybe not the greatest plan. After all, it was basically get the heck out of here and head north to Cole's Mountain.

But at least she had one.

She'd leave Skye a note. Then she would burn rubber out of this town if she had to.

Kelsey rushed back to the alleyway, peeked around the corner, and ran up to the pawn shop door.

A locked steel gate covered it.

"Are you kidding me?" Kelsey murmured. She threw a glance toward midtown.

What should she do? This is where Skye would look.

Kelsey reached through the grate and turned the knob of the main door. Without a sound, it swung part-way open.

Okay, so she just needed to get through the steel gate.

Kelsey stared at the store's floor.

Inside the threshold lay a piece of paper with a smiley

face and a key sitting on it. She grabbed it and pushed it into the grate's lock and softly laughed as the key smoothly turned in the lock.

With care, Kelsey pushed the well-oiled gate to one side. She stepped into the almost pitch-dark store and stopped, trying to listen to the surrounding darkness.

No sound. No rustle, no squeak of a shoe, no breathing.

The store felt empty. It smelled empty too—kind of dusty, but with a bit of dampness mixed in.

Kelsey took another step and shut the door behind her.

On the counter, a tiny lamp made a small circle of light. Beside it, a white piece of paper seemed to glow.

Kelsey tensed. Was this some kind of trick?

But it was so quiet.

She studied the light. It looked solar-powered and positioned so the sunshine would recharge it each day.

As quietly as possible, she made her way to the counter.

In bold, somewhat messy handwriting, the note reassured her that her mountain wasn't the only place with kind people.

It simply said, "Take whatever you need, dude, no probs. Me and mine are chillin' with friends. Hope you get where you need to go."

A small chuckle escaped Kelsey. No one could fake this.

She looked around the store. It was a treasure trove if one disregarded all the ocean toys, including the most extensive collection of boogie boards Kelsey had ever seen.

She turned to the other side of the store where camping and a bit of hunting equipment lined the shelves. If everything went well, she'd be home sometime tomorrow morning. If not, she needed to be prepared.

Kelsey reached under the front counter and grabbed a couple of large shopping bags.

In one, she threw in a selection of MRIs and protein

bars. A lightweight blanket, fire starters, lighters, an ax, a pan, and a few bottles of water were next.

Kelsey stuck two long knives through her belt.

She walked back to the front counter and dug around. With a smile, she pulled out a taser.

Kelsey carried her bags to the door and scanned the store one more time. There was so much more she'd like to bring, but she had time to make one trip to the truck.

Kelsey set her bags down and pulled a piece of paper out of the printer behind the counter and laid it beside the note she'd found.

On it, she wrote her note for Skye, scribbling that she'd made it this far and was fine. She kept it short and unemotional, trying not to give too much away. Neither she nor Skye had time for anything other than the business of escaping.

She ended the note by saying she would see Skye again in almost heaven. Kelsey almost crossed it out, thinking it told too much, but decided not many would realize she meant home—West Virginia.

After, she returned everything to the way she'd found it, including the little smiley paper and the key.

Outside, the quiet street was clear as far as she could see.

Still, she kept to the shadows for as long as possible as she rushed through the ally and turned into the parking lot.

Moonlight gleamed along the side of the truck. It shone like a beacon crying, "Freedom!"

With all her heart, she wanted to run for it. Instead, she stopped and scanned the area.

Slow and steady. That's what Dylan reminded them when they scouted. It was the same here.

Once Kelsey deemed it safe. She crouched and rushed for the truck, her shoes lightly tapping over the concrete.

Her heart thumping, she opened the truck door and threw her stuffed bags into the far seat.

One foot on the driver's side step, she paused.

Something was not right. Someone was out there.

Gravel crunched beneath a boot.

A glass bottle clattered across the pavement.

Kelsey pulled in a sharp breath and clenched the inside handle of the door as the sounds echoed toward her.

The bottle rolled and rolled until ended with a quick pop—like it had burst into a thousand splinters.

They wanted her to know they were here.

Kelsey ignored the icy finger of fear trailing down her spine and jumped into the driver's seat.

She hit the auto-lock and slammed the key into the ignition, turning it.

The truck roared to life. She threw it into gear and stomped on the gas.

The pickup jerked forward.

Kelsey clung to the large steering wheel as she got the vehicle under control, and turned toward the main road.

Behind her, a man shouted.

A bullet buzzed past her window, taking a chunk out of the side mirror.

Kelsey gasped and ducked, cursing the evil people who chased her.

She glanced at the cracked mirror. Three men ran after her, aiming their guns at the truck.

Gripping the steering wheel, she hit the gas and raced through town.

She didn't slow until the men and their guns were far behind her.

28

THE CHASE

K elsey scoured the roadside for highway signs. The sooner she made it to an Interstate, the sooner she would feel safe.

The night's dim light didn't help, and she hesitated to turn on her headlights. They would make her instantly visible.

Her knuckles whitened as she clenched the steering wheel, leaning forward to see better.

Everything had her twitching—the wind moving the trees, a piece of trash blowing across the street.

There would be more of Devon's people out here—she'd be a fool to think otherwise.

When the highway came into view, Kelsey sagged with relief.

Just a little longer and she'd be home-free.

As she turned onto the interstate ramp, she gasped when what seemed like an empty car along the side of the road sprang to life.

They'd waited for her.

Kelsey stomped on the gas. Maybe she could outrun them.

It seemed to work at first, then the car caught up and pulled alongside her.

Kelsey frowned and glanced at it.

A man in the passenger's side pointed a gun at her. He waved her to the edge of the road.

Kelsey's scowl deepened. Absolutely not!

She pushed the gas pedal. The truck surged ahead.

Kelsey snorted. That's what they get for chasing someone in an old man's car.

Unused to maneuvering a vehicle at such high speeds, Kelsey turned her attention to her driving. She was ahead, but not by much.

She clamped her jaw, determined to win this race.

But now what? She couldn't keep this up all the way home.

An exit sign appeared ahead. She needed to get off this road. Here she was, an obvious target with nowhere to hide.

Kelsey continued on the highway and veered into the exit lane at the last minute.

The truck's tires screeched, and the steering wheel rebelled, but the girl kept it in line.

The men blew past the exit before slamming on their brakes, and the passenger stuck his gun out the window and took a couple of potshots at her.

Kelsey ducked, but neither bullet hit the truck.

At a traffic light that no longer glowed, Kelsey looked to her left and right. Buildings to the right—nothing but trees to the left. With no time to think, she chose right and prayed it was the correct one.

Maybe—just maybe—there was a friendly family out there who would help her. Not everyone was a criminal.

Kelsey grimaced. Doctor Evil had probably cleared out

any decent people from these areas long ago. She couldn't count on any help. She was on her own and right back that way she had started this Agflu disaster—scared and alone.

As she drove down the main road, she heard the other car racing down the ramp, trying to catch up.

Kelsey took the first road to her right and drove faster, wanting to get as far down this street as possible before they crossed it. They would be here any minute.

With a groan of indecision, she pulled up to a small snarl of traffic and stopped the pickup so that its front end tipped into a small ditch running alongside the road.

She turned the key and let the car die. Kelsey grabbed the taser out of the shopping bag and sunk deep into the seat.

She put a hand to her chest and willed her erratic breathing to slow. She jumped at every ping the pickup made as it cooled down.

Silence. She needed absolute silence—nothing to give her away. Kelsey already felt too vulnerable sitting here in the open.

She squeezed her eyes shut and listened.

Nothing. Where were they?

Perhaps she should leave the truck. But it was the only safety she had. With it, she was able to race out of here. Her own two feet were not nearly as fast.

She looked at the two paper shopping bags. Right now, everything she had in this world was in this truck.

She'd stay with the truck.

Another minute ticked by with no sighting of the two men. Perhaps they had turned left at the light—hadn't even come this way.

If that was the case, she should use this time to drive further away—not sit here doing nothing.

Kelsey turned in the driver's seat until she was able to peek over the back of the seat.

The road was empty.

Go—or don't go?

She needed a map to guide her down these back roads. She wouldn't be safe on the highway until she was further from these guys.

Kelsey swept her hand through the pockets on the doors, under the seat, and several other nooks and crannies.

Once she'd double-checked the area, she dared to open the glove box. The small light seemed blinding. She quickly shifted through the papers, but still nothing.

Kelsey glanced at the cars.

She didn't want to, but she'd have to check the other vehicles.

Once again, she peered over the seat, and finding no one, reached up and clicked off the dome light.

After drawing the keys from the ignition, she held her breath as she opened the truck's driver side door.

She walked with a light step over the crunchy gravel road to the first car. A blue sedan with the doors shut tight.

Kelsey's foot pushed something deeper into the gravel. She bent and picked it up.

A pen flashlight. She looked around before clicking it on and off. It still worked.

She peered inside the blue car and saw a body. She moved on to the other two vehicles.

One was empty.

Kelsey dragged the door open, hoping the dome light wouldn't come on. It didn't. She searched the entire car, but there was nothing.

Kelsey stared at the two cars with bodies in them and shuddered. But she had to do what needed done.

The yellow car had a GPS on the dash. They probably didn't have a map.

Kelsey turned to the blue car and sighed. "It's you and me, then," she murmured.

She drew in a deep breath before throwing open the door. The stink wafted over her, and she almost choked.

She might as well get used to it—the smell would cling to her for hours.

As quickly as possible, Kelsey searched the car. But again, nothing.

As she stood to close the door, the pop of gravel sounded—as if it were caught between the road and a tire.

She froze.

There was movement at the end of the road.

Kelsey snapped off the penlight and crouched behind the blue car, peeking around its end.

The car drove slow—it was almost silent as it went through the intersection.

The evil men's car stopped, and the passenger poked something out the window.

Although the moon gleamed on the object, Kelsey wasn't able to make it out. Until the bright sweep of a light beam barely missed her.

A spotlight—like the kind people used for deer hunting.

Her heart jumped, and she whipped backward, making herself as small as possible against the wheel of the car.

Would they see the truck—recognize it?

Her gaze darted around the area—her mind jumping from one solution to another until she settled for the best she could do.

Plastic garbage cans sat at the end of each driveway. She army-crawled to the closest drive where a set of bins had tipped over. With care, she peeked into each one. They were almost empty.

Using the truck as a shield, she slid the plastic cans into its bed, making sure they would see them if the light landed on the pickup.

Kelsey walked back and pawed through the larger items that littered the ground. She pulled at some material that turned out to be a large tablecloth.

She dropped it over the tailgate.

Hopefully, that would be enough to make it look like an unfamiliar vehicle.

After having done all she was able to do, Kelsey crouch behind one of the large tires of her truck and watched as the spotlight drew closer.

Her stomach knotted tighter.

The bright beam swept over the yellow car—then the blue one—lingering on each one.

Kelsey held her breath. Had she left anything that would tell them she was right here in front of them?

The light moved, gleaming on the edge of the truck's silver bumper, inches from her.

Her eyes followed it, refusing to budge as it brightened the underside of the vehicle.

She pulled her legs in, putting her arms around them.

Long shadows of the tires appeared on the road. Would the one she hid behind look different from the rest?

Kelsey waited for a shout or the banging of car doors. If she heard that, she'd have to leave everything and run—run for all she was worth.

Kelsey dug the toe of her shoe into the gravel and put her hand to the ground.

The over-bright beam lingered on the truck, then moved on, across the grass and over the houses before it cut off.

Kelsey almost laughed in relief and slapped her hand over her mouth.

She waited until their car moved on before jumping into the truck.

They drove further down the road and turn the spotlight on again.

Her hands curled around the steering wheel. She was eager to leave.

Just a little longer. Slow and steady.

Once they were out of range, Kelsey tossed the garbage cans out of the back of the pickup but kept the tablecloth. It might be of some use.

After climbing back into the truck, she scanned the houses alongside the road. One of them was bound to have a map.

She shook her head as she glanced at the road behind her. This wasn't the place to linger and find out. She'd have to take her chances.

She knew the way north. That would have to do for now.

29

HER TROUBLE

K elsey held her breath as she turned the key. The engine rumbled, then settled into a quiet purr.

Hopefully, the men hadn't heard that.

With a swift glance down the street, she backed the truck out of the ditch and continued up the back road as far as she was able.

When the gravel road dead-ended into a paved street, she turned left. It would take her further away from the Interstate, but that seemed a good thing for now. This larger road may have some amenities. The fuel gauge pointed nearer to empty than she'd like, and a gas station would be a good place to look for a map.

KELSEY DROVE for about fifteen minutes before she hit pay dirt—a gas station.

She scanned the building for any movement.

The pumps lit up the night like a beacon, even though no other lights in the place were on. Someone must take care of the station.

Kelsey passed the building and stopped beside some tall bushes. From here, she could spy on the place.

After about ten minutes with no noise and movement, she took a chance.

After turning the pickup around, she pulled it in beside a gas pump.

Kelsey watched the station's door--sure some irate owner would bust through it at any time.

She yanked the nozzle off of the machine, put it in the truck, and squeezed the handle. Gas flowed into the truck just as if the world hadn't changed.

But it had changed, and this was weird.

After setting the hose to auto, she reached into the back seat and pulled out the taser.

She gripped it with both hands as she stood there waiting for the truck to fill up.

Even before, filling a vehicle at an empty station in the dead of night would've been eerie. Now it was downright terrifying.

Once the tank was full, Kelsey debated her map situation.

She scanned the area. Still no one. Kelsey tried to make out the dim front room of the station but couldn't.

Torn over what to do, Kelsey knew she needed that map. She couldn't let fear stop her or she could end up driving in circles.

There wasn't enough time or fuel to get lost.

Kelsey raced to the front of the small mom-and-pop style store and peeked through the windows.

Her gaze met nothing but blackness.

After glancing at the truck—that now seemed so far away—she went to the commercial glass door and yanked on the handle, taser ready.

Locked.

She almost cried. With one more glance toward the truck and the safety it offered, Kelsey squared her shoulders and ran to the back of the building.

After rounding the corner, she spied a back door.

Kelsey crept toward it as she looked over the back yard. Once she determined it safe, she twisted the doorknob and smiled when the door opened.

The sickly-sweet smell of death rolled over her.

Kelsey's grin disappears as she took a step back and drew her shirt over her nose.

The moonlight over her shoulder revealed a family laid out on the concrete floor. A huge clear plastic sheet covered them. Kelsey's gaze lingered on the flowers, button-down shirts, and pink bows, tears coming to her eyes.

What this world had come to. Had they chosen this themselves, or had someone done this to them?

Stories like this would be lost forever.

Kelsey moved past the decaying family, murmuring apologies and avoiding a second look. The children reminded her too much of her own lost siblings.

She headed straight to the front of the store and found a rack of maps right away. She pulled out one for North and South Carolina as well as Virginia and West Virginia.

Better to be over-prepared.

Beside the map stand stood a cooler with a large vinyl sticker announcing Mountain Dew stuck to the front of it.

Kelsey's mouth watered. How long had it been since she'd had her favorite pop?

Even warm, it would be delicious and help her stay awake on the way home. She opened the cooler door and pulled out every bottle.

Kelsey peeked out the store window at her pickup and cleared the area before unlocking the front door and running for the vehicle. She hopped in and quickly locked the doors.

Kelsey leaned back in the seat and breathed out a sigh of relief before unfolding the South Carolina map. She found her general area but would be sure once she got to a named town. For now, she'd continue north.

Kelsey downed a bottle of Mountain Dew along with two protein bars, both for the substance and caffeine. It was going to be a long night.

She laid the map on the seat beside her and fired up the truck.

It was time to go home.

Three hours later, she'd found her place on the map and slowly edged her way toward the interstate. But Mountain Dew or no—Kelsey couldn't keep her eyes open.

It'd been twenty-four hours since she'd gotten any actual sleep and now, in the early morning, it had caught up with her.

As she uttered yet another yawn, she saw a grassy field with a large, lonely barn. She moved off the Interstate and bumped over the rough terrain until she was on the opposite side of the building.

After locking up, she covered herself, head to toe, with the blanket from the pawnshop. On top of that, she put the tablecloth. Hopefully, if someone wandered past, they wouldn't even see her.

She hugged her taser to herself and drifted off.

When Kelsey woke, the sun perched high in the sky, and the truck cab was warming up. She peeked out of the front window and saw little besides long grass waving in the breeze.

As Kelsey studied the map, she had another protein bar and Mountain Dew. She gave a loud, rough burp and giggled before turning the truck toward the highway.

She settled in for what she figured would be a few hours' drive and smiled as she imagined driving up her mountain.

What she hadn't imagined was the company on the Interstate. It shocked her at first.

Vehicles were admittedly rare, but she'd expected none. Several cars passed her going south. She slowed the first time, her hands clenched on the wheel and ready to swerve if need be. But they just drove on by.

By the time Kelsey came up behind a blue SUV going north, it seemed normal. The kids in the back waved at her, and she waved back. Even the dad gave her a nod and smile when he realized she wasn't a threat.

There were still good people, not everyone was like Doctor Evil.

A couple of hours later, Kelsey was digging around for a bottle of water when she spotted a small caravan of vehicles in the distance traveling opposite of her.

A single car here and there was one thing—but this many together? It seemed like trouble.

She scoured the road for an exit but realized she'd just passed it about a mile back.

Perhaps whoever it was would leave her alone.

Kelsey shook her head. She couldn't take that chance. She was alone—with no one at her back.

She shuddered. Alone was the one thing she'd never wanted to be again. Fenton had been enough.

Kelsey stayed in the furthest right Northbound lane and readied herself to take the truck off-road if need be.

As the caravan of vans and trucks got closer, her breathing quickened. Her heart thumped its fear loud enough Kelsey swore she heard it.

"It'll be okay," she murmured to herself. "They'll continue south—I'll continue north. No problem."

She stared at the line of vehicles as they got closer.

"White van, blue van, blue truck, black truck. Trouble and more trouble."

As if a childhood rhyme, she repeated to herself, "White van, blue van, blue truck, black truck."

Kelsey squinted, trying to see the vehicles better as they sped toward her.

"White van, blue van, blue truck, black truck."

Something about them . . .

They were so close now that they would soon be past her.

And that was just what she wanted.

Didn't she? She held her breath.

The white van blew by her.

She eyed the driver of the blue van.

Kelsey's pent-up air burst out in a shocked huff.

She stomped the breaks and yanked the wheel to the left.

The truck protested, squealing as it left black marks and smoke behind her.

Bumping across the grassy median, she blared the horn over and over.

She'd been right.

They were trouble, but they were *her* trouble.

30

THE QUESTION

Dylan shifted in his seat and winced. When he moved just right, the dang wound still sent a red-hot poker through him.

He sighed. Who was he kidding? Not sometimes, every time he moved. But it was nothing next to the anguish he had over Skye's loss.

Every cell in his being called out for her. The emptiness was almost more than he could bear.

What if he never found her? What if he lived the rest of his life without his darlin'?

Dylan hung his head. He couldn't think like this—it was driving him crazy. He'd find her and take her home. That was all there was to it.

He raised his hand and bit at his nail—his nervous habit kicking in again. At least, he and Jesse had easily caught up with Wade's group. He had to be thankful for that.

But the traveling was hard. Dylan wanted to make plans, feel like he was doing something, anything. But there were no plans to make until he learned the layout of

THE RESCUE: SANCTUARY'S AGGRESSION 5

the place. All he was able to do was watch the trees rush by.

Dylan huffed out a sigh and ran a hand through his shaggy hair.

Jessie, who sat between the two brothers, patted Dylan's shoulder and sighed himself. "It'll be okay, Dad."

Dylan had to smile at the boy as his heart warmed at the boy's new name for him.

Dad.

Dylan had never been sure he'd ever be a father, but he and Jesse had clicked on a deep level. Much of their upbringing was the same, and they understood one another. Dylan wanted to be a strong support for Jesse as he grew—to imitate his own real father and not the stepfather who had been more of a threat than anything else.

"We'll get them back," Jesse said, "I know we will."

Dylan gave him a tight smile and nodded.

Jesse wasn't as confident as he pretended. His round, scared eyes reminded Dylan that he was a kid caught in a world no one understood yet.

Dylan put an arm around his son and squeezed his shoulders. "Yep, we will. We'll be there in no time."

"We'll get 'em both," Jesse said, shooting an uncertain glance at Dylan.

"Of course, we will. Everyone's important, Jesse. We don't leave anyone behind."

Jesse nodded, and his body relaxed some. The boy was sweet on Kelsey, even though she was a couple of years older than him.

Dylan smiled. But someday, in a decade or so, who knew?

When they passed the sign welcoming them to South Carolina, Dylan and Wade glanced at each other.

"Here we are," Wade said.

"I wish we knew how far down the coast they were."

"The road may tell us. It has so far."

Dylan grunted his agreement.

The road had been remarkably clear of debris as they traveled south. Someone had shoved all the empty cars to the side of the road, and from any exits that were apparently used regularly. They had passed a few cars zipping north or south as they'd driven the highway. The men had stared at each one as they went by.

Dylan drummed his fingers against the door. "Still, I wish we had the name of the town to go on."

"You got that right, brother. Anything more than what that lousy miscreant gave would have been nice."

"Look." Jesse pointed to a dark-blue pickup coming up the road on the other side of the median.

Wade's eyes narrowed.

Dylan scanned the vehicle, though little could be seen this far away. It would most likely sail past, its passengers praying for safe passage. But just in case, they kept their eyes glued to it.

The truck seemed to be flying by until it was directly across from them.

Tires squealed as the driver yanked the wheel toward the Southbound lane, then barreled through the grassy strip separating the lanes. The driver blared the horn over and over.

"What the—," Wade said as he pushed back in his seat, reaching for his rifle.

Dylan whipped his head from the crazy vehicle to the scene around them. Was this an ambush?

"It's Kelsey!" Jesse pushed himself to the edge of his seat, pointing.

Wade slammed the breaks so hard they squealed.

Dylan and Jesse grabbed the seat to avoid hitting the dashboard.

The caravan behind them followed suit. Blue smoke and the smell of burnt rubber wafted over the area.

Kelsey's big, blue truck jerked to a stop in the middle of the grass. Her door flew open, and she jumped out.

The girl raced up the small incline, tripping twice as she came. Tears streamed down her face as she shouted for them.

"I'm here! I'm here!"

Wade and Dylan leaped from their seats with Jesse close behind, closing the gap between themselves and the girl. Kelsey wrapped her arms around all of them, clenching them as if she'd never let go. "I found you!"

Dylan wrapped an arm around her. The little thing trembled so hard she could hardly stand. He looked her over, relieved to find she didn't look hurt.

He hoped for news of Skye, but what the girl gasped out was almost incomprehensible. The only thing he understood was her plea, "Please, please don't leave me alone."

"It's okay, Kelsey. We're here. No one will hurt you now," Jesse assured her.

Kelsey nodded and unwrapped herself enough to pull part of her shirt to her face, wiping it dry.

New tears immediately replaced the old, so she took a few slow breaths, hiccuped, and tried to talk, but her tongue wasn't in sync with her mind. Still, Dylan caught some words.

"Man . . . evil . . . Skye . . . experiment . . . help."

Dylan swallowed and crouched in front of Kelsey. He stared at her, asking the question he'd hoped he'd never have to.

"Kelsey, is Skye still alive?" His voice wavered with emotion.

Kelsey nodded over and over.

Dylan sagged with relief.

"Skye is alive. She needs us," Kelsey said with a rush. "She needs us now!"

Dylan ran for the truck.

The rest followed and when Kelsey tripped once again. Jesse helped her up. "Is it okay if I help you?" he asked her.

"Please. I can't seem to walk straight."

Dylan pointed to two men and barked out, "You two. Take Kelsey's truck and follow along. She's in no shape to drive right now."

Dylan and Wade returned to the front seat as Kelsey and Jesse hopped in the back.

"How far away are we, Kelsey?" Dylan asked.

"Not all that far. A few hours."

"Can you show us a good place to stop before we get into their territory?"

"I can do that."

"You need to tell me everything."

"Yes."

Dylan stuck his hand out the window and banged on the side of the truck, then pointed ahead.

He set his jaw and said, "Let's go get her, boys."

31

CHOICES

Skye watched Kelsey as she shimmied down the sheets. It broke her heart to leave the girl. Kelsey was like a daughter to her, and who knew when, or if, they would ever see each other again.

Her heart dropped to her stomach as another knock sounded.

After one last glimpse of the girl, Skye choked back a sob and grabbed up some of the bedding she had just dragged out onto the balcony.

Skye flew back into her room and threw the bedspread over the bed, making sure no one would be able to tell the sheets were missing.

The knock came again, more insistent this time.

"Coming!" Skye yelled as she'd mussed her hair, hoping they would assume she was sleeping.

As quietly as possible, Skye dragged the chair she'd leaned against the door back away from it. She cleared her throat twice as if she'd been sleeping as she turned the doorknob.

Sydney and a male guard stood outside the door. The

male guard looked irritated. "Just getting ready to bust this door down."

Sydney was polite. "Sorry, seems I caught you at a nap."

"Yes, I was." Skye rubbed at her eyes.

"The Doc needs you back at the lab."

Her heart pounded. What did Devon want now? "Mind if I go to the restroom before . . . "

The other guard narrowed his eyes and scanned the room.

Skye glanced over her shoulder, realizing with a start the curtains were open enough to show the bedsheets blowing on the balcony floor.

If either of the guards moved even a few inches closer to her, they would spot it too.

Skye waved a hand. "You know what? I'm fine. Let's go visit Dr. Shade. The sooner I'm there, the sooner I'm can get back to sleep, right?" She smiled at the guards, hoping to ease any suspicions.

"Okay, then," Sydney said, motioning Skye out in front of her.

Skye breathed a sigh of relief when both guards followed behind her. She dropped back to walk beside Sydney. "I thought I was done for the day."

"Yeah. Well, Doc got all excited about something and wanted another blood test."

The butterflies in Skye's stomach slowed down. A blood draw was easy enough. She'd rather fluids be going out than going in. Skye scratched at the spot of the injection Devon had given her earlier. She peeked under the bandage. It was red and blistery.

Sydney noticed. "You doing all right?"

"Yes. This is just a little weird." Skye pulled the Band-Aid open for the woman to look at it.

Sydney winced, then immediately smoothed her expression. "I'm sorry that's happening."

"Sydney?" Skye's voice quivered. Did that mean she would soon be like those others?

"Don't worry. You'll be fine."

But Sydney didn't sound convincing.

When they arrived at the lab, Devon sat on a stool, hunched over a large microscope. He took his time before addressing them.

After a couple of minutes, Devon swiveled toward them. "Skye. We completed the DNA portion of your blood test. Both you and Kelsey had some fascinating results, but I want to rerun it just to be certain. If it comes back the same, well, let's just say you are a fragment more than you ever dreamed you were."

"And that's a good thing?"

He scowled. "It turns everything I believed upside-down. It may, however, be why you've survived. And as I have gotten this result before, I need to face that it is true."

Skye eyed Devon. He'd said Kelsey's test also showed these results. Had he sent someone to her room too?

Devon walked to Skye and put a hand on each of her arms, staring at her.

When Skye couldn't take it anymore, she stared back. "I don't know what you want me to do here, Devon."

"I'm just searching, determining if I can see any differences." He barked out a laugh.

Had whatever he found finally broke him? And what was he going on about? Would his ramblings lead to more of the injections that had ignited the fiery blisters on her skin?

Unsure if she should encourage or discourage him, Skye changed the subject. "The injection site from whatever you gave me is hurting."

Devon made a face. "Yes, it will do that. I'll give you something to help it before you leave. And I think we'll put any more injections on hold for a couple of days."

So encourage it and change the subject back. Skye nodded and tipped her head toward the microscope. "This seems important."

Devon gave a wild chuckle as he readied the needle. "It is. Very important."

Skye sat and waited patiently for Devon to take her blood. He took more than the first time, leaving her light-headed.

She hung her head until, out of the corner of her eye, she saw movement in the hallway.

A nurse pushed a long metal table covered with a sheet out of the room she had snuck into—the outline of a body under the white material.

Which one of those poor victims was that?

"Don't look at that, Skye," Devon said. "No sense in dwelling on the failures."

Failures? Skye scanned Devon. Was that is all he saw?

Devon misinterpreted her gaze and gave her a gentle smile. "We are done for today, Skye. You go back to your room and get some sleep. We'll talk some more tomorrow."

Skye glanced at the receding body. Each day was precious in this place. She scratched her arm. If the testing started back up, how many more would she have left?

As Sydney took her back to her room, Skye watched for any panicked guards searching for Kelsey, but there were none.

It seemed Devon hadn't called for Kelsey this evening—at least, not yet.

Skye had said goodnight to Sydney and sagged against the door in relief. She walked to the balcony and scanned the grounds. When there was no one, she looked out into the distant darkness.

Kelsey had made it! But where was she now? Still in town, or further out?

Skye gathered up the bedsheets scattered across the terrace, ready to throw them over the edge. Should she follow her?

If she did, it might further endanger Kelsey.

Skye closed her eyes and lowered her head, letting the gentle sound of the ocean waves soothe her as she pondered this out.

She ached to leave.

If she left, without a doubt, Devon would scour the countryside for them especially after his excitement over the latest test.

If she stayed, he might be content enough to let the girl go.

She had to give Kelsey the best chance she could.

Only by doing that would Dylan have a chance of finding her.

With a heavy heart, Skye walked back into her room and shut the sliding door.

She remade the bed and laid down, imagining Dylan's strong arms—supporting her, loving her as only he could do.

Tears rolled, unchecked, over her cheeks.

Had he beaten the infection?

Maybe they weren't supposed to be together now, but later—in a better place.

Skye let her mind wander over that possibility and soothe her.

But a part of her rebelled. She wasn't ready to leave this earth yet. And somehow, she knew Dylan wasn't either.

Things needed done. This evil place needed erased

from the face of the earth before either of them would go easy to their rest.

Eventually, her troubled mind released its grip. She hugged her pillow to herself as she drifted to sleep, trying to ignore the empty spot near her heart that only Dylan could fill.

IT WAS STILL DARK when Skye woke with a start.

Someone stood over her—a gun pointed at her head.

WORLDS COLLIDE

S kye gasped, pulling in enough air for a scream. The young blonde woman slapped a hand over Skye's mouth.

"No!" she hissed. "I will not hurt you."

Skye glanced from the slim, blonde woman to the weapon and back again. "You have a gun."

The young woman tipped the weapon up and looked at it. "Yeah, well, it's not a killing gun. It's like a stun gun. You'd just be out for a while."

Skye frowned as the gun moved back to point at her forehead. It didn't look like any stun gun she'd seen before. This one looked more like the real thing—though the dark blue color and the longer, thinner barrel was a bit off.

The young woman narrowed her eyes. "So are we good here? It makes me sick to point this thing at you. It's not something I'd normally do."

"Then why are you?"

The blonde waved her arm toward the door. "It's just this place—it's never what it seems to be."

The statement seemed to sadden her, and her beautiful features turned downward.

Ok. So she wasn't happy with what this place did either.

Skye nodded. "I know what you mean—and yes, we're good."

The girl dragged the office chair over to the bed and plopped down on it as Skye sat up.

When Skye threw her legs over the side of the bed, the woman brought the gun up again. She waved at Skye to move her legs back up. "I'm sorry. I can't really trust you yet."

Skye quickly complied.

Yet. So, there may be a chance this young woman would help her.

"Who are you?" the blonde asked. "And why are you here?"

"My name is Skye Jackson, and I'm from the West Virginia hills. They brought me here against my will."

The blonde woman brought a hand to her forehead.

Skye studied her. Though smaller than Skye, she had the advantage of a weapon.

Besides, if she had skulked in here like this, she certainly wasn't a friend of the infamous doctor.

The enemy of her enemy was Skye's friend.

"Can I ask your name?" Skye asked.

"Oh, sorry. Of course. Sonora. Sonora . . . Orca."

"Orca? That's an unusual name."

"Well, I'm from the Orca Clan now." Sonora waved her hand and murmured, "Not that you'd understand any of that."

She was right. Skye didn't understand. Was it native? Local?

"What are you doing here?" Skye asked.

Sonora threw her arm out. "I came up here for a stupid

necklace, a few family things we left behind when we went
—Well, when we left."

Sonora ran a hand through her hair. "This isn't
supposed to be happening! Ian is going to be so mad. There
is a cure! What happened to the cure?"

"You mean the one Doctor Shade is working on?"

Sonora's mouth dropped, and she gaped at Skye.
"Devon? Uncle Devon is free?"

Skye startled. This young woman was related to that
monster? "He's here, in charge of whatever this is."

"I'm not talking about his—" Sonora rapidly swept her
hand through the air. "—evil nonsense. There is a cure. We
left a real cure here with the military. They should have
delivered it to everyone."

Skye shook her head. "I've never heard of another cure.
I mean, there were a few crazy ones tossed around on the
news. One even supposedly from Atlantis."

Sonora's eyes widened, and she pointed her finger at
Skye. "That's the one! What happened to that one?"

Oh, great. The girl was as delusional as her uncle. "I
don't know. Nothing came of it."

Sonora stood and paced as she again ran a hand
through her straight hair. "What? I don't even know . . . how
this happened. I have to go."

Skye jumped to her feet and grabbed for Sonora's arm.
The blonde woman stepped back and almost tripped but
still managed to raise her gun.

Skye raised her hands in surrender. "Please don't leave
me here! Take me with you!"

"I won't be long. I'll be back within twenty-four hours—
with help. You can't go where I'm going. I don't have the
extra equipment. And if you leave, it will alert them something's up." Sonora reached out and gave Skye's hand a
quick squeeze."I'm sorry."

"What help?"

Sonora glanced out the window, and Skye followed her gaze. The sea was in a rare mood. The water tossed and turned as if it were as restless as she felt. Spray flung high into the air as two waves crashed into each other.

"You're not going to believe this. And when you see them, it'll seem crazy until it doesn't anymore," Sonora explained. "My husband, Ian—his people—are big and strong. They'll save you." She flung out her arm. "They will save everyone here. I promise!"

Skye closed her eyes, praying that even a little of what the woman said was true. "How will I know them?"

Sonora giggled. "Oh, you'll know them. They will be unlike anything you've ever seen."

She gave Skye's hand one last squeeze and walked out the door, locking it behind her.

Skye dropped back onto her bed and covered her face with her hands. What had just happened?

Almost nothing about the interchange had made sense, except the young woman's promise to come back for her. And even that was strange.

But the brief conversation gave Skye hope. Every day she was here, she was closer to death. She could feel it.

She prayed that Sonora, the conversation, and the rescue were real. It could come even sooner than anything Kelsey could bring.

Skye tossed and turned for the rest of the night. She would've sworn she didn't sleep at all, but she must have.

Because when she woke, it was to the sound of sirens.

3 3

ALARM BELLS

Skye jolted upright. Were the alarm bells for Kelsey? Or Sonora?

Sydney and two other guards burst into Skye's room, guns raised.

Skye pushed back against the bed's headboard, hands raised.

The guards scanned the room, balcony, and bathroom.

She watched them in silence, her heart thundering.

A guard walked over to Skye and grabbed her hair. "Where is she?" he shouted.

"Who?" Tears of pain flooded Skye's eyes.

"You know who!" He shook her for emphasis.

"I don't! I really don't!"

She couldn't tip them off about either Kelsey or Sonora.

The guard leaned closer, almost spitting his words. "The girl! The little girl in the next room!"

Skye wished he had meant Sonora. She didn't know where *she'd* gone. "I don't know where Kelsey is."

He tightened his grip on her hair, and Skye's scalp burned. She pushed at him. "Please! I don't know!"

"Cliff," Sydney said as she stepped closer. "I don't think she knows."

Cliff stared at Skye before glancing at Sydney. "She does," he said.

Cliff turned his attention back to his victim. "It's Sydney who will be punished for this, and you know how he is. Sydney will be fortunate if she lives a month."

"I'm sorry." Skye glanced at Sydney's pale face. "Kelsey could be anywhere. I don't know where she is."

Sydney moved toward Skye. "Kelsey is important, so important. We need her—both of you—for the cure. Doc will be irate when we tell him she's gone. I can't even imagine his reaction."

Skye dropped her gaze to the floor.

Still clenching Skye's hair, Cliff shook her head.

She moved her hands to his wrist, hoping to slow him. But Cliff slid a hand under her jaw and pulled Skye off the bed. She gasped. Her skull flared with pain.

Dylan's lessons were instinctive now, and she raised a knee.

The guard jumped back, pulling her with him at first, then pushing her away when she tried again.

A chunk of hair ripped from her head. Skye yelled and flung out a fist.

It caught Cliff beside his eye.

The three came after her, and she scrabbled back onto the bed, practically hugging the headboard.

She looked for a weapon, but there was nothing.

They had all the power here.

"Wait," Sydney said, "we can't hurt her without his permission."

Cliff waved her back. "When he knows what she did, he won't care as long as we don't hurt her too bad."

"I don't think she knows anything," Sydney said. "And I don't want to do this. She's my responsibility."

"You're too soft on them. That's what got you into this mess. You go on outside and I'll take care of this."

Skye shot the woman a pleading look. "Please, Sydney, don't let them hurt me. I really don't know where Kelsey is!"

"Ignore her," Cliff growled. "It's her or you. And she's dead meat, anyway."

"I'm sorry, Skye," Sydney's voice wavered as she apologized. "In this place, a person needs to look out for themselves."

Skye's heart fell.

Her arms flailed as Cliff and another guard grabbed her and pulled her to the end of the bed.

She struggled to sit up.

Cliff sharply slapped the side of her face, slamming her back onto the bed.

They hauled her up and landed another blow. Skye grunted as she fell.

"Sydney, help me! Please!"

Sydney kept her eyes glued to the floor and ignored her.

They pulled Skye up, again and again, each slap harder than the last.

On the fifth, Cliff's iron grip held her shoulders as he shouted, "Where. Is. She?"

When Skye only shook her head in denial, he curled his fingers and punched her in the face.

Skye puddled at their feet, her head ringing.

He pulled her up and balled up his fist again.

This time red fire burst from behind her eyeballs. Pain —unlike any she'd felt before—rushed through her skull.

When Cliff shook Skye, her head wobbled. He let go of her. She dropped to the floor into darkness.

·   ·   ·

195

WHEN SKYE WOKE her clothes were soaked through to the skin. Her head ached. Everything seemed wrong.

She moved a hand, sloshing water. What was she doing in the tub?

She frowned and looked up at the three guards standing over her.

"No, no!" she murmured.

Cliff glared down at her. "You have two minutes to decide what's going to happen next."

Skye raised one of her wet hands to the side of her throbbing head and winced.

The guard crouched to the edge of the bathtub. "It's you or us, girl. And we will have answers."

Skye sobbed. "I don't—"

"If you finish that with 'know nothing', it starts now."

Skye sank her head to her sodden knees. There was no way out of this. She had to give them something. "I saw her leave. That's all," she whispered.

"Good girl. Now tell us more."

"There is no more."

The brawny guard wrapped a hand around Skye's throat. "There is more." He smiled. "I don't want to do this. *You* are making me do this."

Skye took in his expression of delight. It wasn't true. He enjoyed torturing.

When she stared at him, he tightened the hand around her neck and pushed down toward the water.

Skye flailed.

Water slapped the sides of the tub and splashed over the edges, soaking Cliff.

He held her head just above the water. It edged along her cheeks.

He pushed her closer.

Water crept toward her nose and mouth. Skye clawed at his hand.

At a nod from Cliff, a second guard held her legs.

"What else do you have to say?" Cliff barked.

Skye shook her head.

"What else? Last time."

Skye pressed her lips together. There was nothing she could say that would make him happy.

Cliff shoved Skye until her head hit bottom. Her already shaken brain pounded. She let out an unheard scream. Bubbles floated to the surface.

Cliff's muffled voice drifted to her. "I wouldn't do that. I'm keeping you down no matter how much air you let go."

Skye wrapped her hands around his thick arm, clawing at it.

The hard man's image waved above her. Would he kill her? Would Devon even care? The scientist could get all the blood he wanted if it no longer needed to sustain her.

Skye's lungs strained. She resisted the need to inhale, but she didn't have long. What could she tell them?

Nothing about the note Kelsey left at the pawnshop. Never that.

But something—enough to satisfy them.

The need to inhale grew almost unbearable. She tightened her grip on Cliff's arm.

He chuckled.

Her body begged for a breath. Skye flailed, kicking the stomach of the guard who held her feet.

Cliff's eyes brightened. He raised her head and banged it against the iron tub again.

Skye almost gasped. Her brain swirled. Her lungs burned with need.

Her body began its fight for life, Skye felt it shudder

and buck. She banged on Cliff's arm, hoping for some kind of mercy.

There was none.

The man watched her with intense interest, his face covered with glee.

She lost focus. Skye's nose and mouth quivered.

Left with no choice, she inhaled—not precious air but an invading enemy—water.

Liquid filled her nose and ran down her throat.

Her body trembled. It seemed odd and out of sync with the rest of her. As if an entity of its own, it shuddered as it realized what was happening.

She was dying.

Strangely, something like relief filled her. It was out of her hands now.

On Skye's third quake, Cliff raised her limp body out of the water and laid her over the side of the tub, hooking her ribs over the edge. He pounded her back so hard that some small part of her, somewhere in the recesses of her mind, was sure her ribs would break.

Skye didn't move, but drifted in and out of consciousness, certain Cliff's banging would only hasten her death.

How she wished she could have seen her Love one more time. Hear his rumbling voice calling her darlin', telling her everything would be okay.

Cliff thumped her back again. What did he think would happen? She was too far gone for this to help now.

Skye slipped head-first toward the floor.

Cliff pulled her limp body over his knees and thumped on her back some more.

When the liquid came, it came all at once—just like with the AgFlu. Water streamed from her mouth and nose, hitting the floor with such force it bounced back at her.

Skye pushed against the floor with weak arms.

Cliff shoved her back down.

Skye choked and sputtered, but only pulled in a tiny ribbon of air. She stilled, careful not to lose that lifeline.

Gradually, she choked out the water. Her lungs still burned, but this time it was a good burn—it meant she would live.

Again, she pushed against the floor and away from Cliff. This time he allowed it.

After a few minutes, she used the lip of the tub to stand.

"Where do you think you are going?"

Skye waved toward her room.

Cliff crossed his arms and laughed. "We're not done here yet. You're going back into that tub."

Skye wilted and shook her head.

"Skye, you haven't told me what I wanted to know yet," he said, scolding her as if she were a child. "This won't be over until you cooperate."

Skye covered her mouth to stop the sob that threatened.

Cliff reached toward her.

She flinched.

He ran a finger down her wet hair. "It's simple, honey. Just tell me something, and this will be all over."

Skye stared at the floor.

"Fill the tub. Cold water," Cliff told the other guard.

Skye listened to the rush of water, tears rolling down her cheeks.

Something. She had to give him something.

She felt his eyes on her, waiting for her to break.

When the tub was full, Cliff stood. "Come on. Get in there."

If he thought she would voluntarily step in there, he was crazy.

She refused to budge.

With rough hands, he pulled her up. When she fought him, he slapped her until her head rang.

He slammed her into the frigid water. "Tell me!"

Panic overtook her.

He recognized the instant she broke. A satisfied gleam lit in his eyes.

Cliff pulled her head from the water. She reached for him. She would have reached for anyone to get out of this situation.

"Please," she begged, her teeth chattering, her mind screaming. A wrong move on her part now would mean she would go under the water again. Cliff was waiting for any excuse.

He held a hand to her throat. "You know what you have to do."

"Please." She wrapped her arms around his. "Let me out and I will tell you everything."

"Tell me now."

"I'm afraid you'll kill me, anyway."

"Oh, honey. Where's the fun in that? Almost killing. That's where the fun is."

Skye laid her head against his arm and cried.

Cliff ran a hand over her long, dark hair. "It's okay now. Just say it and I'll get you out of here. Okay?"

Skye nodded. She couldn't do this any longer. She needed to say something now.

Skye's raspy voice quivered. "We said if we escaped, we would go home."

"Where is home?"

Skye hesitated. She needed to stay close enough to the truth that he would believe her, but far enough away for Kelsey to be safe. Her hesitation earned her punishment.

His hand tightened around her throat.

"West Virginia!" she gasped out.

"Where in West Virginia?"

"Fenton." Skye almost mumbled the word. The Interstate forked at Fenton. If everything went well, Kelsey would have made it past there by now.

The guard stared at Skye.

Tears started again, flooding her eyes. "That's all I know. We didn't have a plan. We didn't, I promise."

Skye stiffened as Cliff pulled her close to him, his breath drying the wet skin on her face. "Devon thinks you are his, but you're mine now, you got that? *I* broke you."

She wanted to fight and punch and scream that it wasn't true, but that would only get her further punishment. Instead, she stayed still, as if happy to be there. Let him think what he wanted.

Sonora had promised to be back within the day. Kelsey was out there trying to get home. Someone would help her, even if she could not help herself.

Cliff rested his hand on the back of her bruised head, smoothing his hand along it as if the movement would stop the hurting.

"Come on, let's get you up and out of these wet clothes," he said.

She tried to stand twice, but her shaky limbs refused to work.

Cliff smiled, happy with his results.

"It's okay," Cliff said as he and the other two guards removed her wet jeans and t-shirt, leaving Skye in her underwear. He wrapped a large towel around her, picked her up, and carried her to the bed where he gently laid her.

"Here." Cliff shoved a glass of water and some pain medicine into Skye's hands. "You'll want this."

Skye wanted to resist every supposed kindness. The man was trying to condition her. But she had no strength, and she needed the medication.

Skye glanced from one guard to the other as they settled into chairs.

A knock sounded at the door, Cliff opened the door to two more guards. One he ordered onto the balcony and the other to stand outside in the hallway. Sydney stood across from the bed, eyes on the floor.

Tears rolled over Skye's face, soaking her pillow.

Five guards? How would she ever get home to Jesse and Dylan now?

Skye closed her eyes and imagined Dylan's arms holding her tight.

She drifted to sleep, to the sound of his voice telling her everything would be okay—he was coming for her.

34

THE TABLE

Skye woke to Cliff standing over her, his rough hand shaking her shoulder.

"Doc wants to see you," he said.

An icy shiver ran down her spine.

She threw Cliff a glance and mumbled, "Don't touch me."

He burst out laughing. "Make me stop." But he walked away.

With care, Skye stood, making sure the towel Cliff had wrapped around her stayed in place. She picked up some clothes and went into the bathroom.

Cliff stared at her but didn't stop her.

Once she'd closed the door to the bathroom, Skye let the towel drop as she looked in the mirror.

Her forehead had a large bruise as did the side of her face and her neck.

Skye ran a hand over her stomach where light bruising had started. She poked at it and winced.

After examining her tender scalp, she gingerly combed her knotted hair.

Outside the door, the guards talked and laughed. Skye sighed. She'd done everything she could so they would trust her, hoping for less supervision, and now this. Four guards. And Cliff.

Skye clung to the sink, refusing to slump to the floor in despair.

How would she get through this? Was day after day be like this, at the mercy of Devon and Cliff, until she ended up like the people on those metal tables?

Skye tried to push away her depressing thoughts. Other people had gone through worse. She'd handle what they threw at her somehow. But her fears pressed back, refusing to leave.

Skye raised her teary gaze to the mirror and imagined Dylan there.

She ached for the vision to be real—yearned to turn and feel his firm embrace around her.

She couldn't have that—not right now. But she could still take strength from him.

"What's done is done," he'd say. "Now, what are ya gonna do about it?"

She couldn't wallow in her feelings. She needed to move ahead. Skye would have to regain trust somehow.

"I hope I make the right choices, love," Skye whispered as Dylan's image wavered. "The ones that lead me back to you."

"Stay alive, darlin'. I'm coming for you."

Skye sobbed as he disappeared, leaving only her beaten face in the reflection.

After wiping her tears away, she pulled on her jeans and t-shirt while berating herself for losing focus.

She needed to keep Dylan shoved in that little corner of her mind until she was ready to let him out. A clear head is what she needed. The emotion he evoked was overwhelming.

But even as she scolded herself, memories of him flooded her.

His slow smile, the way his eyes brightened when he saw her, evenings by the fire.

Skye pressed her lips together and held back the sadness.

She told herself that Dylan was fine, he was on his way, and soon she would be out of this evil place. Then they would go to the mountain together.

That was it. That was the story—their story. She just had to get through one hour at a time until she heard his voice.

She pushed against the countertop, standing as straight as her hurt stomach would allow.

After making sure she tucked Dylan away, Skye walked out of the bathroom.

Cliff stood just outside the door.

Skye almost vomited.

Of course he was.

"We will not tell Doc about our little fun here. You got it?"

She narrowed her eyes at Cliff. "I want some breakfast."

Cliff nodded his head at one of his underlings, who handed her a protein bar.

Skye looked at it with a wry expression. "You'd think the world would be out of these by now." She tore the wrapper open and choked the dry granola bar down.

Cliff motioned everyone toward the hallway and positioned two guards in front of her and two in the back as if she were a dangerous criminal. Cliff walked beside her.

Skye kept her eyes on the floor as she steamed. It was a show of force. Cliff wanted her impressed.

She was not.

As they got closer to Devon's lab, two guards broke off while the other two escorted her in.

Devon eyed the group before his gaze landed on Skye.

"Where is Sydney?"

"Sick," Cliff answered.

Devon nodded before going to Skye and taking her hands. His gaze slid over her bruised face, then ignored the injuries.

"Skye, dear, I have such news to tell you! Sit, sit." He pulled her to the desk, waving her into a chair. Devon scooted another chair from behind the desk closer to her.

His eyes were bright, almost feverish. "Do you remember our conversation about the Atlantians?"

Skye wanted to sigh, but pressed her lips together and nodded.

This again? But if it made him happy to prattle on about imaginary beings, she would let him.

"Of course you do," Devon continued. "We all have common DNA with them. They are, after all, mostly human, though I am loathed to admit it on most occasions. However, as I mentioned before, Atlantians also have DNA humans don't have. But then, some humans like yourself have more DNA in common with them than others."

Devon's explanation seemed disjointed. Was he sliding further into his delusions?

He frowned. "I'm not sure how that happened, though I have my suspicions. But you, Skye, you share some of that same mysterious DNA."

He waited—as if she'd won the lottery and should jump up and down—before going on. "People like you will help me clarify the mysteries of the disease."

Oh, really? Clarification. Was that what we were calling torture?

Skye rubbed at the fiery boils lingering on her hand.

Perhaps if she could dissuade him from this fantasy, he would stop the experiments.

"Devon, how would I have gotten this DNA?"

"From an ancestor, of course."

A memory flashed, but she scoffed at the idea and pushed it away. "But that makes no sense. I'd know about something like that."

Devon waved his hand at her. "Leave those things with me, dear. I'm an expert. Just know you'll be treated like royalty here because you, Skye, are going to save humankind."

Skye's stomach clenched. "And how am I going to do that?"

"We are going to see how strong you are."

"Strong?"

"I'm going to give you every disease known to humankind and chart each one. I'm going to see if you are closer to them or us."

Sickness rose in Skye's throat. "How long will this take?"

"Years, dear." His eyes shone as he answered. "It will take years."

Skye's gaze grew wider as she scanned the room. Already syringes lined the countertop. A tray full of scalpels and other shiny medical tools sat on a wheeled cart beside the dreaded metal table.

Skye jerked in a breath and held it. Then spoke in a rush.

"Devon, what use is this? Most people either had the AgFlu, or they haven't. Soon, it will go just as so many other types of flu left. We don't need a cure."

"Yes, Skye, we do." Devon shook his head, a grave look in his eye. "I know we have lost a lot, but we can still save most of humankind."

He still thought the world was full of people. When was the last time he'd left this building?

"No, we can't. Most of the world is empty now. I've been out there. I know."

Devon chuckled. "Tsk, tsk, Skye. There is no getting out of this. We cannot delay." He rose and walked to the metal table. He patted it. The table gave an ominous ring. "Hop up, Skye."

Skye jumped to her feet. Her chair scraped backward as she glanced at the door.

Cliff and another guard barred her path.

"No, Devon. Let's talk about this," Skye gasped.

"I've never felt that talking solves anything." Devon nodded to Cliff, and the guard moved toward Skye.

She scrambled backward. "You can't allow this, Cliff. He will murder me."

Cliff shrugged. "I don't care what he does to you as long as me and mine do okay."

It was useless. She knew it. But it wouldn't stop her from trying.

Skye turned and ran down the long room toward the door Devon often disappeared into. Maybe there would be a way out there.

Cliff and the guard's footsteps slapped the tile floor behind her.

Skye focused on the door. She was almost there. Reaching out a hand, her fingers grazed the cool silver knob.

Something hard exploded against the back of her head.

Skye dropped into darkness.

35

A SLIM CHANCE

Skye blinked her eyes at Cliff's image as it blurred above her. Her head still rang from the blow.

Cliff grabbed her trembling body from the floor, walked to the metal table, and dropped her onto its surface.

Skye's head bounced, the steel and her skull ringing. Her ankle caught the bottom lip's edge. Pain radiated around it.

Skye let out a scream that became a groan as darkness swirled around her.

She fought the blackness. Who knew what they would do to her if she passed out?

Skye tried to pull her foot up over the table's edge.

A guard reached out and took both legs, holding them down.

Skye cried out, "My ankle. I think it's broken."

"It's okay, dear. You won't need to do much walking."

Regardless of his words, Devon pushed the guard out of the way and looked at her foot. Skye ground her teeth and moaned as Devon rotated it.

"No. Not broken." He patted her leg when he released it.

"But it hurts so much."

"It's fine. Pain can be good for us sometimes."

The guard returned to his position and took her legs again. This time he seemed to have a sliver of empathy for her, and with a loose hand, held her hurt ankle.

Devon walked up to the head of the table, trailing his hand along it as he moved. "We've never had a female of your species here before. This is going to be interesting."

"What are you talking about? I'm human!" Her voice broke.

Devon picked up a scalpel and inspected it. "Hold her down."

Skye fought as the guards moved to either side of her.

With little effort, the big men pushed Skye back onto the table and held her there.

She squirmed, wrenching her arm from the guard on her right.

Cliff grabbed her head, squeezing it between his hands. "Each time you cause trouble, I cause trouble. Do you want me to show you?"

Skye glanced at Devon, hoping for help, but he simply waited for Cliff's demonstration.

After everything Cliff had already done to her, she had no doubt he could hurt her.

"No."

"Be good then."

Skye squeezed her eyes closed. The metal instruments clacked against the tray beside her as Devon decided what to start with.

When it stopped, she opened her eyes.

Devon was coming at her with an IV stand. A bag with dark, almost ink-colored liquid swung from it.

She groaned as Devon wrapped a tourniquet around her arm, searching for options but finding only one.

She didn't have to be awake for the cutting.

Skye gathered up as much saliva as her dry mouth could produce and spit in Cliff's face.

For a moment, everything was still. Then Devon laughed. The other guards followed suit, chuckling under their breath.

"She's a tough one," Devon said, sounding like a proud father.

Cliff raised Skye's head and shoulders off the table and slammed them down with such force Skye was sure her skull had broken in two.

Her brain flashed as if short-circuiting—everything came in pieces.

"See," Cliff's disjointed voice whispered during a flash. "I do what I want. He won't stop me now."

Everything turned dark—then light and dark again.

IN THE NEXT FLASH, Devon stuck her with the IV needle. "Did you know, dear, that your people have larger hearts and lungs than humans do? It's going to be interesting to find out if you also have them."

The light left and returned.

SHE TWISTED HER HEAD, trying to examine her body. What had happened while she was unconscious?

But did it matter? She was as good as dead. She'd be a lifeless corpse soon.

If Devon didn't kill her, Cliff surely would.

In fact, she would anger Cliff until he did. Then she wouldn't suffer years of experimental torment.

Skye eyed the ominous IV now attached to her arm.

"Don't worry," Devon said, "only a bit of pain medicine. You see, I can be merciful."

Skye eyed the grey-black bag. Pain medicine? Doubtful.

The scientist leaned closer to Skye. "I'm going to be digging a little deep today, so I thought you might need it."

Her stomach turned, and a moan escaped her.

Something. She had to think of something.

"Devon, I'm not Atlantian. I have my—my family tree thing at my house. I can take you there. It goes back hundreds of years."

"No need. DNA doesn't lie, dear."

Tears rose, flooding her eyes. She shook her head from side to side. "They aren't real. Atlantian's are not real. This is part of a disease. You have a mental disease, Devon. I'm a physiological doctor. Remember that."

Devon stiffened. "It's not my imagination!"

"Devon, I'm sorry. Atlantians aren't real—just like Martians aren't real."

"They are!" His face flamed. "You just haven't seen them!"

Cliff raised Skye's head and waited for a signal from Devon.

She had one chance to say the right thing. "Then show me! You are going to do all this to me? I want to see one!"

Devon waved a hand. "Ask the guards, they know."

"Have they seen one?"

The room got quiet. The guards shook their heads.

Skye threw down the challenge. "Show me an Atlantian, Devon. Not a picture of someone on a table. A real, live Atlantian swimming in the water!"

"Then you'll cooperate? No problems?"

Devon continued his work, injecting an orange liquid into the IV bag. The color dissipated into the black.

Skye seemed queasy already.

Devon picked up a second vial.

"Yes," she barked—anything to get him to stop. "I'll cooperate." Skye didn't like to lie, but these were extreme circumstances.

Devon put down the vial. "Let her up, boys."

Two guards hauled her over the lip of the table and dropped her on her feet.

Her ankle gave way, and her head swam.

Cliff reached for her.

Skye pushed him away. "Put me down! You make me sick!"

"You just wait until he gives me full leeway with you." Cliff gave her a hard stare as he swung her up into his arms.

Skye suppressed the urge to vomit, ducked her head, and refused to look at him again.

As ill as Cliff made her, he wasn't the biggest problem at the moment.

She needed to convince Devon he was mentally ill—seeing there was no substance behind his belief of Atlantians may do that.

Skye twisted to look at Devon. "How many people have seen an Atlantian?"

"Millions. They were on the Internet!"

Skye sighed. There had been some odd pictures circulating during the AgFlu crisis. "Devon. That was a hoax."

"No. It was not."

"Most people believe it was a prank. Some of your own people could be laughing at you."

Devon glanced at the guards.

"Perhaps," Skye pressed, "if you want your people to believe in what you are doing here, all of them should see this Atlantian."

One guard uttered a low chuckle.

Devon came to an abrupt stop and narrowed his eyes.

"Seeing is believing, they say," Skye added, hope rising.

Devon gave a quick nod. "Maybe you're right. This place has grown since the pandemic's beginning. It would be helpful for new ones to understand our primary purpose is to find a cure. That this isn't only a place to find good shelter and abundant food. We are more than that."

Devon started walking, his pace quickened.

Cliff zeroed in on Skye. "What are you up to?"

"You don't want to look at one?" Skye mumbled.

The reality was she didn't know what she was doing or if this would work, but it had gotten her off that table. Her best hope was that everyone would see that this so-called Atlantian was fake and revolt.

Skye's heart soared as Devon waved a guard over and said, "Go on ahead of us. Tell them to gather everyone by the big tank."

She had a chance. A slim one, to be sure, but it was something.

36

SO CLOSE

Dylan hiked his crossbow a little higher on his shoulder. He, Wade, and Kelsey stood on a small hill overlooking the town of Seaside. He'd left Jesse behind with Paul and the others, and the boy was spitting mad about it. But this wasn't the time to troop the entire group through the brush. This was a scouting mission.

Dylan scanned the area. Seaside wasn't a big place and could just as easily have been a small mountain town if one judged it by size alone.

But it was much more colorful or had been. His gaze lingered on the broken pink and orange umbrellas strewn across the streets, the bright blue window shutters hanging haphazardly by what looked like a single screw, and the overturned brilliant green lawn furniture.

A storm had gone through here. A bad one. But a while ago.

Dylan ran a hand over his chin. Apparently, there weren't enough townsfolk to clean up, or they didn't care anymore. Either way, there would be no help from this town. His men were on their own.

Kelsey pointed to a large concrete building sitting so close to the ocean that the blue waves almost lapped at its gray walls. "It's there."

Dylan nodded. It didn't surprise him. The huge dome seemed out of place—much like an eerie house on a hill. It was imposing—and would be tricky to get into.

Dylan crouched and picked at the short seagrass with his fingertips as he examined it.

There were no windows on this side—only four large double entrance doors and a couple of single glass doors. Large wood planks sat on the right side of the building, presumedly to cover the glass. No doubt these people would lock this up tight if they sensed danger.

And activity—way too much activity for sneaking in on this side.

He blew out a breath. Maybe the other side?

Kelsey had told him about the rooms with balconies facing the ocean. Maybe if they waited until evening, they could get Skye out that way.

Dylan ran a hand through his hair and groaned inwardly. It was killing him he was this close and wasn't able to storm in there and get her.

His eyes narrowed. Who knew what they were doing to her in there? Kelsey had spoken of experiments.

Ice slid down his spine. He couldn't think about that now. He needed a clear head.

Kelsey moved to sit cross-legged beside him, patiently waiting for his take on the place.

"This doesn't look good," he said. "Remind me of the back again."

Kelsey made a face. "Our rooms are three stories up. We'd need a grappling hook to throw up there."

Dylan grunted. No better than what she'd said the first time.

Wade shifted, scraping his foot against the sandy soil. "Maybe we could get Skye's attention. Have her throw out some sheets and shimmy down like you did, girl."

"They may expect that now." Kelsey rubbed her cheek. "What about going in the front? I could act like a captive. Once we're in, I know where to go."

Both men bristled at the idea. "Ain't no way, that's happening," Wade blustered. "You just get that outta your head right now, you hear?"

Kelsey threw a hand toward the building. "But look! We don't have many choices."

Dylan understood. The front doors were open, and people trooped in and out of them on a regular basis. More than once they'd seen victims dragged into the building by scruffy-looking men.

Dylan looked at Wade and himself. They'd fit in, but there'd also be problems. Dylan shot a glance at Kelsey. "And what if they take you away when we get in there? Then we'd need to be tracking you down too—and you'd be no good gettin' us around the place."

Kelsey sighed. "Well, then, you're going to have to come up with the idea."

Dylan chuckled. The way the girl said it was like they hadn't been doing that for years. Dylan patted her on the shoulder. "It'll be okay, Kelsey. We'll manage to piece somethin' together."

"Brother," Wade said as he looked over his shoulder. "is this going to be one of those long stakeouts you like to do? Cause if so, I'm gonna need me a Coke. I saw a machine up there, and I'm fixin' to get me a bottle."

Dylan didn't answer at first. Wade always did get antsy when he didn't have something to do, but it'd be nice if occasionally his brother would give a man a minute to think.

He waved at Wade. "Go get it, if you want. Get me a water. And Wade—don't go anywhere else."

Wade blew out an irritated breath. "I ain't a little kid you gotta boss around." He scuffed his feet as he walked away.

The corner of Dylan's mouth curved. Once Wade had his Coke, he'd settle.

"Get me one too, please," Kelsey said to Wade's retreating back.

He waved a hand at her.

Dylan watched people come and go from the Marine Center. A group would go in, there'd be a lull and another group would drive into the parking lot.

Kelsey was right, it was their way in, but Dylan didn't want to put her in jeopardy even if the girl was sure it was possible to slip into the hallways and rescue to Skye.

Dylan winced. It hurt to even think of Skye's name.

Who would've guessed that he'd ever be so hung up on a woman? But he hugged those feelings close to his heart, clung to them as if he was a drowning man grasping at some last bit of driftwood.

It didn't matter that he'd been brought up to think love was a weakness. That was wrong, and he knew it now, even if it did try to crawl back into his head from time to time.

Skye had shown him there was strength in love, not weakness. And she was his love—his everything.

He would save her. Or die trying.

He was here, and she was right there in front of him. He had to get into that building and bring her home.

"Here, D," Wade said as a heads up right before a bottle of water came sailing Dylan's way.

Wade noisily sat on the ground with his legs out in front of him and handed Kelsey a Coke.

"So I had an epiphany," Wade said as he twisted the cap off his bottle, smiling at the rush of air.

Dylan looked over at Wade and frowned. "An epiphany?"

"Yeah, it means a big idea." Wade took a long drink of his soda with his eyes closed and sighed in contentment.

Dylan scoffed. "I know what epiphany means. I just wondered if you did."

When Wade put the soda to his lips again, Dylan stopped him. "What? What's your idea?"

"Kelsey doesn't need to be a captive. But she's too clean to fit in with the rough crowd down there. We need to dirty her up some, rip her clothes a bit, stick a cap on her. Then she could walk right in too."

Dylan glanced at Kelsey.

Epiphany. This idea may just have been that important —close enough, anyway. Wade's idea would be saving lives.

"Okay," Dylan said. "Let's go with your epiphany."

Twenty minutes later, Kelsey walked beside Dylan loaded with weapons and more unkept than the two brothers put together after a long winter's hunting trip.

No one would be messing with her.

Dylan eyed the large front doors, happy they'd driven the truck in and it sat behind them in the parking lot. It'd be a quick getaway if they needed it.

He swapped a glance with Wade as he murmured to Kelsey, "You stick close and keep your eyes open, ya hear?"

She nodded, her knuckles white on the rifle she gripped.

"Let us know where to go when we get in here." Dylan switched the box he held from his right to his left arm.

Most people took in something. If they didn't have captives, they had boxes. Of what, Dylan didn't know. But they'd stopped by a pawn shop Kelsey pointed out and picked up a few things that would, hopefully, be good enough to get them through the door.

The gray wall of the building seemed to grow taller as they got closer. Once he got a peek into the entrance, his heart fell.

People swarmed the lobby—many more than he expected. He'd planned for some small force of resistance. Twenty, maybe thirty men. Something his group could handle. Nothing on this scale.

The best he could hope for now is to sneak in and get Skye out, and that would be a lot trickier than being in control of the situation.

They were at the front doors when someone peeked out and yelled, "The Doc wants everyone in here. He's gonna show us one of the mermen!"

Dylan shot a surprised glance at Wade. His brother's eyebrows rose almost to his hairline.

After the brightness outside, the inside of the Marine Center seemed dark.

Dylan gave his eyes a minute to adjust, then continued into the building. The lobby was massive—two stories high — and echoing with the noise of excited people. They had pushed old props and tables against the walls to make room for the crowd.

To their right were the ticket counters and restrooms. To the left was a solid wall that opened onto a large tank filled with murky water. Everyone gathered there.

Dylan set the box on a table and pushed it toward a woman.

She flustered. "I was just going to watch—" The woman pointed to the crowd.

Dylan nodded. "That's fine. We'll check in after."

The woman agreed and rushed away.

Their little group hung around the edge of the gathering, ready to bolt if necessary.

People continued to flood into the room from connected hallways. Dylan reckoned there were already about a hundred people, and he hoped it stopped soon.

He scanned the crowd, looking for Skye. If he didn't find her, maybe this would be the opportunity to slip away to her room.

The crowd murmured, "The Doc's coming." As one, they turned to watch the hallway doors.

Through it came five men and Skye.

Dylan's heart went into overdrive, and he vaulted forward.

Wade's grabbed his shoulder, his fingers digging in as Dylan tried to shake him off.

"Steady, D. Steady," his brother said.

Dylan clamped his jaw and stepped back—the hardest thing he'd ever had to do.

He watched, tracking every movement Skye made.

A man carried her. Why?

She had a hand to the side of her head. Was she hurt?

She was pale, so pale.

When the group surrounding the doctor reached the front of the crowd, the man who held Skye put her down.

She stumbled, and Dylan steeled himself not to run to her. The man beside her took her waist and arm to steady her.

Dylan practically growled as Skye pushed him away.

When he didn't release her at first, she pounded his arm until he did.

Dylan's face turned thunderous. It appeared the man was trying to help Skye, but something was going on. The look she'd given him was pure hatred.

It was clear the men were the doctor's muscle.

Dylan quickly identified and dismissed the infamous Devon Shade from his perfectly groomed hair to his shiny shoes. Separate him from his guards and the Doctor would go down with one blow.

Someone handed the doctor a megaphone, and he began to speak.

Dylan paid little attention, he needed to figure out a way to get to Skye.

A guy to his left glanced at him, then Wade. "Hey, do I know you two?"

Dylan hardly spared him a glance. "No."

He didn't have time for distractions.

3 7

THE REVEAL

Skye eyed the large water tank as they weaved through the crowd, hoping it would somehow be her salvation. Calling out Devon's belief in Atlantis could backfire on her, but it was the only move she had.

Once they stood in front of the glass, Cliff lowered Skye to the floor. She gasped and stumbled as her injured foot met the tile.

Cliff grabbed Skye's arm to help her, but she shook him off. She would have none of that.

She slugged his arm. "Let me go!"

Cliff dropped his hand and rubbed the spot. "I'm helping you."

"I don't want you touching me. Most especially in front of these people—acting like you have some empathy instead of being the goon you are! I'd rather walk on a bare nub then have your help! You caused these injuries!"

"I can arrange that." Cliff's eyes narrowed. "You don't need limbs for what Doc has in mind for you."

Skye's gaze widened, and she stepped away. The man

was vile. "I've never said this to anyone before, but I would erase you from this earth if I could."

"Same here, baby. But I'd send you off screaming."

Skye edged away from Cliff, backing toward a blonde guard. Anyone was better than him. At least this one had done nothing to her.

Devon looked over his shoulder, shooting Skye and Cliff an irritated look. "Stop bickering. My goodness, you two are like competing siblings. Don't worry—I have time for both of you."

Skye shuddered. Did he really think that was what was going on? The man was becoming more and more delusional.

Devon waved Cliff to his side. "You stay here with me now. I need you to keep the crowd away. The others can watch her."

Skye couldn't believe her good fortune. Her biggest watchdog was relieved of duty.

She glanced at the large glass doors across the room leading to freedom. Could she somehow inch her way there and make a run for it? And would she make it on this ankle?

She had to try. It was her last chance at life. She had to go for it—or die trying.

Skye stepped closer to the blonde guard next to her, bumping her arm against his to make him think she was right where she should be.

She gasped as she put weight on her ankle. He looked down at her. "You okay?"

"Yes. I'll be fine," Skye said as she bent to rub her leg. Booking it out of here was out of the question.

She put some weight on her toes and found that less painful.

When Devon waved for someone to turn down the lights, Skye straightened and looked at the tank.

According to the placard, the massive aquarium had once held a pod of dolphins. But it was empty of sea life now, and cloudy. Evaporated water had left marks on the glass, and peering through its foggy depths was not as easy as it must once had been.

Movement at the top of the water drew Skye's attention. Four guards surrounded a giant of a man. They poked at him with cattle prods, forcing him to walk onto a platform jutting a few feet over the pool.

The man struggled away from the guard's weapons—but feebly—with much less strength than a man his size should have had. His slack features suggested they had drugged him.

A shimmering tattoo ran over one shoulder and down his bicep. When the light caught the design, it seemed illuminated. Even his skin seemed to glow as if he were the pinnacle of health instead of the emaciated form that stood before her.

Skye frowned. He was different—there was no doubt about that. Could Devon's stories possibly be true?

She scoffed at herself. Of course not. And she couldn't get sidetracked by this nonsense.

Excited cries came from the crowd and they surged toward the tank, taking her with it and almost pushing her into Cliff.

Skye glanced at the outside doors. They had gotten smaller as she'd tried to work against the crowd, but got nowhere.

A black light in the tank caught her attention. A guard waved it over the giant man's skin.

Skye gasped when a colorful pattern emerged

reminding her of a tropical fish. The crowd erupted in chatter.

Skye froze.

Sonora had said her husband's people were huge, and like nothing Skye had seen before.

But how would Atlantians be possible?

Skye shook her head.

They weren't.

But this odd man explained why Devon believed him to be some sort of mythical creature.

Coming to life, the captive man jerked from the light. When one of the guards screamed at him, he knocked the guard to the ground.

Devon raised a small controller and hit a button.

The giant dropped. His body quaking uncontrollably against the ground until Devon raised his finger from the control.

Skye groaned in empathy.

Devon chuckled.

Cliff turned toward Skye, his eyes bright. "It's an implant for the troublemakers. You're next."

Skye shuddered and took a couple of steps away from Cliff.

Devon turned to him. "Stop scaring her, or I'll put one in you."

That sobered her tormentor up.

Skye moved closer to the blond guard. After a moment or two, she took one step backward. Then another.

No one stopped her.

The captive man lay on the platform as his guard continued to yell at him.

Where did Devon find these vile men? Were they always here? Or had the change in this world released the evil in them?

Skye knew the answer, but it wasn't one she liked.

There had always been evil in this world, just waiting for the right moment to reveal itself.

But she refused to believe it was stronger, or in more abundance, than the good.

Good would always win. She had to trust that. Or she might as well give up right now.

38

IMPOSSIBLE

W hen the guard finished bellowing, the giant man crawled to the water that gently lapped at the platform and slid in without a splash.

Bubbles appeared around him, almost hiding the large man from view, then dissipated, lazily floating to the top.

The anguished expression left. Peace and joy replaced it.

The water roused the man, and he swam, zipping from one side of the tank to the other much faster than Skye would've imagined possible. He undulated through the water, feet together, arms at his side. The tattooed man's muscles strained with the effort, but it was clear he savored it. The sight was mesmerizing.

Devon tapped the button.

The captive jerked—his gaze shooting to the scientist.

Devon waved him to the front of the glass.

The giant man made his way forward, staring at the crowd. Did he look them over, searching for some sympathetic soul?

He closed his eyes as if disappointed and seemed to become one with his watery surroundings again.

Skye stepped backward again and again until a woman gave a small cry when she stepped on her foot.

"I'm so sorry!" She mumbled as she shuffled to the woman's side.

Skye quickly looked toward the guards, hoping the woman hadn't drawn attention. But to Skye's delight, they were further away than she'd thought.

The woman gave her a quick smile of forgiveness and continued to stare at the captive. "Amazing, isn't he?" she said.

Skye nodded and took another step backward. She glanced behind her. She'd come about halfway.

There were so many more people between her and freedom.

She straightened her shoulders—she would make it. With everyone's attention focused on the giant man, she would be out of here in no time.

Devon held up a stopwatch and brought a megaphone to his mouth. "Five minutes without a breath!"

There was a murmur through the crowd.

Five minutes? Had that much time really gone by?

Skye narrowed her eyes as she examined the large captive hovering in the water. It couldn't have been more than a minute or two. That was the average time a person could hold their breath.

Skye tried to move again, but the knot of people around her tightened.

She changed direction, inching her way across to the wall. From there it might be easier to fight the crowd. She made it a few feet before she was stuck again.

Skye tried to scan the room, but her height worked against her. She swiped at her sweaty neck. Any minute

Devon or Cliff could realize she had left their side. One order to the crowd and they would immediately find her.

Devon held up the stopwatch again. "Ten minutes without a breath!"

Skye stared at the captive hovering in the tank. He showed no sign of distress.

Devon knocked on the glass and motioned for him to swim.

Back and forth, at greater and greater speeds, he went. Skye stood transfixed. How was this possible?

The swimmer changed his pattern, circling the water in the huge tank. The water worked its way into a whirlpool.

Skye shook her head, trying to deny what was right in front of her. The man had no way to breathe, and yet he was able to do this?

And the speed! She'd never seen a person swim that fast.

"Ladies and gentlemen, I introduce you to The Atlantian!"

Another quick tap by Devon on the control and the man stopped and returned to the glass. The water swirled around him, but he held steady.

Skye stared at the captive. His size, his skin, his strength. They were everything Devon had said they would be. Her eyes zeroed in on his brawny chest. It should heave with exertion.

It didn't.

His chest didn't move at all.

Impossible.

The crowd surged ahead, taking Skye with it despite her attempt to stand her ground. This was her chance to go.

Hoping her ankle would hold out, she lowered her head and pushed through the crowd, squeezing past person after person—until someone too solid blocked the way.

One large hand wrapped itself around Skye's mouth as an arm snaked over her ribs.

"Shh," someone murmured in Skye's ear.

Skye's gaze widened.

The crowd thinned as the man carried her backward.

She kicked with her one good foot—almost catching the man's kneecap.

"Settle, ya little she-cat!" The man uttered a deep, relieved chuckle. "It's me, darlin'."

Skye sagged with relief, wanting nothing more than to turn and drink him in.

Could this possibly be true? Dylan here, holding her as she'd dreamt of all these days?

His woodsy scent surrounded her, and Skye breathed it in.

When he readjusted her in his arms, she wrapped hers around his neck and stared at him to reassure herself he was real.

Dylan carried her back to the wall where Wade and Kelsey waited.

The girl was so dirty, Skye needed to do a double-take to recognize her. The white teeth of Kelsey's grin shone in her grimy face and Skye smiled back, comforted to see her.

"You made it!" Skye whispered to Kelsey.

Dylan lowered Skye but kept an arm around her. Wade lined up on her other side for support.

"Hey, Sis," he said with laughter in his eyes. "You gotta stop runnin' off like this."

Skye gave him a wide grin. "I'll try."

She couldn't stop the tears flooding her eyes when Dylan put a hand to his own injury. This trip had cost him. She hoped not too much.

The four of them stayed inched against the wall past the crowd.

As they reached the outer doors, Devon yelled out, "Twenty minutes!"

Skye threw a glance at the captive and looked at Dylan. "Do you see that?"

Dylan stared at the tank dumbfounded and shook his head. "I don't know what I'm seeing."

The four of them slipped out of the door and ran across the parking lot—Skye between the brothers.

Wade helped Skye into the car while Dylan rushed to the driver's side of the truck.

Once the vehicle doors slammed shut, Skye glanced back at the Marine Center. No one had followed them. Yet.

Dylan squeezed her thigh. "How hard are they gonna be looking for you, darlin'?"

As he started the truck and maneuvered toward town, Skye answered. "Pretty hard. They think I'm like him."

Puzzlement covered everyone's face.

Skye put up a hand. "Yes, I know. I'm not. But Devon is convinced. So we need to. . . "

"Get the heck out of dodge, I'd say," Wade said.

"The faster, the better," Dylan added before clamping his jaw and hitting the gas.

39

BACK WITH YOU

Dylan sped through the town with little care. If any guards had been posted out here, they were probably at the Marine Center for the big show.

He leaned into Skye, breathing in her scent, as she wrapped her arms around him. His heart floated now instead of being sunk somewhere in his middle, hard as a rock.

They'd done it.

Skye and Kelsey were out of that place and now they could head home, back to his green hills as fast as they could.

Skye hugged him a little tighter. "I was... Dylan, I can't even express everything I'm feeling right now." Her voice trembled.

"I know, darlin', I didn't fare too well myself. I worried that I'd never find you, especially when I found out you were states away."

"Just you and Wade came?"

Dylan shook his head, a smile spreading across his face. "No, darlin'. I couldn't hold those mountain men back.

There's a bunch of them up ahead. We were only supposed to be scoutin' this time, but it was too good an opportunity to pass up."

"How in the world did you get here so fast?"

Kelsey piped up from the back seat. "Wade ran into those jerks who kidnapped us and beat it out of them."

Wade puffed his chest. "Yep, left 'em tied to a tree. I hope they're still stuck there."

"Well, Wade, I'm glad you found us, no matter what it took. And I won't feel sorry for men who trade others as if they were no more than a bushel of potatoes."

Skye's gaze turned back at Dylan and kissed his cheek.

He glanced at her, a smile on his face. "Can't wait to welcome you home properly. Get that ring back on your finger."

Skye gave a wide grin. "I'm glad Jesse and the ring made it home safe. I can't wait to see my boy."

"He's spittin' mad we left him behind with the other men. But one kid was enough."

"Hey!" Kelsey said, "I did good, and you know it."

Dylan glanced at her in the rearview mirror and chuckled. "You did great, but it's an extra responsibility. I'd hate for something to happen to a young 'un on my watch."

Skye twisted in her seat to grab Kelsey's hand. "Without you, I'm not sure they would've found me. You were so brave!"

"I'm glad I caught Dylan and the others on their way down here. And I'm not sure brave is the right word. I was terrified is what I was."

Skye searched Kelsey's face. "What happened?"

"Obstacles," the girl said, refusing to divulge more, "but I overcame them." The girl gave a wan smile and glanced at Wade. "Gotta roll with the punches, right Wade?"

"You got it, girl! The bigger they are, the more you roll. You did awesome."

Skye turned back and snuggled against Dylan. "It was awful in there. The things he is doing to people." She rubbed at the Band-Aid covering her hand.

"What did he do?" Dylan frowned as he glanced from her hand to her face.

"That doctor. He's doing awful experiments on people —supposedly for a cure to the AgFlu. But medical torture is what it is. In one room . . . " Her voice trailed off, and she shuddered. "It's what Devon planned for me and Kelsey. He showed me a file of what he'd done to one Atlantian. It was awful, Dylan. Terrible."

Dylan pushed his fingers through his hair. This guy, Devon. How long would he get away with this?

A niggling started somewhere in Dylan's gut, but he tried to ignore it.

It didn't help when Wade offered from the back seat. "We need to go back tomorrow and take care of those guys, D. They're nothing but trouble."

And if what Sue Ellen thought was true. That these men were poaching people all the way up on Cole's Mountain—his mountain. That they were the ones who shot him.

Dylan's jaw hardened.

But he didn't have enough people. And no matter how much he wanted to take these people down, he wasn't at his best. Far from it.

No. They lived states away from Seaside. Once they left this area, the mad scientist wouldn't be an immediate concern. The best way to save the community was to high-tail it home and close ranks. Make sure those scouting for this place recognized the mountain was off-limits.

Behind him, Wade continued to bluster, but Dylan ignored him.

He had to.

Dylan's hand moved to his own injury as a fiery jolt went through him when they hit a pothole. It was still healing—still hurting more than he let on.

He wasn't up to a fight—not yet anyway.

The best he could do right now is hunker down with his loved ones until he was full strength.

He changed the subject. "So that's what we're calling them then? Atlantians? Are we believing that?"

An open window tousled Skye's hair, and she brushed it back as she answered, "I don't know what else to think. Here's the thing. I saw the file, and I didn't believe it, but seeing that tattooed man in person, seeing what he could do—how can we deny it? And there's something else."

Dylan raised an eyebrow.

"A young woman, Sonora, snuck into my room early this morning. She seemed to know the place and was shocked it was still there. Devon is her uncle, and she said he was in jail. Sonora said there already was a cure. And get this—it was the one we saw on the news, the Atlantian Cure."

Skye frowned when Wade was about to interrupt, stopping him. "I know! I know it seems crazy, but she was credible. She said she and her family had left. So I wonder, where did they go? Atlantis? She said she came up here for some things they left behind. Up here? It all fits."

Dylan rubbed a hand over his jaw. "So, you're thinkin' she's one of them? An Atlantian?"

"I don't know. She was no bigger than me unless it's just the men who are larger. I supposed it's possible, I mean look at some of our basketball players, they're tall." Skye bit her lip. "I doubt they are aware one of their own has been left behind."

"Well," Wade said, "We don't know them. Maybe they just cut their losses and left him there."

"I don't think so," Skye disagreed, "because Sonora said she'd come back for me, and she doesn't even know me."

"She's coming back to rescue you?" Dylan asked.

Skye nodded. "And bringing her husband and his family. She said they were all big and fighters."

Dylan squinted his eyes and looked out the side window. If that girl came back looking for Skye and got hurt because of it . . .

Still not his problem. If she had a big, powerful army to back her up, this Sonora would be fine.

Dylan gnawed on a fingernail. He sure couldn't fight worth anything if he wanted to, not with this wound. He just wanted to go home.

Dylan turned into the driveway of the house where the rest of the group waited. He got out of the truck and walked to the back yard overlooking the ocean and the big gray dome that the mad scientist called home and others called hell.

From here, it looked no bigger than a coffee cup—but it still looked like trouble.

And the more Dylan heard, the worse it got.

The door of the house sprang open and Jesse flew out and down the porch stairs. He ran into Skye's outstretched arms and hugged her tight.

Skye squeezed the boy close, her eyes closed, pure happiness warming her face.

"Jesse," she breathed out his name. "I worried so many times over the last few days that I'd never—I'd never— "

She pulled him tighter as she cried.

"I wanted to go with them and find you, Mom, but they made me sit here and twiddle my thumbs."

Skye kissed the side of his head and ran a hand over his hair. "I know, Jesse. But it's fine now. Everything worked out just fine." Skye put a hand on either side of his face and gave him a watery smile. "I'm just so happy to see you."

40

THE LOVE OF HIS LIFE

L ater, the group sat in the backyard of an abandoned house. They gathered around a low campfire hidden by trees and ate vending machine food they had scrounged up.

Even though Wade continued to rally the troops for a fight, the decision had been made to leave in a couple of hours, traveling by the dark of the night. Most agreed that any battle they began could only be won with more men and weapons than they had available. For now, they kept a lookout for anyone searching for Skye.

Skye slumped in her lawn chair, exhausted from the past few days, and dozed as the others discussed the problem.

When Skye stirred, Dylan took the chair beside her, handing her some aspirin and a bottle of water. "Here, darlin'. We'll get Doc to look at you the minute you get home."

Skye nodded as she swallowed and sipped—her eyes on the ground.

He stared at her. Something wasn't right. "What is it?"

"Nothing."

"There's something. Is it your face? That'll heal, darlin'. It just needs some time."

"It's not my face."

Dylan brushed her hair to one side and kissed her bruised forehead. "What then? It's okay to tell me."

"It's just... all those poor people under Devon's control —hurting so badly. I wish we could help them now."

"We ain't got enough manpower. The few of us against one hundred or more. You saw them. We gotta go home. Get safe. We'll come back when we can."

"I understand. But that kind of evil," Skye pointed to the domed building near the ocean, "doesn't just go away. It grows larger and larger unless it's exterminated. It will catch up with us."

Dylan looked at the ground. It already had. She just didn't know it yet.

Dylan's gut writhed with every thought of the place and what those evil people had done, both here and in their invasion on Cole's Mountain, but he couldn't do anything about it right now.

"Skye." He steeled himself for what was coming.

"I want to go back."

And there it was. Dylan sighed and pulled away. "Naw. We're goin' home."

Skye stared at him. "You didn't see them. People are suffering terribly because of what he's doing."

"You really think we outta go back after them now with the odds so stacked against us?"

"Don't you?"

Dylan's gut screamed yes, but he raised an eyebrow. "How many can we really help?"

"Does it matter if it's two or two hundred? They need us.

I can't even describe to you . . ." She swiped a tear rolling down her cheek.

Dylan's expression fell as he pulled Skye toward him. How could he fight her on this? She'd almost been one of them. Everyone in that building had someone who worried about them as much as he'd worried about Skye.

"There's a lot of firepower in there."

"You don't think we can beat them? Can we think of a way?"

Dylan stared into her big green eyes that begged for his help. This wasn't just about that place down there. She'd never actually gotten over the fact that she had let Calvin go and still considered herself responsible for the people he'd killed because of it. No doubt, if they walked away now, she'd feel the same, no matter what he said.

He put an arm around her and pulled her to his side.

She groaned and put a hand to her bowed head.

"Skye, what is it?"

"You're not going to like it." She pulled away and put a hand on her ribs.

"Tell me."

"I wasn't a cooperative patient. That guard, Cliff, banged me up pretty good."

Dylan's face hardened as his gaze skimmed over her. So, her bruised face wasn't her only injury.

"The back of my head." Skye gingerly felt the back of her skull. "I passed out more than once. And this." She lifted her shirt enough for him to see her purple stomach. "But that isn't all." She bit her lip.

Dylan's eyes narrowed as she scratched at her hand for what seemed like the millionth time. "Did he inject you?"

"Yes." She nodded, tears in her eyes. "Something—I don't know what. But that roomful of dying people had this all over their body. I don't know—I don't know what that means for me."

Fury ignited a red-hot flame in Dylan's belly. He swallowed some of it down just so he could speak.

This was no longer some nameless, faceless victim. This was the love of his life they had hurt. His body went rigid—his muscles like bands of iron.

Through a clamped jaw, he growled, "They need ended."

41

INTRODUCTIONS

H ope flared in Skye. The sooner Devon was taken down, the better. She wrapped her arms around Dylan. "I know, love," she murmured as she laid against him. "You'll make sure Devon and Cliff never hurt anyone again."

"And make sure he tells us what he injected you with so we can get it treated."

She tipped her head toward Wade. "You should talk to your brother."

One glance and a nod of Dylan's head and Wade was at his side.

With Dylan's declaration of war, Wade uttered a single word. "Finally!"

The three stared at the moon-lit dome below them.

"I'm so fired up I wish I could tear through the building right now," Dylan said.

"I hear ya, brother," Wade agreed.

Dylan looked at Wade, then threw a glance at the good men around the campfire. "We have fighters, but not enough."

Wade nodded. "And if we go in with explosives, we might hurt some good people."

"We need to be careful," Skye said. "We're there to help them."

Dylan and Wade continued to throw out options. When the driveway gravel crunched behind them, everyone instantly became quiet.

Everyone whirled toward the sound, weapons drawn.

Standing in the drive was a dark-haired, very tall, muscular man, dressed in a dark blue uniform. A weapon similar to a rifle hung over his shoulder. He held one hand up in greeting while holding a small blonde woman behind him with the other. She struggled to get by him.

Skye smiled when she recognized the woman and started forward. "Sonora!"

Dylan grabbed her arm to stop her.

The younger woman waved, a big grin covering her face. "Hi! I'm so happy—"

The man in front of her barked something in a language Skye didn't understand.

Sonora made a face and continued. "—you're out of that place. Are you okay?"

"I am. I think."

Sonora almost made it around Ian, but he swatted her back again. She punched him in the arm and complained, "You big brut."

Dylan looked at Skye with a raised eyebrow.

"It's Sonora," she explained. "The woman who said she'd save me. They're friendly."

"We don't know that. He has a weapon."

"Of course he does. But he hasn't drawn it. But you two continue to aim yours at them."

"He could have others with them."

"Dylan! They are friends."

Skye almost laughed when Sonora succeeded in escaping the large man, only to have him grab the back of her knee-length sky-blue dress. She stopped immediately, and Skye didn't blame her. It didn't look as if the light material would survive a tug-of-war.

"Woman!" The large man said, "You make a dignified entry impossible."

"Ian, you don't need to impress them. They are friends." She shook her dress. "Now let me go."

Skye watched the war of wills. "Are you okay, Sonora?"

"Oh yeah, this is my husband. He doesn't always play nice with Humans—including his wife." Sonora turned to scowl at him. "He's still upset with me for coming up here without him," Sonora pretended to whisper to Skye.

Ian gave an exaggerated sigh. "I had reason to be upset. You put yourself in danger. However, I will release your dress if you vow to stay by my side."

Sonora threw up her hands. "Fine. If that will help things move along."

"It will, *Jata Ara*. I appreciate your cooperation."

Ian turned to Dylan and Wade, scanning them from head to feet. "I am Caspian of the Orca Clan," he proudly introduced himself, "though most call me Ian, and from Atlantis. Do you know of my people?"

The brothers stared back at Ian.

Wade scratched the scruff on his chin. "Well, maybe?"

Ian's eyes lit with amusement. "That is a start." He nodded toward the Cole's weapons that still pointed at him and his wife. "Can I assume we will not be firing upon each other?"

Dylan and Wade glanced at each other and lowered their weapons.

"I'd also like to introduce my lovely—and impatient—bride, Sonora. Originally from the town of Seaside, though,

245

I have persuaded her to be my mate. Not an easy task, I assure you. As you can see, it can be quite exhausting to keep her at my side."

Sonora threw Ian an irritated glance, but when he turned a gaze of utter devotion toward her, the irritation faded, and adoration took its place. She wound her arm through his and patted him.

"May we approach?" Ian asked.

Dylan nodded, and the couple approached as he introduced himself. "I'm Dylan Cole. This here is my fiancé, Skye Jackson, our son, Jesse, and my brother, Wade. The others are our friends."

Wade waved back the group that had gathered behind them. "Let's give 'em room, boys. They're friendly."

As Ian reached Dylan's side, he stared down the hill at Seaside. "Gentlemen, I'm assuming you are discussing the situation below."

"Yeah," Dylan said, giving Ian a cautious look.

"My family and I would like to help with that. We believed the situation under control until recently. We would like to help finish what we started. Let me explain what I mean."

While the men talked, Sonora made her way over to Skye. "Did my uncle do this?" she asked, pointing to Skye's bruised face.

"One of his henchmen, Cliff." Skye could barely utter his name.

Tears sprang to Sonora's eyes. "I'm so sorry. We had him arrested and thought he was in jail. I mean, he was, but with everything that happened, he must have gotten out somehow."

"What he's done isn't on you." She hoped the young woman believed her because she was about to find out a lot more about Devon's evil side.

4 2

ATLANTIS

More than once as the group talked, Ian's gaze lingered on Dylan and Skye. Eventually, he spoke his mind. "Both of you are injured. Are you able to fight?"

"I'll do what I need to do, don't ya worry about that," Dylan blustered.

"Your willingness is not in question," Ian said, his expression earnest, "your physical ability is—and only because we can fix it."

"He was shot and barely survived it," Skye said. "How can you help him?"

"Did you bring a healer?" Sonora asked her husband and explained that it was a doctor's tool.

"Unfortunately, I did not. But I believe a trip back to Atlantis may do us all good. Skye is not only bruised. Something deeper moves inside her. Do you feel it, Skye?"

Tears came to her eyes. A dark shadow had taken up residence in her since Devon's final injection. As hard as she tried, she couldn't banish it. Instead, it had grown and with it had come pain. Ian was right, something was wrong with her—very wrong.

247

"Can you help me?" Her voice came as a whisper, as if afraid the thing inside her would hear and bury itself deeper.

"Our doctors are the best in the world," Ian assured her.

Sonora walked over and hugged her. "Oh, Skye! They really are the best. They will help you. I just know it."

Ian stood. "Then that is what we will do. Go to Atlantis, see the doctor, and gather our army and return ready for war."

Wade stood, looking stunned. "Wait. What? Not Atlantis—like under the underwater Atlantis?"

"The very one."

"I ain't going." He folded his arms. "I'll just wait right here."

Dylan stood, groaning a little as he did so. "I'd be doin' the same, but for Skye and for this wound in my side, that's getting worse by the hour. Ian is right—I can't fight like this, bro. Just can't do it. I'd be more of a liability than anything else."

He patted Wade on the back. "I understand if you want to stay, but I sure could use you at my side."

Wade ran a hand over his face and shuffled his foot. "Of course, brother. If you need me, you know I'll be there." He threw a glance at the dark water below. "I ain't looking forward to this one though—not at all."

"It's better if we all stick together," Dylan explained.

"That means I get to go?" Jesse asked, his eyes bright with excitement. "This is awesome!"

The group gathered their things and piled into their vehicles—some with dread, some with excitement. But one thing was clear, anyone who had scoffed at stories of Atlantians before was a firm believer now.

43

THE SEA

Dylan had never disliked the water until now. Raised in the mountains, he'd had little experience with anything much bigger than a large pond, but he did know how to swim—in regular water.

But this ocean he stared at now was nothing like the pools of water back home. This first glimpse of the sea would be memorable in more than one way. Not only would he see the topside but the underside too.

His shoes sunk into the soft sand as he walked from the parking lot to the water's edge, the suction reminding him a bit of mud.

Dylan stopped where the sand mixed with water and became firmer and took in the sight before him.

From where he stood to the horizon, the blue liquid rolled and twisted before it kissed the land, only to pull away from the very place it'd been trying to reach.

He dipped the toe of his shoe in a small pool left behind. He'd heard people say the ocean was calming. It didn't seem that way to him.

Instead, it reminded him of how he'd felt when he and Skye were separated—anxious and unsettled.

Ian stepped up beside him. "First look at the sea?"

"Yep."

"She's amazing, isn't she?"

Dylan stared as a large agitated wave blindly smashed onto the beach, throwing spray and foam into the air.

"It's something, all right," he said.

Jesse rushed by him straight to the water's edge, running alongside it and waving his arms as he tried to yell louder than the crashing waves.

Dylan smiled. It was good someone was enjoying this.

Skye entwined her arm with his. "What do you think?"

"I don't know." He kicked at the sand.

"You don't have to like it. It's not a requirement," she said, the corner of her mouth turning up.

"It's too—I'm gonna use a big word here—turbulent. It seems uneasy."

Ian nodded, a solemn expression covering his face. "You have read her well. Our sea has many moods, and each day is different. Today, she is uneasy. No doubt she senses the evil residing so close and is eager to see it gone."

Dylan looked down the beach to his left, where the glint of lightbulbs could be seen. Did the mad scientist actually need to generate that much electricity? Or was it a lure to draw more innocents in?

"Eager as I am, I'd say." Dylan's jaw hardened.

The group of humans startled and moved backward as five Atlantians surfaced from the water, walking toward them.

Ian raised his hands. "It is fine, my new friends. These are my people."

He turned and talked with the new arrivals in a gentle

language, then interpreted. "They have brought us vehicles."

When the group muttered uncertainly, Sonora reassured them, "They are very nice. Kind of a cross between a mini-van and little submarine."

Ian sent her an exasperated look. "It is not a mini-van."

"I know, dear. I just want them to understand they will be comfortable."

As the Atlantians waved them toward the water, Dylan took a moment to put his hand to a massive red rock wall beside. The plaque on it read, "Spire Cliff."

"This is what I'm used to," he said to Skye. "Solid around me. Solid under my feet. Dependable." He bent back, looking to the top. "It looks as out of place as I feel."

"If it makes you feel any better," Skye said as she laid her head on his arm, "this makes me nervous too, even though I have been on the ocean before."

Dylan's gaze zeroed in on hers. He'd been so concerned about himself he'd given her worry no thought at all. "I'm sorry, darlin'. I didn't even ask about your nerves. But I'm thinking that if this heals us, it will be worth it."

"It will." Skye nodded and pulled him toward the water.

Getting to the vehicles was both easier and harder than Dylan expected. The Atlantians had brought the vehicles as close to shore as possible, and into an area protected from most of the waves. However, everyone needed to wade out to them.

The Atlantians made their way through the choppy water with ease, but the Humans had more trouble.

Skye clung to Dylan as they trudged their way through waist deep water to the vehicle, but she quickly lost her strength.

As Dylan bent to pick her up, two large Atlantians appeared beside them. "May we assist you."

Dylan's gaze narrowed at them. It was *his* job to make sure his woman stayed safe. He ignored them as he lifted Skye only to feel pain shoot down his side so intensely that he almost dropped to his knees.

"We understand," one Atlantian said. "We will treat Skye with respect and have her at your side as soon as possible."

"It's okay, love. I'm sure I'll be fine," Skye added.

Dylan reluctantly surrendered her but kept an eye on her as they moved away.

When he arrived at the water vehicle, Dylan grabbed the edge of the hatch and hiked himself in. Beside him, the tall Atlantian gently set Skye on her feet and asked about her health.

"I did well. Thank you," she replied.

The Atlantian's gaze lingered on Skye a little too long for Dylan's comfort, and he hurried to her side. "I'll take care of my fiancé from here."

The man gave Dylan a quick nod and stepped away.

SONORA OFFERED THEM FRESH, dry clothing. Dylan found it tempting since his jeans now seemed heavy and uncomfortable. He eyed the dark blue uniform most of the Atlantian males wore. Though their clothing looked like it had already dried, the thick material seemed to clingy for his taste.

Skye took a dress from Sonora and changed in a small room she pointed out.

When she emerged, Dylan caught his breath. The light material seemed to float down her body and around her bare calves. The green color brightened her eyes.

Dylan helped Skye into a window seat and took the one next to her. "Lookin' good, darlin'," he murmured in her ear.

Skye giggled. "Thank you. Are you sure you don't want dry clothes?"

"I think I'd rather stay in what I have on then go around in one of those ballerina suits."

DYLAN PEEKED around Skye at the watery scene outside the windows and almost shuddered. He sure hoped this place didn't take long to reach. Dylan grabbed Skye's hand, then loosened his grip as he realized he had squeezed her fingers harder than he intended.

"It's okay," she assured him. "We are safe—truly safe down here. Devon will never find us. Let's just enjoy that feeling for now."

She was right. For the first time in a long time, no one could hurt them.

His tension evaporated, and he put his arm around Skye's shoulders and kissed the top of her head.

He gave her a slow smile. "When you're right, you're right, Doc."

She nodded and returned the quick hug.

Jesse and Kelsey jumped from the water onto the rim of the hatch and smiled.

Jesse rushed to take the seat across from Skye.

"Mom, that was pretty awesome!"

"It was."

Wade followed close behind him as Kelsey took the opportunity to change out of her wet clothing.

"I ain't gonna say it was awesome," Wade said, "but it was better than I thought it'd be."

He waved a hand at Jesse. "Am I gonna have to fight you for the window seat, boy?"

"Nope. Cause I've already got it." Jesse laughed and ducked when Wade threatened to pick him up and move him.

"Hey," the boy said. "You can't pick me up so easy anymore. And besides, I got here first. You're taller than me, so this is better, anyway."

"Not that much taller, boy. And that big head of yours is in the way."

Skye laughed. "Share nice, boys."

"Yes, ma'am," Jesse replied as his eager gaze turned to the water again.

44

QUITE THE ADVENTURE

Skye took in the underwater scene. Blue—maybe blue-green, if she were precise.

Bits of seaweed and small sticks floated through the water close to the vehicle, while below sand stirred from the ocean floor. Visibility only went so far. It would have made her uneasy, if she hadn't been out here with experts.

She'd always wanted to take an underwater tour, but had never gotten around to it. She'd imagined she'd be able to see a long way, just like a nice day on a hilltop. But that wasn't the case. It was a few yards at the most before everything faded away into a darker hue of turquoise.

IAN ZIPPED by the window on something similar to a motor-cycle and took the lead of the caravan.

Jesse sat straighter, craning his neck for another glimpse. "Whoa, did you see that?"

"I did. Pretty cool, huh?"

"Way cool! Isn't it, Dad?"

Dylan nodded. "I gotta admit if I were into under-the-sea riding, I'd like to try that bike."

Wade twisted around to stare out the front window to where Ian had stationed himself in front of them. "Well, I'll be! Wonder if that Ian would be willing to give a lesson on that thing."

"He might," Sonora said, "if we have the time. But be warned, he is very possessive of the vehicle."

"Course he is! All men like to keep an eye on their rides," Wade said.

"Especially one as awesome as that. I want a lesson too," Jesse added.

"Uh, huh," Skye replied. "Like Sonora said, if we have time. There are other matters to take care of first."

Jesse sobered up. "Yeah, I know. But," he said with a glint in his eye as he looked at Sonora, "we can visit again, can't we?"

"Of course you can, as often as you'd like."

Jesse sat back in his seat with a satisfied expression on his face.

AFTER A WHILE, Sonora sat forward. "You'll see the city soon."

"What I want to know, " Wade asked, glancing at Ian again, "is how often that husband of yours takes a breath? He's been sitting in the water now for quite some time."

"It's unnerving at first, isn't it? I think, once an hour or so."

"How the heck is that possible?"

"Over time, their bodies adapted to their environment. They developed the ability to drastically conserve oxygen."

"Evolution?"

"No. Adaptation. The two are often confused, but adaptation happens in many species of plants and animals—even humans."

A flicker of light against the deeper blue of the ocean caught Skye's eye. As they drew closer, she pulled in a breath and sent Dylan a surprised glance.

"Look at the size!"

He leaned across her for a better look. "Just how big is Atlantis?" he asked Sonora.

"As large as a medium-sized Human city, but I think it seems bigger since there's nothing around it to compare it to. It does take about twenty minutes to drive from one end to the other in a vehicle though."

"Good lord," Wade exclaimed. "How is this kept hidden?"

"As we get closer, you'll see what looks like a fine net dome over Atlantis," Sonora said. "That device can scramble any fish or depth finders, making the ocean floor appear very shallow and rocky so people avoid the area."

"And this had been going on for how long?"

"For centuries. Atlantis isn't their only city either. They have many, spread over the oceans."

Wade slapped his knee. "Well, I'll be. This is—it's just too much."

Dylan shook his head, agreeing with his brother.

"I understand." Sonora gave a soft smile. "I thought I was going crazy when I first saw this city. But that was almost a year ago now." She smiled. "The place grows on you."

Skye leaned forward. "What can we expect?"

"Don't worry. It's nice, really nice and so, so safe."

Skye leaned back in her seat. That is what she wanted to hear. She didn't care if they hovered in the water in suits twenty-four/seven as long as they were safe.

She tried to ignore the burning itch of the bubbly rash

on her arm. It was getting worse, and it was all she could do to stop herself from clawing at it.

The redness was beyond the bandage now, running up her arm with small blisters forming along it.

When she moved, something behind her stomach sent pain moving through her body. Whatever Devon had put inside her was growing—changing.

The sight of those tortured people came to her. Had her body started to decay even before death as those patients had?

Her heart skipped several beats, then rushed to catch up.

Was that because of nerves? Or Devon's deadly cocktail?

She would've broken down in despair if her family were not around her. For them, she would put on a bright face and act as if nothing were wrong—nothing at all.

Skye gave Jesse an over-bright smile and raised her eyebrows. "This is quite the adventure, isn't it?"

45

THE BEST THING

Skye wasn't fooling him. Dylan felt her tenseness and noticed the many times her clawed hand reached to scratch her arm only to jerk it away.

Tears of pain crept from the corners of her eyes as she tried to distract herself by talking to Jesse.

Dylan stared at the underwater city in front of him. No matter what else it held, it had better hold the cure for whatever ailed Skye.

He'd finally found her, he couldn't lose her again.

Two armed guards waved the driver through a large silver gate—the only way into the thin, netted dome.

Water moved freely from the outside to the inside of the dome. The city was more vertical than horizontal, with a watchtower rising high above it all. Because of that, roads seemed high rather than wide so that a vehicle was more likely to be above or below them rather than beside them. Not that there were a lot of vehicles. It seemed more people would rather swim.

The buildings and houses looked like something Dylan

would have seen out of a history book. Old, some even ancient—though well taken care of.

The vehicle slowed near a building, giving it a light tap before shuddering to a stop. The driver stood and addressed them. "I have brought you directly to our hospital as instructed."

Some murmured, a worried expression on their faces until Dylan spoke up. "Best thing you could've done. Thank you." He meant it. The sooner Skye got the care she needed, the better.

Dylan pushed out of his seat, groaning as he did so. He wasn't in the greatest of shape himself. He'd taken a peek under his bandage. The wound was starting to pus up again.

A side door on the vehicle slid open and two Atlantians stood beside it. One man held a hand to help Dylan out of the vehicle.

Did he look that bad?

Dylan scoffed at the man and took the step down on his own but without his usual confidence. He was weaker than he would've liked.

"Help her," he instructed the Atlantian, jerking his thumb over his shoulder before turning and also helping Skye.

"Thanks," he said, nodding to the man. Not only was Dylan grateful for his aid, but Sonora had mentioned that Atlantians were very polite and appreciated others following their example.

The man smiled and tipped his head. "It was my pleasure to be of service."

Unsure what response he expected, Dylan just gave him another nod and moved on.

Skye clung to Dylan as they moved down a dry, oxygen-filled corridor. A few of the city's residents spread out along it, watching them. Dylan narrowed his gaze.

But when Skye stumbled and Dylan struggled to catch her, two women rushed to their side to help and stayed close.

Dylan and Skye thanked them, and Skye sent a relieved glance to Dylan.

He understood then that the Atlantians were posted there to help them if needed.

Of course, he and Skye would be suspicious. It had become instinctive and necessary for their survival. Maybe here they could relax a little.

They guided the Humans into a large room where a woman invited Skye to sit in the nearest chair.

The area was massive containing several beds for patients. It reminded Dylan more of a Star Trek movie Wade had once dragged him to than any proper hospital he'd been in.

Skye pointed out her family to the medical staff, and they assigned the Coles areas near each other. When Dylan opted to stay at Skye's side instead of going to a bed of his own, there was no discussion. The staff accepted it without complaint.

A few minutes later, a tall, thin woman with straight, jet black hair strode into the room and took a minute to scan the patients before turning to one of the staff.

The two women conferred for a moment before making their way over to Skye.

"Hello, I am Mako of Cirrina Clan," the thin woman said and came right to the point. "I hear you are both injured. Others will deal with those wounds as they are more than capable. I am an expert on what you call AgFlu, and I'm here to examine Skye."

Mako bent over Skye, looking her over. Then she

attached a type of bracelet to Skye's arm and consulted a readout on the wall behind her.

"Um, interesting." Her curious gaze turned to Skye. "Tell me anything you can about the injection they gave you."

Skye looked startled. "Oh. I hadn't mentioned—"

"Ian has told me everything. That so-called scientist also tortured him. And now I hear the Humans failed to distribute the cure we left for them. Oceans help us!" Mako folded her arms. "Not surprising to me—I *told* the council we needed to take care of it ourselves."

A man walked through the door and overheard Mako's complaint. "The council thought we should allow Humans the opportunity to help themselves."

She threw him an irritated stare. "And see what it has brought us? They infected this poor child with things not even the mighty waters could wash out of her. Yet, I am expected to do so. This has become the maelstrom I warned you about, Jorah. It is good I continued with my research."

"With which I have every confidence you will save this young woman."

He stepped up to Dylan and Skye and shook their hands. "I am Jorah of Orca Clan, leader of the council and father of Caspian, who brought you here, as well as two lovely daughters. I am sorry to interrupt your time with Mako, but I needed to inform her there will be a meeting of the council tonight."

Mako put a hand to her hip. "How am I expected to complete my work with these interruptions?"

"The evil is great," Jorah replied. "It must be dealt with swiftly."

Mako's expression changed from irritation to determination. "I will be there."

After Jorah left, Skye told Mako what she could about what Devon had done to her.

Mako nodded as she pulled out a small tool and waved it over Skye's body.

Dylan looked over the woman's shoulder, trying to read what it said, but even the letters were strange to him.

Mako called two of the other medical people over and spoke to them in Atlantian before turning to Skye.

"I am afraid this will be a little more invasive than I like to be. Not too bad though, rather like those IVs that your people like to poke others with."

"And it will cure me? Of everything?"

Mako held up the small device she had just been using. "Our word for this is "healer" in English. It is small and good for small injuries. There is a larger one. You will lay on the table below it and it will move over you."

Mako paused as if reading Skye's reaction. When it seemed Skye accepted the course of treatment, she continued.

"We will also give you a medication that will rid your body of all the poisons the crazy Human gave you."

"And then I will be cured? For real?"

Dylan squeezed Skye's hand.

Mako gave Skye a strange look. "Of course, for real. What else is there? I do not pretend to cure people."

"I'm sorry," Skye stumbled over her words. "I didn't mean—I saw people dying horrible deaths and thought that was my future."

Mako smiled and patted Skye's shoulder. "I understand. That is because you come from up there." She shuddered. "Here in the sea, we do miraculous things. Don't worry, little one. You will be cured—in less than an hour."

"Thank you!" Skye turned to Dylan, collapsing in his arms.

Dylan dropped into the closest chair, taking Skye with him. Relief had left his legs weak.

He buried his face in Skye's silky, dark hair, and whispered, as much to himself as to her. "It's gonna be okay. It's all gonna be okay now."

46

FREE

Dylan watched Skye climb up on the healing table, smiling when she gave him a little wave. The ache in his stomach had evaporated like a morning fog when Mako said they would cure Skye. And it wouldn't be a long drawn out procedure, but quick and easy.

Who knew what else these strange people could do?

Once Skye settled in for treatment, Mako moved to a nearby table and waved Dylan over. "Could I examine your injury?"

Dylan nodded. As he grabbed the bottom of his shirt, a familiar bite of unease slid over his skin. He never liked displaying the scars covering his body.

Mako's eyes narrowed, her gaze instantly going not to his fresh injury, but the old ones. The scars that told the sad story of childhood. She reached out and lightly traced the thickest of them, the knife wound that ran from his back to his belly, but she said nothing.

Instead, she removed his bandage and examined the bullet wound.

The hole in Dylan's side looked every bit as bad as the

last time he looked at it. Pus oozed from the inside and redness encircled it.

Dylan prepared himself for the pain of being poked and even worse, getting it cleaned out.

Mako grabbed the small healer off a side table and held it over his injury. She looked at the wound a few times as she tapped the healer's small screen, then held it a couple of inches from the liquidy mess.

The gaping wound shrank in size.

Dylan jerked, almost jumping off the table. What was this thing doing to him?

"Was there pain?" Mako asked in a surprised tone.

"No. It surprised me, is all".

"You must be still," Mako commanded.

Still unable to believe what he was seeing, Dylan asked, "What are you doing?"

"Clearly, I am healing your wound."

"Just like that?"

"Yes, just like that. Now, be still."

"Yes, ma'am."

Dylan watched as the hole the bullet had torn through his body got smaller and smaller. "Well, I'll be," he murmured.

"I'll be what?"

He looked up at Mako, confused for a moment, and laughed. "No, just I'll be. It's something we say."

"It makes no sense."

"Nope. None, but it fits."

Mako shrugged off her confusion.

When she lifted the healer, Dylan ran his fingers over the small ridge still left on his stomach.

"It's like it was never there."

"Clearly, it was there. A scar is still left. But I can erase that too if you wish."

"Yeah, erase it."

"I was unsure as I have heard that Human males take great pride in their scars, and you seem to have many."

Dylan looked down at what his lifted shirt revealed.

Cigarette burns, thin whitish strips, and that thick long knife scar. Battle scars, yeah. But not the type she assumed.

He had survived his step-father's abuse, and that was something to take pride in, but otherwise, he hated the marks. Each one a horrible memory forever engraved on his skin.

For as long as he could remember, Dylan had avoided mirrors. Looking at them made him sick.

"These ain't anything to be proud of."

Dylan tried to console himself for the millionth time the only way he could. They were part of what made him— him. Without them, who was he?

"Dylan."

He didn't want to look at the doctor. Dylan couldn't hide the shame he knew would shadow his eyes, and the only person he revealed that to was Skye.

"Dylan." Mako's usual clipped tone became warm and understanding. "The healer can erase them all if you wish."

His gaze flew to hers. Could that be true? Would he be able to stand proud before Skye without the sins of his father written all over him?

Tears flooded his eyes and though he tried to contain them, one ran down his cheek. He scrubbed at it, lowering his head.

"Tears do not need to be hidden from me. Emotions are something all people share, especially Atlantians. Did you know that we literally share each other's emotions? Can even send ours out to others? So, you see, I feel your pain as if it were my own, and your desire to shed the past." Dylan

267

looked up to see the tears in her eyes. "You have powerful emotion, Dylan."

He gave a weak chuckle. "Yeah, I have a hard time reining them in sometimes."

She tipped her head. "Who are you, Dylan Cole?"

He understood what she asked.

"I'm a father who'll be better than the one I had. Someone who tries their best to love, care for, and cherish not only my beautiful Skye but my entire family."

"A good man." She nodded. "A family man." She leaned a bit closer. "What do you want?"

His voice wobbled a little as he answered. "To look in the mirror and see that man—not the one my step-father tried to create."

"Then lay back and allow the healer to reveal that man."

Mako started with the bullet wound, erasing that from his skin as easily as his teacher had wiped a chalkboard. Then she moved on.

With each one, a memory returned. The belt that broke the skin, the scorching burn of a cigarette, the swipe of a knife that narrowly missed killing him.

As Mako went from one to the other, the memories lingered. He let them, thinking on them one more time before he put them all away forever.

When the doctor finished, he ran a hand over skin as soft and taut as a newborn babe. And where some men would have been ashamed of such fine skin, Dylan smiled with pride.

"Thank you," he whispered. "I ain't ever going to forget this. Never."

Mako put a light hand on his arm and gave him another warm smile before going back to her normal quick manner. "Just doing my job. Isn't that a human saying too?"

Dylan gave her a quick grin, knowing it had meant more to her than that. "It is. Seems to me, you've got a pretty nice job."

"I agree, Dylan," she whispered to him. "But do not let others in on that secret. The harder I pretend it is, the more the others leave me to it."

She straightened, put a hand to her hip, and scanned the room. "It looks like some of our guests are ready for the rooms I had prepared. Skye is still undergoing treatment. If you wish, you may go to her side, and when her treatment is completed, we will give you a room where you can wash and change clothes. I need to prepare for the council meeting."

Mako clicked her tongue. "Oh, a woman's work is never done." She looked at Dylan. "Sonora taught me that one, and I am in total agreement with it."

Dylan laughed and sincerely thanked her again before making his way over to Skye.

As he strode across the room, Dylan wondered at the difference in himself. He felt taller with each step, like a man who had broken the chains of his past.

He felt free.

47

GRAND PLANS

S kye eagerly awaited the last long swipe of the healer. The darkness hovering around and in her, the last few days was gone.

She smiled up at the medical assistant who ran the machine, grateful for these people and this technology— neither of which she had known anything about a few hours ago.

It still boggled her mind that an entire race of people had lived on this earth for centuries, and almost no one had known.

Skye eyed a weapon a guard left leaning against the corner of the room. If they had this kind of medical technology, what was their weaponry like?

Skye turned her head toward Dylan as he walked toward her. There was something different about him— though she couldn't put a finger on it. Happier perhaps?

When he reached her, he took her hand and kissed her forehead.

She locked gazes with him. The dull sadness that always lingered in the back of his eyes was gone. Not

THE RESCUE: SANCTUARY'S AGGRESSION 5

tamped down, not pushed to the side so he could enjoy the happiness of the moment, but truly gone.

"Dylan?"

"Yeah, darlin'?"

He still leaned over her, grinning at her as he ran a hand along her hair.

"Something is different," she said.

"Sure is, but we'll talk about that later. Right now, I want to be sure this thing completely healed you."

"I feel good."

"That's what I wanna hear, darlin'."

There was a click as the nurse returned the healer to its original position.

"It is finished," she said with a smile.

"Will I need any kind of follow-up?" Skye asked the nurse as she sat up and ran her hands over her arms and stomach.

"No. It is gone now—completely gone."

Skye shot Dylan a joyous glance before enthusiastically thanking the nurse. She refrained from jumping off the table, but put one foot then the other onto the floor with care, testing her damaged ankle. It was as strong as it had ever been.

She took Dylan's arm and leaned against him, not because she needed to, but because she wanted to.

LATER THAT EVENING, Skye and Dylan sat with Wade, Jesse, and Kelsey in an apartment-like dwelling given to them for the duration of their stay when Ian and Sonora stopped by.

Skye invited them to sit around the thick, wooden antique table that she couldn't get enough of. She ran her hand over its pristine surface.

"Did you enjoy your meal?" Sonora asked, seeming a bit anxious.

"I sure did," Wade replied. "After I made sure I wasn't going to be fed anything still wiggling."

Ian chuckled. "I can assure you most of our food is well cooked."

"Good to hear."

Ian changed the subject to the matter at hand. "The council has met, and as expected, we will join the battle against Devon and his army. We have made the decision to leave in the morning."

"I would've liked to be at this meeting," Dylan said, with a frown.

"It is rare for an Atlantian other than a council member be admitted to a meeting, let alone a Human. And there was not much of a question of what the decision would be."

Skye grabbed Dylan's hand and squeezed it. "We are grateful for the help. A larger force means fewer injuries on our side."

"With so few of us, it would've been a hard fight," Dylan admitted.

"There is one thing we need to discuss," Ian said, eyeing Dylan. "Our weapons."

"Okay."

"We will set our weapons to stun—unless forced to use stronger."

"Stun?"

"A person stunned will remain that way for hours. It will give time to get them jailed."

Dylan's frown returned. "I don't want to sound merciless, but what do we do with them then?"

"We ask that you let us care for the situation. Those who can be rehabilitated will be. Those that refuse will be dealt with."

Dylan disagreed, but Skye stopped him. Remembering Sydney, she told him, "There are good people caught up in this mess that I think will be just as relieved as we are when it is over. We should give them one last chance."

"My people will handle this. You will be free to go back home as soon as you would like." Ian eyed Dylan, waiting for his answer.

Dylan looked at Wade, who said, "I got less mercy than my brother, but if Skye says there are some good ones in there—I believe her."

"I agree with Wade," Dylan added. "Jesse?"

Jesse, who had closely followed the conversation, perked up. "Yeah. I agree."

"Kelsey?" Dylan asked.

"Same here."

Dylan nodded at Ian. "Reckon we're all in agreement then."

"That is good," Ian said. "Let us review the battle attack."

The plans were simple. The Atlantians had more power behind them than anyone would ever have dreamed. They would attack from the front—straight on and plow their way through the building.

Dylan's group, along with another group of Atlantians, would pick off stranglers.

Skye stood. "Now that's taken care of, why don't I bring out the dish of what I can only assume is a dessert that someone left in our refrigerator—if that is what you call it."

SOMETIME LATER, Ian and Sonora left for their own home, and Wade, Jesse, and Kelsey went to their rooms, leaving Skye and Dylan in the living room.

Dylan turned to Skye with an almost shy expression.

"Darlin', we haven't had a minute to ourselves, but I have something—Mako did something I never thought possible at the infirmary today."

Skye moved closer. Whatever this was, it meant a lot to him. "What did she do?"

"It's better if I just show you." Dylan raised the edge of his shirt.

Skye's gaze followed the edge of the material to the bullet wound—or what used to be the bullet wound. She touched her finger to the spot. It was nothing but smooth skin.

"Wow, it's like it was never there. That's great, Dylan."

"That's not all." He raised his shirt higher.

The thick scar that had curved around his back had disappeared too.

"Dylan?"

His smile of absolute delight was contagious and had her grinning too.

She ran a hand over his once damaged skin, pushing his shirt out of the way so she could see his entire chest, then back.

"The scars are gone—totally gone!"

"Yep."

Skye sobered for a moment. "How do you feel about that?"

"Kinda amazing." He ducked his head. "I keep checkin' to make sure I didn't dream it."

"Oh, Dylan! I'm so happy for you!"

He nodded, a smile still lighting his face as he scanned the room's furnishings.

"Things are nice here. Best I've ever seen. The people are good too."

Skye followed his gaze, appreciating the gleaming antiques that Ian had explained were castoffs from the world above that Atlantians lovingly brought back to their former glory. "It's true."

"And all the technology they have. It would sure make livin' easier, especially now our world is no longer . . . right."

"A few of their inventions could really make a difference."

"And it's safer here. Safest place on earth, I reckon."

"I feel like it is."

Dylan was quiet for a moment as he studied Skye. "You deserve this. I see Sonora—how happy she is here, how secure. You deserve that too."

He stood and moved to the large window, staring out into the sea. "I just don't know if I can do it."

"What are you talking about, love?"

"Ian took me aside. Told me how close you were to dying and said you could be safe here. For our entire lives, if we want. It's all you've ever wanted. Don't tell me it's not."

Skye's heart skipped a beat. Dylan was right. From the moment the AgFlu had started it was her only goal—get to safety and stay safe no matter the cost. But she hadn't yet achieved that—maybe never would up on land.

But here? She stared into the ocean, then slowly turned to scan the beautiful home again. Something comparable to the lovely home her mother kept and could afford to with all their millions.

The opportunity to stay overwhelmed her. Jesse and Kelsey could heal from their trauma. The calm atmosphere would also be good for Dylan and Wade.

Her sweep of the room eventually brought her back to her fiancé and what he offered.

Dylan, clad in jeans and a t-shirt with his scruffy face and shaggy hair, the way he stood, the way he talked. Everything about him proclaimed his heritage.

Mountain man. Her mountain man.

He glanced at the water outside the window and his expression seemed sad.

"I just don't know if I could do it," he repeated. "But I'd try for you. I'd try anything for you. You know that, darlin', don't you?"

Her eyes flooded with happy tears. This man, who had risked his life and braved the enemy to rescue her, was now willing to turn his back on his beloved home to make her happy.

"Oh, Dylan. I love you."

Skye wrapped her arms around him. When she pulled back, she caught his resigned expression as he threw another glance at the ocean.

"You, love, are the best man in the world. I can't believe what you are offering me. But this is an under-the-sea home."

Dylan's eyebrow rose. "Yeah."

"I want an on-the-mountaintop home, preferably in West Virginia. I want the warm sun on my face and the soft breeze brushing at my hair. Most of all, I want my strong, dependable, nature-loving husband happy by my side."

Dylan laid his hand on Skye's shoulders and put his forehead to hers. "Are you sure, darlin'? Look at everything you're giving up."

"Look at everything you've already given me. Home, family, love."

"It ain't enough. I can't keep you—it—safe, not like here."

"We can make it safe. You and me, Wade, and the kids. We can make our own safe place."

Dylan gave her an uncertain stare, so she pressed on, "Love, you are as good as the warm sun, as unstoppable as the hilltop breeze, and if you decide you're going to do something, you will." Skye brushed a bit of hair off his face.

"But you're right, we've been surviving. It's time to start living."

"How? How do we do better than what we've always been doing?"

"Look at what the Atlantians have. They can help us, teach us. Then we can make our own world better."

Dylan pulled Skye into a warm embrace. "We can make Cole's Mountain as safe as here."

"We can start there."

Dylan's chest rumbled as he chuckled, and Skye smiled at the sound, snuggling deeper.

"You have grand plans, darlin'."

"Better grand than none, I say."

Dylan pulled away just enough to tip his head back to Skye's. "Grand it is, then."

He brought his lips to her, brushing them with his before saying, "Cole's Mountain—here we come."

48

SCARS

The next morning, when Wade entered the kitchen, Dylan sipped at something the Atlantians drank for breakfast instead of coffee.

"That stuff Ian suggested any good?" he asked, nodding at Dylan's cup.

Dylan grimaced. "Naw. I'm drinking it mostly out of habit."

Wade leaned against a cupboard and crossed his arms. "This is an amazing place, no doubt. But I have yet to eat or drink anything decent."

"You got that right, brother," Dylan said, laughing. "Give me a rabbit burned over a campfire any day."

"Well, give me a cup of that anyway. I need somethin' or my whole day will be off-kilter."

Dylan waved to the wall beside him. A spout and buttons extended from its smooth, stone-like surface.

"I just pushed things until something came out," he said.

Wade grumbled as he grabbed a cup off of an open shelf and started punching the buttons for himself. He stopped when liquid began to flow out of the nozzle. When it stopped, he sniffed the brew and made a face.

Dylan understood. Their normal cup of strong black coffee had a dark, earthy scent. Whatever this was, it smelled lighter and sweeter. It threw a body off.

"Just imagine it as something different, and it'll go down better," he told his brother.

"But where's the kick? I need my kick." Wade stared at his cup with a woeful expression.

Dylan shrugged. "I'm still waiting."

A dolphin swam by the window, drawing the men's attention.

"Every time I look out a window, I'm surprised I'm under the ocean," Wade said.

"Not me. I can't forget we are under tons of water."

"It's eerie."

"Skye says it's beautiful."

Wade shot Dylan a glance. "You better get that woman of yours home. She's gettin' weird."

Dylan, who had been drinking the last of his "coffee", choked a little as he laughed. "I plan to."

Dylan turned to Wade, changing the subject. "Brother, there's something I wanted to talk to you about."

Wade raised an eyebrow.

"These people," Dylan continued, "sure can do some amazing things."

"Sure can."

"They got rid of the scars."

"What? How?"

"They just waved that little machine over them. I got skin like a baby now."

"Now that's hard to believe."

Dylan pulled up his shirt.

"Well, I'll be," Wade murmured.

"That's what I said. I still expect them to be there, they've been on me so long."

"Part of you."

"I assumed so, but I'm doing just fine without them. I feel like a new man."

Wade folded his arms and leaned against the counter. "I noticed somethin' was different. I just reckoned it had to do with finding Skye."

"I wanted you to know. In case, you wanted the same before we left."

Wade turned and looked out the window, glancing toward the surface—toward the sun—an almost unconscious check for the time. But it was impossible to see the sun this far down in the water.

Dylan waited. It was Wade's way to make quick decisions, even on something as big as this. When his brother turned back to him, he'd made up his mind.

"I'm thinking I'll keep 'em," Wade said. "They aren't as bad as yours. And yeah, he was your father, but he wasn't your blood. He was mine, and sad to say, these scars are the only thing he left me." He ran a finger over a burn mark on his forearm. "They remind me to settle down when the more unkind personality traits he handed down to me start takin' the lead."

"You sure? "Dylan gave him a hard stare.

Wade chuckled. "This sparkling personality is hard work." His expression turned serious. "We got kids now, and I don't ever want to treat them like he treated us."

"I know, brother." He put a hand on Wade's shoulder.

Dylan understood. No one knew Wade or their upbringing better than he did. When it came to battle, or fighting of any kind, Wade was fierce. That hard gleam would flame in his eyes, and he was ready to mix it up— whether he should or not.

"And if you ever change your mind, the Atlantians will be here," Dylan assured him.

Waded nodded. "Now let's stop this lallygagging and get us some bad guys."

WITHIN THE HOUR, they were all back in the water vehicle, heading for the surface. But this time an army surrounded them.

Kelsey bumped Jesse's arm. "Look!"

Atlantians stretched as far as the eye could see. Some rode the same type of water motorcycle as Ian, and some traveled in larger open sea vehicles holding twenty to forty of them.

Dylan smiled.

That mad scientist would never know what hit him.

49

TO BATTLE

The entire company rose out of the sea as one. If any human would've been standing there, Dylan was sure they would have needed to change their pants.

He'd been in more battles than he could count, and no matter how often it seemed weighted in their favor, there was always that small doubt saying his side wouldn't be the winning side.

But not today.

There was no way he and the Atlantians would lose.

Dylan smiled as he stood in the midst of the army, strapping his weapons onto his body.

Skye scanned the sea of warriors gathered in the parking lot by the beach as they prepared for battle. Somewhere in that bunch of men was Dylan, and she wanted one more glimpse of her fiancé before he left.

She raised on her tiptoes, straining to see him. Just when she was about to give up, a line of men jostled each other to one side, creating an opening.

Dylan broke free of them and strode toward her. Head up, shoulders back, and giving her that slow smile of his.

Her toes curled into the sand.

"Darlin'."

"I was hoping you'd come over and say goodbye."

"Of course. Wouldn't leave without this." He bent, molding her lips to his, and ignoring the teasing calls of the men behind him.

Skye relaxed into him. After today, they could go home, and she could expect this every morning.

Dylan pulled away and tipped his head to hers. "You'll stay here, right? So I'll know you're safe."

"Of course." Skye took in the small contingent of Atlantians assigned to protect Sonora, Kelsey, and herself as well as any injured. While she had been more than willing to stay at Dylan's side, Kelsey was happier on the sidelines, treating the wounded. And Sonora's husband was barely comfortable with her on land.

Now Dylan was asking her to stay here for the second time today. She understood. Too much had already happened to them.

When he gave her a doubtful look, she said, "I will stay here, I promise—really promise."

He pulled her tight again and gave her a quick kiss. He ran a finger down the edge of her hair and gazed into her eyes. "I love ya, darlin'."

Then, with a soft groan, he turned and walked away.

Feeling bereft over the sudden loss of his muscular arms, Skye wrapped her hugged herself as she watched him disappear into the army of men.

Kelsey walked over to her. "Don't worry. It won't be long. Devon has nothing compared to these guys."

The two women leaned against each other, as the company started its short walk to the Marine Center.

. . .

Ian once more sent his love to Sonora, wrapping her in it as he walked behind his father, Jorah, who led the army. Beside him were the Cole brothers and a few of his father's most trusted warriors, but Ian kept his eyes forward, lost in thought.

Devon Shade. The man who tortured him for months in the guise of medical experiments. Ian barely survived it.

Even now, it haunted him.

His people may be able to get rid of physical scars, but the mental ones had to be taken care of the old-fashioned way.

Ian tried to keep the worst from Sonora, but she knew. He often woke in the middle of the night with tears rolling down his face. It was her soft embrace, her sweet kisses, that helped him get through those black times.

Ian would have been happy to kill the man before they had returned to Atlantis months ago, but he'd refrained. Though his wife and her family were horrified over what Devon was, they hadn't been ready for such drastic action. And it seemed Devon would spend the rest of his life in jail.

Ian let that be enough for him.

But somehow that evil man escaped the tight bands of justice.

Perhaps that is how it was supposed to be. To give Ian the chance to have sweet revenge for himself.

Ian tightened his hand on his weapon.

Devon Shade would die on this day.

JESSE WALKED alongside his mountain brethren, his eyes bright. He'd hoped to be part of this momentous battle—had held his breath as he asked—and whooped like a crazy man when Dylan said yes.

Of course, like everything with Dylan, he needed to

agree with a million cautions. His father made sure he took the battle seriously and went over every likely scenario and even made Jesse swear to do everything he or Wade said.

After that, they talked weapons.

Mom was not so happy.

She was, in fact, livid. Livid was a word they recently discussed in reading class, and it fit her feelings over the matter perfectly.

When Dylan told her he'd given Jesse permission to walk with them, her lips thinned and lost all color. Her eyes had gotten a bright, hard look.

She'd grabbed Jesse and held him to her and said, "No!"

Dylan gently pried her off Jesse and pulled her into the bedroom where they "talked"—with loud voices.

But when they emerged, she seemed at peace with it.

"I gotta learn sometime, Mom," he'd said. "This battle will be better than most. Everyone thinks so."

"So I keep hearing. And I realize you're bigger and stronger now but, Jesse, you're my boy. This isn't ever going to be easy for me, not even when you're a grown man."

Jesse gave her a lopsided smile. "I know. You love me."

Skye ruffled his hair even though she needed to raise her hand almost to her eye level to do so. "You know I do."

He never tired of hearing her say it. His new family was the opposite of the severe conditions Skye had saved him from. Hearing her proclaim her motherly love for him meant the world was right and good.

It's what made him want to take part in the battle—so the world was good for other people, too.

Devon needed to be stopped.

Now, Jesse marched along the rest of them—Human and Atlantian—so excited he wasn't sure his feet actually touched the ground.

On top of that, he replayed the warmth of Kelsey's quick hug before he'd left and felt his heart thump extra hard.

Much as he'd like to start up something with her—if she liked him too—Dylan had explained that a man needed to learn a lot before he could protect and care for a woman nowadays. Dating was a serious business, not just for fun anymore.

He may be too young now—but he was learning, and someday . . .

SONORA PUT down the bandages she had arranged and walked over to Skye and Kelsey as they stood seeing the men off.

She searched for a glimpse of her husband's dark hair and found it—maybe. It was so hard to see the front of the line.

But it didn't matter so much. She could still feel Ian's emotion as he marched away from her. His love surrounded her like a warm, fuzzy blanket.

Sonora would've smiled except for that hard edge of darkness hanging just beyond his love for her. The blackness had been a part of him since she had helped rescue him from Uncle Devon's lab.

She shuddered, remembering her first sight of him sitting in the too-small cage, injured and sick.

Her beloved uncle had done that to him. To this day she couldn't believe it, even though her uncle had admitted it himself.

Sonora knew what the darkness in Ian meant. Her uncle wouldn't make it through the day.

She was okay with that. The only judgment left in this world was the judgment they made for themselves. Uncle

Devon was an evil man. There was no doubt about that. And evil needed to be destroyed.

Even though her small amount of Atlantian blood didn't allow her to share the full strength of her emotion with her husband, she sent it anyway. Her husband needed to know she was on his side and would forgive any action he needed to take today. They were *Jatta Arra*—together forever.

He sent his immediate response, so overwhelming she gasped.

Relief that she would accept the inevitable. Appreciation and love in wave after wave.

"Be careful, my love," she murmured.

Skye reached for Sonora's hand, squeezing it. "This is hard, isn't it? Seeing them off like this."

"It is, but when this day is over, we will be home and the world will be a better place."

"It will," Kelsey added. "And we can be proud of making it that way."

The three women watched until the last person faded from their view. They pushed their worry aside and turned toward the infirmary tent sitting on the blacktop under the shadow of Spire Cliff and prepared it under the guidance of the Atlantian doctors.

INTO THE FRAY

Dylan and his group of mountain men had found a high place. From there, they could see the major battle and anyone who tried to escape it.

This suited Wade just fine. From what those Atlantians said, they'd be through the building in a few minutes and that would leave him nothing to do. And there wasn't anything he loved more on God's green earth than a good ole man-to-man fight. And from what Skye had told them, getting rid of the jackasses in the Marine Center couldn't happen soon enough.

Wade blew out a noisy breath. And people thought he was bad.

He dug into his front pocket for a few pieces of candy he'd stashed in there earlier and popped one into his mouth before handing another to Jesse.

"We're gonna have some fun today, boy."

Jesse sent him a thin smile as he took the candy.

Dylan scowled at Wade. "We're here 'cause it needs doin'. Not for fun."

"You think what you think and I'll think what I want."

Wade rubbed his hands together. "I ain't gonna rough anyone up too bad unless I have to. It's a way to let off some steam is all."

"I wish a fight didn't make you so happy. But your rowdiness does always help." Dylan looked down and kicked at the ground. "I can't say I ain't feeling some of that myself. But we don't need to pass something like that on to the boy. We only fight when it needs doing, and that's it."

"Of course, brother, of course. Jess knows that, don't ya, Jess?"

Jesse nodded. "I do. And the butterflies are swirling so thick in my stomach, I'm feelin' more sick than anything else. I'm not sure I'm going to consider fighting fun."

"That's good," Wade said as he chuckled. "No worries, D. The boy had his head on straight."

"That's good, Jesse." Dylan clapped him on the back. "That's real good."

Jesse threw a glance back toward the beach. "I wish I could see Mom and Kelsey from here. I'm worried about them. Can you spot them, Dad? Your eyes are better than anyone's."

Dylan scanned the beach. "Seems all quiet." He turned back to the boy. "Worrying is part of battling, but you need to keep your mind on what you're doing. As much as you can, anyway. Even a slight distraction can cost ya."

"Speaking of—," Wade said, "heads up."

Below them, Ian and Jorah's army broke free of the brush and trees to cross the parking lot to the domed building. Their dark blue armor shone in the early morning sun, and each man carried a rifle-like laser weapon.

Ian had explained that his army would have their weapons set to stun. That way they could fire at will and sort the good and the bad out later. It would make for a quicker and cleaner attack.

Wade could understand that, but it seemed to take the fun right out of it. He was glad he was up here looking for the stragglers.

The Atlantians closed in on the front of the building, dropping the few Humans standing in the parking lot.

One scraggly group ran, pulling along their five tied-up captives—no doubt on their way to feed the evil scientist's experiments.

Jorah's men fired, deliberately missing the innocents. Most fell, leaving the captives standing there with disbelief written all over their face.

This was their lucky day.

Jorah nodded and two of his men walked to the captives and moved them to safety.

Jorah's army now stood at the front of the building, a row of patched-up commercial glass doors the only thing standing between them and the enemy.

At a signal from Jorah, the first line aimed their rifles at the doors. The blast sent wood, glass, and metal flying into the air.

When everything settled, the barricade had disappeared.

Inside the lobby, people scattered. Some tried to scoot out the side doors, but they didn't stand a chance.

The guns blasted, and the enemy fell.

Wade grunted, hardly believing what he was looking at.

The night before, Ian had proclaimed they would be through the building in no time, and that sounded just about right.

"Head's up," Dylan whispered, nodding to their right.

Something—or someone big moved through the bushes. Wade got a flash of plaid. Definitely Human. "Here we go."

Dylan waved, indicating the group should move

together. He put Jesse between himself and Wade before leading the way.

When the man in plaid saw them, he tried to make a run for town.

Dylan sent two men after him. They had the weaponless man pinned and tied in no time.

Wade walked up to him and stuck a rag in his mouth. "In case, he starts squawkin' and warns others."

One after another, they grabbed those trying to escape. Wade was pretty sure most of them were on the wrong side. A couple of them seemed confused and didn't put up much of a fight, and he wouldn't be surprised to find they were the innocents they claimed to be, but there would be more time to sort that out later.

Before long, they had gathered a small group of prisoners. Dylan left two armed men with them and took the rest of his company to search for others.

After returning to their high spot, they scanned the area for movement. They saw none.

Dylan and Wade shared a satisfied glance until a bullet buzzed by them and buried itself deep in the tree beside Wade's head.

51

ONWARD

Dylan ducked, his heart pounding as he grabbed Jesse's arm and pulled him down beside him.

He scanned his company, making sure all his men crouched against the sandy ground.

It'd been too easy. There was always something.

"Stay low," he mumbled to his son.

On their far left, several tall bushes swayed. Someone—several someones—forced their way through them.

Dylan signaled for his men to keep low and follow him.

They moved toward the enemy, using the thick brush along the beach to hide their advance.

Slow and steady. Watch and wait. The last thing Dylan wanted was to walk into an ambush.

He looked over the land. As far as Dylan could tell, the people ahead were the only ones out here.

He picked up the pace, turning to Jesse as they got closer.

"When we catch up with them, you find somewhere to lie low, ya hear? You had some fun with the others. But there are more in this group, and I'm not risking you."

Jesse opened his mouth to argue, and Dylan threw him a stern stare. The boy closed his mouth and nodded.

"Good man," Dylan said.

He narrowed his gaze and hardened his jaw as he focused on the group ahead of them. Tightening one hand on his rifle, he waved his mountaineers onward with the other.

When the enemy slipped around a small curved hill, Dylan looked back the way they had come, his stomach tightening.

This was taking them further out than he'd expected. Soon the Marine Center would be out of sight. If he couldn't see that building, he wouldn't be able to keep an eye on Spire Cliff where Skye and Kelsey were.

Dylan stopped, peeking around the small hill at the enemy ahead.

The enemy seemed relaxed, slowing from a trot to a leisurely walk as if they didn't realize someone followed them.

Wade waved for him to continue forward, that eager light in his eyes. When Dylan didn't respond, Wade whispered, "What's the problem, bro?"

"Something doesn't seem right."

"What?"

"I don't know. It's not something I see—it's something I feel."

"You sure you just ain't feeling lonely over Skye."

Dylan shot Wade an irritated glance, but his heart thumped in agreement with Wade. Not lonely, though. Worried.

He'd promised to keep her safe, and he couldn't do it from this far away.

He shook his head. Now wasn't the time for distraction.

Skye had two giant Atlantians at her side and weapons of her own. She'd be fine.

"I ain't lonely," Dylan growled at his brother.

Wade chuckled. "I kinda like the lovesick Dylan."

"Shut up."

"He's so cute and cuddly."

"I said shut up. Keep your mind on the job."

"Oh, are we finally going to get to that? Here I was thinking we're gonna let those boys skip on out of here."

Dylan gave Wade a deep scowl which caused his brother even more amusement. Dylan ignored him and went back to scoping out the scene ahead.

Dylan perked up when the men from the Marine Center moved to an area the trail widened.

He broke his men in two, four on either side, telling them to stay well behind the enemy as they followed them until he gave the order to attack.

Each man slipped silently through the brush and grass with the care Dylan had taught them.

Dylan nodded approvingly at Jesse. The boy had done well so far but it was time for him to find a safe place. Dylan pointed to a hollow behind a tree.

Jesse pulled a face, but he did as he was told.

After making sure his men were all in line, Dylan turned his gaze on the enemy ahead and made sure his weapons were ready to fire.

When two of Devon's men bumped their shoulders together and started laughing, Dylan knew the time was right.

He raised his crossbow and fired.

As soon as the bolt had left the shaft, he loaded the second one.

Within seconds of each other, the two men dropped.

Dylan and his men shouted an earsplitting battle cry.

The enemy startled and raised their weapons.

Dylan reloaded. When he raised his weapon, he saw the mountain men had Devon's men surrounded.

"Drop your weapons, ya filthy varmints," Wade shouted at them.

Dylan's stomach hardened when, for a moment, it seemed they would refuse. A firefight this close would have casualties.

He couldn't allow this to escalate.

Dylan stepped forward and raised his gun to the head of the closest man. Deadly serious as he stared at their leader. "Drop 'em. Now."

The man's expression changed from defiance to distaste. He spit on the ground as he dropped his gun. "Do as he says, boys."

Then he turned to Dylan. "Look. We were just trying to leave this place—not cause any trouble. Look at it. It's going down—it's already over. None of us are White Coats. Just let us go."

Dylan's gaze scraped over the dirty, heavily weaponed group. There was only one reason men like these would be on this property. They were the ones who dragged the innocents to this awful place. Maybe the very ones who had brought Skye and Kelsey here.

"No," Dylan said.

A man toward the rear of Devon's group reached behind his back.

For Dylan, everything slowed to a crawl. He jerked his rifle up and zeroed in on him.

"Don't do it," he warned the man.

"We just bring them here. I'm not taking the blame for something someone else did." He raised his gun so quickly it almost seemed a blur.

Dylan didn't think—he squeezed the trigger.

The man huffed as the bullet hit his shoulder, burying deep. The gun dropped from his slack fingers to the ground with a thud. He grabbed his shoulder and yelled.

Wade shook his head as he patted the rest of them down. "We warned ya. It didn't have to be this way, but you didn't listen."

Dylan waved Jesse out of his hiding place and handed him some strip ties. "Help Wade tie them up."

Jesse took the ties, an urgent expression on his face. Dylan was glad to see him take his job seriously.

Once the enemy was secure, some of Dylan's tension left him.

Now they needed to take these guys to the Atlantians and meet back up with Skye and Kelsey.

5 2

ALMOST

Skye sighed as she released her bottom lip. How was Dylan doing? And Jesse?

She glanced up—then higher still—at the Atlantian beside her. He was tall and muscular, almost a twin to the one standing on the other side of the small medical camp. She was glad they were on her side.

They had introduced themselves, explaining they were brothers and given names her tongue could never reproduce.

When the tall, brown-haired man beside Skye gave her a reassuring grin, she returned it with a quick, half-hearted one and turned her worried gaze toward the Marine Center.

Even this far away, and over the roar of the ocean beside them, the screams and cries of the enemy were heard.

"Do not worry," the Atlantian assured her. "Those are only cries of fear. They will harm no innocents, and the guilty will have a trial. Jorah and the Counsel have decreed it."

"Will the trial be here or in Atlantis?" Skye asked.

"Here, of course, kind lady. Never would Jorah allow Humans such as those into our most precious city."

Skye nodded. If she was Jorah, she wouldn't allow anything to mar that beautiful home either.

The cries gradually faded, and only occasionally would one slice through the morning air, silencing the chatter of small animals and birds.

"It is almost over now," the brown-haired Atlantian said.

"Good," Sonora replied as she stared toward the building and folded her arms. "Good."

Kelsey walked over to Skye and leaned against her. "It sounds like our side won."

"Yes, it does. Now all those suffering from Devon's experiments will be helped." Skye's heart lifted a little. It was what she'd wanted—what had started this entire battle.

Was Dylan's group having the same sort of success as the Atlantians?

She imagined his bullet-riddled body lying across a trail. Jesse by his side, crying—or worse . . .

Skye shook her head to dislodge the horrible vision.

SKYE'S GROUP WAITED, sure there would be some injuries.

Eventually, two Atlantians showed up reporting that everything had gone well. Some warriors continued to round up the enemy while others followed Dylan's men, searching for any stragglers or escapees.

He predicted any minor skirmishes would soon be over and that any injuries would be small. Then both Atlantians disappeared back into the tall seagrass.

. . .

TIME DRAGGED by as Skye eagerly awaited her family's return, and when the two Atlantian guards stood taller, their eyes searching the beach and tall grass, she started looking around too.

"You hear something?" she asked.

"Someone comes. Several Humans."

Skye's heart soared. Dylan and Jesse!

The Atlantian beside her swayed, then fell with a thud, unconscious at her feet.

Skye blinked in confusion and turned to look at the second Atlantian, who bounced against the sand when he dropped.

Skye gaped before she pulled her scattered wits together and realized someone had stunned them with an Atlantian gun.

As she drew her weapon, she yelled, "Kelsey, Sonora, fire! They have Atlantian lasers!"

Sonora held her laser gun and fired into the tall seagrass.

Someone on the other side gave a loud grunt. There was a dull thud as they hit the ground.

As Skye sent Sonora a triumphant glance, the blonde woman fell to the sand as graceful as a ballerina.

Skye fired at the enemy and grabbed the back of Kelsey's shirt, tugging her backward. "We need to run!"

Skye's arm jerked down as Kelsey fell to the ground, her eyes closed.

Skye refused to let go of the girl. She dropped to her knees, making herself as small as possible against the sand. Skye stuck her gun into her waistband and put her hands under Kelsey's arms, dragging her back to a large rock behind them.

She glanced up at Spire Cliff. If she could get Kelsey

between the rock and the cliff, they would have some protection.

Then what?

One thing at a time.

Skye tugged, making more progress than she'd imagined she would.

Her gaze darted from one side of the tall grasses to the other.

Why hadn't they fired at her? Maybe they had moved on. Not considered her a threat.

Still, she kept on dragging Kelsey to the rock. They could hide there until the girl woke up or help came.

A long, deep chuckle came from the grass.

Skye froze.

The tall blades stirred and someone stepped from behind them.

"Oh, Skye dear, this is indeed my lucky day."

Skye starred back in disbelief. Her stomach turned.

Devon. Devon Shade.

Beside him, Cliff and two of Devon's guards emerged.

In a flash, Skye pulled her weapon and fired it at the guards holding laser weapons.

The first and the second went down, screeching and clenching their wounds.

Cliff raised his gun, aiming at her head, his finger curled around the trigger.

"Don't hurt her!" Devon screamed. "I need her!"

Cliff changed his aim.

Before Skye could move, the bullet came at her like an angry hornet. Fire ripped through her hand.

Her gun fell to the sand with a thud.

Skye screamed and brought her hand to her stomach, cradling it.

When Cliff started toward her, Skye turned and ran.

She stumbled but pushed against the sand and continued as fast as she could go.

Cliff's breath huffed behind her.

A few steps later, she felt his steel fingers digging into her collarbone and twirling her around.

Cliff's glee-filled expression filled her line of sight before he wrapped his fingers into a fist, drew back his arm, and punched her in the face.

Her vision flamed red as her skull reverberated with the bone on bone contact.

Skye's bad hand hung useless at her side. Her good one shoved at him but was too weak to do any harm.

Some small part of her brain still worked, and it screamed for her to do something—anything.

Instead, she slipped into darkness.

The sand was soft and warm. As her brain shut down, she allowed herself to enjoy that small bit of comfort.

It may be the last she would have.

53

NOTHING

P ain woke Skye. She pulled in a ragged breath.

She was slung over Cliff's shoulder. Her bullet-riddled hand spiked with pain as it collided with Cliff's back with every step he took.

The entire side of her face ached, and jolts of pain flashed through it.

Skye groaned and pushed against Cliff, wanting away from him. The thought of his hands on her made her sick.

Cliff laughed and slid his hand from her knee to her thigh.

Skye jerked and pushed harder, straightening at the waist a little.

"If I let you down and you can't walk, I'll punch you again and carry on."

"My feet are fine." Her voice came out weak and trembling. She hated that she sounded that way.

"Let's see how your head is." Cliff held her legs up, letting her slide lower on his back.

Skye yelled and grabbed his shirt, trying to hang on.

He cackled as he shook her up and down.

Her brain swirled, and she choked with nausea.

Cliff dropped her.

Skye avoided landing directly on her head by letting her arms take the worst of the fall. Her hand exploded in pain. She turned her head and vomited.

As Cliff's hands reached for her, Skye pretended to choke again. Everything had happened so fast, and she needed a minute to assess the situation.

She looked around. She must have only been unconscious for a few minutes. They hadn't gotten far—only further into the beach's parking lot.

Scattered across the blacktop were a few vehicles. Two looked like they had sat there a while. The other van and trucks were the ones her group had arrived in.

Where was Dylan, Wade, and Jesse? Were they close?

It didn't seem like Cliff thought that was a possibility. He'd made no attempt to keep quiet.

He towered over her, watching her every move. It limited how openly she could scan the area.

Devon pushed Cliff aside and knelt beside her.

The scientist clucked over the damage to her face and admonished Cliff. "You use too firm a hand with her. I have repeatedly told you not to harm her so much."

"I remember you saying I could do whatever I wanted as long as she was still able to undergo the experiments. A bruised face doesn't bother them."

Devon didn't reply, instead he mumbled something Skye couldn't make out.

Skye kept her eyelids lowered as she let her gaze trail across the parking lot and into the brush, trees, and tall grass that surrounded it.

There was a trail on the far side, wide enough for a car —if only she could get to her feet and run.

Something on the other side of the parking lot caught her eye.

A glint. It lasted only a second, if that.

Was someone out there? Or had the sun hit a patch of sea glass?

She prayed Dylan was there, waiting for the perfect time to ambush Cliff and Devon.

The scientist picked at her injured hand, muttering about it. He prodded it, almost kneading it.

Skye screamed as pain like a hot iron radiated through her hand. She pulled her arm away from the evil scientist, cradling it to herself.

When Devon came at her again, she pushed his fingers away.

"Now, dear, stop fussing," he said. "There is dirt in your wound."

"It hurts, Devon. Please, just leave it be for now." Treating him well had always worked in the past, she'd try it again now even if it did seem as if he'd lost even more of his hold on reality. "I'm sorry. I'll be braver later."

"If it gets infected, it may cost your life, and I can't have that. You're too valuable to me."

He moved toward her hand again, even though Skye tried to hold him at bay.

Devon stopped. "Unless—oh yes, that may be interesting."

Skye gave him a wary look. "What is interesting?"

He ignored her, a sign that he was seeing a medical subject and not a real flesh-and-blood person he should have empathy for.

"Cliff," he said, "this may give us a new opportunity. Let us see if she is vulnerable to infection. If not, we carry on like before, but with some added knowledge. But if it does become infected, we can see if she had the same regenerative powers as a starfish."

Cliff raised an eyebrow. "What do you mean by that?"

"We cut off the infected arm and see if it grows back."

Skye reeled back in horror, her heart racing.

"I've never thought to try that," Devon continued. "Why, I don't know. Clearly, an interesting experiment."

Cliff chuckled as he stared at the horrified Skye. "Clearly. But I want some time with her before you start pulling her apart. Promise me that and you'll have all the help you need."

"Of course, Cliff." Devon waved his hand at him. "Same set of rules, though. She must be able to carry on with the experiments."

"Don't worry. I'll leave enough of her for that."

Skye stumbled to her feet and ran. Her head spun, and the ground seemed to move with every step.

"Go after her!" Devon ordered Cliff.

"Look at her. She's not going far. I need to get into one of these vehicles first."

It gave Skye time. She narrowed her eyes as she tried to see clearly.

Glass shattered, tinkling onto the pavement. A false start or two of an old engine and then a roar as it caught.

It didn't help that their group often left the older mountain community vehicles keyless and always hot-wired them.

Skye redoubled her efforts, concentrating on putting one foot in front of the other as she weaved across the parking lot.

Cliff's shoes slapped pavement as he easily caught up with Skye and pushed her to the ground.

Her chin caught the hard, pebbled surface. She bit her tongue and blood spurted into her mouth.

Cliff stepped on her back.

Skye fought, clawing at his legs with her good hand and trying to drag herself away from him.

He quickly tired of his game.

With a foot still on her back, Cliff reached down and grabbed her good hand, pulling it up toward him until she yelled.

"You never listen," he retorted. "Are you going to listen now?"

"Yes," Skye whimpered. "I will."

"You can be a one-armed woman or a no-armed woman."

"I'll listen. I will!"

"If you don't, I swear I'll take this arm. You got it."

Skye raised her head and nodded.

Cliff grabbed Skye around the middle and hauled her to her feet. He kept a tight grip on her arm as he dragged her to the van he'd already started.

He opened the side door of the vehicle and threw her in.

Skye choked back a sob. This van should take her to her beloved mountains, not wherever these evil men were going.

When Cliff backed away to slide the van door closed, he saw her eye the door.

"If you try it, I'll come after you. I'll get you just like I get you every time." He stepped closer and put his face to hers. "And I'll enjoy it. You know I will."

Skye dropped her gaze to the floor. Her last hope of escaping died when Cliff found a zip-tie and secured her ankle to a steel bar under the front passenger seat.

As Cliff slammed the door shut, Skye took stock.

She was tied to the vehicle, had one usable hand, couldn't go two steps without dizziness.

If she somehow got loose in the time it took Cliff to walk to the driver's seat, could she make it across the parking lot and beyond?

The answer was obvious.

Cliff would catch her like he always did, just as he'd said. Then he would beat her. How much more of that would she survive?

Cliff strutted around the outside of the van, past the passenger seat window and the front windshield as if he had done something he could brag about and not just beat up a defenseless woman—again.

Devon waited in the front seat, not caring what happened to Skye as long as he got enough of her to slap onto an exam table and torture.

These men were in charge of her life now.

Her stomach dropped and the deep, bone-numbing fatigue of defeat overcame Skye. She crumpled to the floor of the vehicle.

There was no way out, and no one to help her.

This was her life now.

Skye lay like a lifeless husk, her eyes dull. She had nothing left—no fight, no emotion.

Only the tears running over her cheeks showed she had any life left at all.

54

FALLING

Devon uttered a short, odd cry.

Skye jerked up from the floor.

The scientist fumbled with his seatbelt, his eyes wide.

Skye looked out the front window.

No Cliff.

"What happened?" she asked, but Devon didn't acknowledge her.

Skye tried to turn onto her knees, but the twist-tie didn't quite allow it. She pushed up the best she could and looked outside the van, her gaze darting from one end to the other.

Still no Cliff.

She reached down to her ankle and worked at the zip-tie.

Something slapped the driver's side of the van.

Skye looked up.

Cliff clawed at the window with bloody hands. A bolt ran through his body below his shoulder from back to front. It scratched against the glass.

The door handle rattled.

Skye scrambled toward the driver's chair. She needed to

lock that door. She crawled onto the seat and stretched as far as she could.

Cliff stared at her. "Help me!"

Skye stared back as she pushed the lock down.

"What are you doing?" Devon yelled at her. "We need to get out of here."

He pushed at Skye, and she fell to the floor of the vehicle. Devon stood to unlock the driver's door.

Skye grabbed his pant leg with her good hand and pushed her free foot into the back of his knee.

With one good yank, the man fell onto the floor beside her.

Skye reached for her ankle, glancing out the window as she did so. She gasped as joy filled her.

Dylan and his mountain men ran straight for the van.

Skye jerked at the zip-tie and scanned the van for anything to remove it.

Beside her, Devon pulled a small scalpel from his pocket and held it to her face.

Skye stilled.

Quickly, Devon dropped his hand to her ankle and sliced the plastic holding her. He brought the scalpel back to her face and held it there as he maneuvered himself out of the van.

Then he motioned Skye out.

Devon grabbed her arm and dragged her across the parking lot.

"No!" Skye struggled. "Devon, let me go! You can't win this. They're coming."

He whirled to see Dylan's group gaining ground. His gaze darted across the parking lot as he looked for a way out.

There were only two ways—across the parking lot to the trail or onto the path for Spire Cliff. Everyone knew the path for Spire Cliff ended at an overlook five hundred feet above the ocean waves.

There was only one logical way to go.

Insane Devon did not go that way.

She pulled away, surprised at Devon's strength as he forced her to stay beside him.

Skye curled her good hand into a fist and punched Devon square on the nose.

Devon reared back, but he clenched Skye tighter.

Skye threw another punch.

He yelled and let go of her for just a moment.

Skye whirled around—a mistake with a concussion—but quickly regained her balance. She trained her eyes on Dylan and ran toward him.

Devon followed her, his shoes tapping against the pavement.

She felt his hand in her hair.

He yanked her backward.

Skye's scalp burned as hair tore from her skin. She fell but scrambled back up.

Devon curled his hand in her hair, gaining another handful, and jerked her close to him.

"I know just what to cut on you so you'll never walk again," he threatened as he held the small sharp knife in front of her.

Skye stopped fighting. If Devon crippled her, she wouldn't be able to run.

Devon held the scalpel to Skye's neck, turning her right and left so Dylan could see he had control of her.

The mountain men slowed.

Devon backed himself and Skye up the trail.

Across the parking lot, Ian broke from the trees and ran toward them.

Skye smiled. There was nowhere for Devon to go. He'd have to give up now.

Devon continued to step backward—up Spire Cliff's trail—pulling her along with him.

Dylan continued to close in and was now close enough that Skye could see his frantic expression.

"Skye. Skye, darlin', it'll be okay."

She started to nod, but Devon's fingers still held her head tight. "I know, love."

"Is this your mate?" Devon asked. "How disappointing! I'd hoped if you were already attached it would be to one of your own kind."

Skye's blood boiled. "For the last time, Devon, I am not Atlantian."

"You are—a little. That is why you are the secret to the cure."

"Devon!" Skye argued as she tried to slow their progress. "The Atlantians already have a cure. One they will share with all of us. You don't need to search for one anymore."

Devon screamed at her. "The cure is mine to find. I must! The world is suffering."

"Most of the world is dead."

Devon jerked her head back and touched the blade to the side of her neck. "Shut up! You don't know what you're talking about!"

Skye kept quiet, taking a step backward when forced to, but she locked her gaze with Dylan's. It is what gave her strength.

She sent a worried look to Dylan as they passed the last trees on the trail and headed toward the overlook.

"Fall," Dylan mouthed to her.

Skye pretended to stumble.

Dylan raised his rifle and aimed.

The scientist pulled Skye up as he made himself small behind her.

"Very clever," he said. "But not clever enough."

When Skye struggled, he put the blade to her neck and pressed hard enough that blood ran down her neck.

Dylan lowered his rifle.

"Thank you," Devon said as pleasantly as if Dylan had passed him a cup of tea.

"What you don't understand, Skye dear, is that I must find a cure and will do anything for it. Anything. Do you understand? It is my entire motivation in life."

"I do understand. But Devon—"

"We cannot trust the Atlantians! I do not care if they say they have a cure. I don't believe it. It is more likely a poison designed to wipe the rest of us from the earth. I started this disease as a weapon against them. Why would they help us?"

Devon weaved both of them through the end of the safety fence that surrounded the overlook and stopped.

Skye kept her gaze on Dylan and, with her one good hand, grabbed the top of the thick metal railing.

"Devon. Where are we going?"

"Why over the edge, dear."

Skye's heart hammered. Barely able to breathe, she said, "We won't survive that."

"We will, dear. We will. The Atlantians jump it all the time and survive."

"We are Human, Devon. Human!"

"So it would seem, and yet we are not, are we?"

"What are you talking about?"

"I guess I can finally reveal one final truth to you. After all, we are going on this little adventure together." Devon cleared his throat.

"I also have Atlantian DNA." He sighed. "There, I said it.

I don't mind telling you, I went a little crazy when I found out."

A little crazy?

"I ran the blood test fifty times before I believed it. Literally."

Devon took a step back.

Skye kept her grip on the fence, stretching her arm to the limit.

Her fingers slipped from its slick surface.

"Don't worry, dear—only a couple of steps left."

Skye looked at Dylan, the love of her life.

His face turned ashen and his gaze darted from one side of the cliff to the other, looking for a solution.

There wasn't one.

If Devon was determined to go over the edge, he'd take her with him.

"I love you," she mouthed to Dylan.

"No!" he roared.

"You are everything to me. Everything," Skye said aloud. "Tell Jesse, Wade—everyone how much I—"

Devon's arms locked around her—one around her middle and one around her throat.

"See you at the bottom, Skye dear. Then we will start anew."

Skye felt Devon take another step backward. His foot slipped against the edge of the cliff.

He squeezed her tighter.

She stared at Dylan. She'd take this last look with her. Her eyes filled with tears as she fell backward.

Dylan raced to the edge, throwing his rifle to the side as he ran.

Skye raised a hand to him.

Their fingers grazed.

"Skye!" One word screamed Dylan's anguish.

The wind rushed past her ears as they free fell.

She would have screamed except for Devon's arm around her throat, restricting any intake of air.

Instead, she watched the side of the red rock cliff zip by.

It was both longer and shorter than she expected.

His heavier body hit first. It bucked as he hit the water.

There was a crunch Skye both felt and heard as a hundred bones in Devon's body broke at the same time.

His body protected hers.

The warm water surrounded her, and his lifeless arms released her.

Skye shuddered with shock.

A wave lapped over Skye's head, and she kicked upward to break the surface again.

Nausea, dizziness, and pain returned in full force. Skye struggled to keep it at bay as the ocean sent a barrage of waves toward her.

Each push of water sent her further downward.

Skye kicked and pulled at the water, trying to reach the surface.

Two waves collided with her in the center. The tumble sloshed her already bruised brain.

The water's powerful surge forced her down.

Skye was too weak to push back.

She slipped under the surface and watched the light darken.

55

WALK AWAY

Skye woke, sputtering and coughing, only half aware of her surroundings.

There was a sharp pain in her damaged hand.

She jerked it to her, but someone held it fast.

Skye's chest tightened with panic, and she fought.

"Hush, darlin'. It's all right now."

"It's almost over," Sonora added.

Skye opened her eyes and glanced around. She was in the medical tent she had helped set up for the battle.

Ian held her arm as he ran the healer over it. Sonora stood beside him.

Dylan was on her other side, cradling Skye's other hand in both of his. Her gaze searched his.

"Ian thought it was best to heal up that hand before you woke. He knew it would hurt some."

Skye gave Dylan a tight smile as another sharp pain ran through her injury. "I'm just glad he can heal it. It felt so bad, I was afraid to even look at it."

"Look at it now," Ian said with a smile.

With a bit of hesitation, Skye raised her hand and flexed her fingers.

No pain. No sign of any injury. She almost wept. "Thank you!"

Ian nodded. "We will send two healers with you when you go back to your mountains."

Skye beamed as she pushed herself into a sitting position. "Oh, Ian. That will help our community so much."

Dylan agreed. "Sure will."

"I am happy for that," Ian said. "Your people and mine work together now. My father will also have other items for you."

Outside the medical tent, a group of people stood. In the middle of the circle, someone in a dark blue shirt laid on the sand.

"Is that him?"

"Yes, darlin', but he's gone now. You don't have to worry."

Skye bit the inside of her cheek, then said, "I want to see him. I need to."

Dylan helped her out of the cot. As soon as Skye got her footing, she was able to walk on her own over to the group.

Ian and Sonora stood beside Skye, arms wrapped around each other as they stared at the body.

Each one of them had seen Devon differently—from a loving uncle to a prejudiced killer.

All felt relieved he no longer walked this earth.

Skye stared at the evil scientist. In death, he looked small—powerless.

She shook her head, wishing for all their sakes the man's life had gone better.

In another world, Devon may have been a better man.

In this one, he had been a monster.

Beside him laid Cliff—a broken bolt shaft still protruding from his body.

He had inspired true terror in Skye, and if she could've chosen his death, she wasn't sure she would've been merciful enough to give him such a quick one—not after the torture he'd inflicted on her and doubtless many others.

She stared at the two evil men for a moment.

They had fallen.

She had survived them both.

Skye turned away, secure in the knowledge they would never harm anyone again.

Dylan stood beside her.

She slipped her hand into his.

Together, they walked away.

5 6

REST

Later, Skye, Dylan, and Wade sat with Jorah, Ian, and Sonora inside the coffee shop Sonora frequented before the AgFlu had begun.

"Time will be needed to develop more of the cure, but it will be done as quickly as possible," Jorah promised them. "Since I had thought I left the distribution safely in Human hands the last time and it failed somewhere along the line. I hope you understand if I wish to lead the effort this time."

Dylan raised his hands. "Have at it. I'm satisfied leaving it to you. I'd like to take some home to Cole's Mountain."

Jorah nodded. "Of course."

"Dylan," Skye asked, surprised at his willingness to hand over the project, "will we deliver any as we head home?"

"To my father and his people. We'll leave the rest to someone else."

Before she could say another word, Dylan answered her unspoken question.

"That's work for others to do. You and I—we've done

enough, darlin'." He squeezed her hand. "We're still aching over what's happened."

Skye glanced at the Atlantians. They all nodded in agreement.

"Our place is on Cole's Mountain, standing side by side, making it better," Dylan continued. "I'm not risking you or this family ever again."

"The greatest blessing in life is family," Ian said. "And the greatest challenge is their safety. Dylan, you have done well. It is time for you and your family to rest now."

Dylan grinned. "You heard the man, darlin'.

He was right. Although their physical wounds were healed, their emotional ones needed more time.

"My family owes you an enormous debt after everything Devon put you through. This is your time to heal." Sonora said, "It is our time to work at fixing his evil mistakes."

Ian nodded. "Atlantians the world over will rise and distribute the cure. I assure you, Humans will be saved."

"Now hang on a dang minute," Wade blustered. "If they want to take a rest, well, I reckon, they earned it. But I plan on being part of this. Don't be leavin' me out."

"Of course," Ian replied, "any Humans who wish to join us will be welcomed."

Jorah stood. "Humans and Atlantians working together. It is a new day! May it continue for as long as the seas kiss the land."

Skye smiled. Warmth filled her as she imagined a new, better world.

Ian, Sonora, and Jorah watched Dylan's people drive away, heading back to their home.

"They still look at us as if they can't believe we are real," Ian said with a chuckle.

Sonora looped her arm through her husband's. "I'm married to you, and sometimes *I* have trouble believing it."

"I wonder what their reaction would be if they knew about the time-travel?" asked Jorah.

"Don't tell them," Sonora said. "Their heads may pop—at least some of them."

Jorah looked at her with a worried expression.

She quickly reassured him. "It wouldn't literally. It's just an expression. It means it would be too much for them."

"Then we must keep it to ourselves. We do not want our new friends to explode."

"Good idea," Sonora said, a little too quickly.

"What have you been up to my dear little wife?"

"Nothing, my love. Nothing at all," she said as she waved at Skye.

57

CABIN ON THE MOUNTIAN

S kye sat on the front porch of their cabin, taking in the spectacular pink sunrise making its way over the mountain.

The door beside her opened and Dylan handed her a cup of steaming coffee.

She took a sip as he seated himself in the wooden chair beside her. When he settled, she took his hand.

Skye tightened her hand around his. "I had given up hope of ever seeing this again—ever sitting here with you again."

Dylan grunted his agreement. "Had a few shaky moments myself. It's why we needed to get back here. To prove to ourselves all that was really over."

"This cabin has always been your safe place—your place to heal, hasn't it?"

"Yep. It's yours now too."

"Yes, I believe it is," Skye said with a happy sigh.

Sue Ellen popped her head out the front door, rubbing one eye. "I was gonna start breakfast if that's okay with you.

Tricia taught me an awesome biscuit recipe I wanted to make for you. Well, me and Kelsey."

Dylan winked at her. "I'm always up for biscuits."

"That sounds wonderful, Sue Ellen. Thank you," Skye added.

Once the girl had gone back inside, she turned to Dylan. "I can't believe the change in her. What did you do when I was gone?"

"Had a few heart-to-hearts is all. She just needed to realize she was safe—that we have her back. And Tricia has given her a purpose now, too."

"I love that she helps Tricia make and deliver food to the older ones. They all love Sue Ellen so much."

"I ain't sure if it's the food or those blonde curls of hers they look forward to more."

Skye laughed.

"Speaking of changes, you're a morning girl now, uh?"

"Well, I'm not promising to stay that way, but I just can't stay in bed when I know I have a beautiful new day to start with you." Skye leaned against Dylan's shoulder.

"I like hearing that."

Dylan kissed the top of her head and stared out over the mountains. "Darlin', I'd hoped to be more patient with this, but I can't be."

Skye raised her head, a puzzled expression on her face. "Patient with what?"

"Our wedding, darlin'. I've been wanting to say those words to you for a while now. I say it's past time."

"We've hardly been home a week."

"Yeah, but we're settled back in now, and Wade's gonna be heading back down for more of the cure now that's he's delivered it to all the communities around here. They may not send him back up this way, and I'd like him to be here."

"Of course. I hadn't thought of that."

Skye laid her hand on Dylan's rough cheek. "I'm as eager as you are. Name the day."

He gave her a slow grin. "As soon as we can get this thing together."

"Okay." Skye giggled. "Let's see. I have that gorgeous dress Sonora gave me. I could wear that. We could hold the wedding outside if the weather is good and inside the courthouse, if it isn't. Perhaps, everyone will bring a dish."

"Course they will. That's the way we do things here on Cole's Mountain. Always have, always will."

"I love that."

"I love you."

Someone cleared their throat, and Skye pulled away from Dylan.

Travis stood beside the porch. The young man had somehow won Sue Ellen's affections and was often at the cabin. "Sorry to—well, I didn't mean—" He cleared his throat again. "Sue Ellen said to come for breakfast. Is that okay, sir?"

Dylan waved him in. "Sure, she's in there cookin' now."

Travis rushed into the house.

"The third piece in Sue Ellen's change of personality," Skye said with a smile.

"He's a great kid, but if he doesn't stop callin' me "sir", I'm gonna refuse to let him in the house."

"No, you won't. We need him to keep Sue Ellen nice."

"That's the thing that confounds me. When I left, all she did was spit at him like an angry wet cat."

"Some relationships start that way. I wasn't all that happy with you when *we* first met."

Dylan ran a hand down Skye's hair. "I sure was taken with you. I was just too scared to admit it."

"I'm taken with you now. Does that count?"

"It sure does, darlin'."

Sue Ellen's voice rang out. "Breakfast is ready!"

The smell of fresh biscuits enveloped them as they walked into the kitchen. Travis held plates as Sue Ellen plopped eggs onto them. Bacon sizzled on a cast iron pan.

Jesse waved Skye over and patted the seat beside him. Kelsey, who spent as much time here as the Doctor's house, sat on Jesse's other side.

Wade sat at the end of the table, rambling on about some story or another.

The entire scene wrapped around Skye like a warm, fuzzy blanket. She needed to pinch herself to make sure it was real. Tears sprang to her eyes.

"Darlin'?" Dylan leaned toward her, a concerned expression on his face.

Skye waved a finger in front of her face. "Happy. Happy tears."

He smiled as they took their seats at the table. Everyone quieted.

Dylan looked at everyone. "Well, I'm kinda surprised I'm saying this, but I think sayin' Grace is in order. I'm feelin' real appreciative. How about that?"

Everyone agreed.

"If there's a day to start showing our appreciation, today is a good one. This here is the beginning of a new, better life," Wade said. "We got each other, and we got the Atlantians who are willin' to help us. And there's a cute little Atlantian girl I got my eye on. I could use some help with courtin' her."

"Wade. It doesn't work that way with them!" Jesse said.

"Yeah, that's why I need some help."

The group exploded into laughter.

"I'd be more worried about you, Wade," Skye said. "But I know there are several ladies on this mountain with an eye on you."

Wade raised an eyebrow. "There are? Well now, that's something to consider, ain't it?"

While Wade mulled over his romantic possibilities, the rest of them dug into their breakfast as they sent him amused glances.

58

A BETTER WORLD

Every resident of the mountain had shown up for the wedding. There were even a few visitors. Ian and Sonora. And Dylan's father and family had made it, too.

Dylan proudly stood in front of them all.

They hadn't gone far for their special day, only the front yard. But the day was beautiful, bright and blue, and the view was the old mountaintops. What more did one need?

He pulled at his collar, still surprised that he had not only consented to wear a suit but actually suggested it. He'd even trimmed his hair and shaved. That's how much this day meant to him.

It's what he'd always dreamed of—but never thought he'd have. He'd been sure he wasn't good enough, and he didn't know the first thing about doing right by a family.

Until Skye had shown up. She'd burst into his life like the sun rising over the mountain. Every bit as beautiful, every bit as blinding.

Look at her now, coming down the aisle toward him, Jesse at her side. They were a package deal, and Dylan loved the boy as if he were his own blood.

Every day he thanked the Lord for her, for all of them. Wade, Sue Ellen and Kelsey too. They were all part of the big happy family he had yearned for.

Somehow it would seem that much more real when they said the words, made those vows and slid on the rings.

Their marriage would be a forever one—just like Atlantians'.

Dylan knew it every time he stared into Skye's green eyes. They were made for each other.

Dylan watched Skye take one delicate step after another until she was face to face with him. Her beauty overwhelmed him.

From the bright wildflowers that wreathed her dark hair to the small light-green shoes that matched her delicate dress.

She smiled at him, her entire face beaming.

It was almost more than he could take. He swallowed—once, twice, then three times—before he got himself under control.

But she knew.

Skye's gaze never left him. "I feel the same way," she whispered.

SKYE SMILED as she sunk deeper and deeper into Dylan's gaze.

This was her day—their day. And if they wanted to stare at each other for half of it, that's what they would do.

It was Tricia's giggle that broke their gaze. Skye sent her an amused glance. She supposed if she were in the audience, she'd want things to move on too.

There would be time and more time for long gazes after the wedding.

Skye turned and hugged Jesse, happy he walked her

down the aisle. He was as much a part of this marriage as she was.

She handed her bouquet of wildflowers to Sue Ellen and kissed her on the forehead. The girl was quickly becoming a treasure.

Then she turned to Kelsey, who stood beside her and wrapped her arms around her.

"My girl. We made it!" she whispered to her.

The girl beamed and hugged her back.

Turning back to Dylan, she slipped her hands into his. She smiled and nodded at her cousin, Tom, who stood ready to marry them.

With such a shortage of government, it had been decided that Tom would become the town's magistrate and could now perform marriages.

Tom smiled and began.

The words rolled over Skye, making the already beautiful day more perfect. When it was time to say her vows, she stepped closer to Dylan to make sure he heard every word of them. Her voice shook with emotion.

It was her forever vow. There was no doubt in her heart and mind about that.

Dylan's deep voice quivered a bit as he recited his. He ended them with, "I love you more than life, darlin', and I always will."

Skye couldn't have wished for a more perfect vow—for a more perfect wedding. When Tom introduced them as man and wife, she couldn't be more proud to stand by her husband.

THE NEXT MORNING Skye was the first to wake. She smiled at the sleeping Dylan, then wrapped a blanket around herself and walked to the window, allowing him to sleep.

As if he'd noticed her absence, he woke and came to stand beside her.

She held out part of her blanket, and Dylan stepped into it, folding it around them both.

The sun was low in the sky, but shining bright.

"Another beautiful day," Skye said.

"Yep, sure is."

"I want every day to be just as beautiful as yesterday."

"It sure would be nice."

As much as Skye wished for that, she wasn't a fool. Absolutely perfect days did not exist in an imperfect world.

But things were looking up.

The Atlantians continued to hand out the cure and seemed to enjoy the travel.

The cure had been given out to most, if not all the communities in this area. And some who had been in the late stages of AgFlu were now free of the disease with the additional help of the Atlantian's healers.

At first, most communities were suspicious of the Atlantians, but they quickly got used to their kind, mannerly ways. And communities who thought to take advantage of the undersea people quickly learned that Atlantians always had the upper hand.

Once people got used to them, the Atlantians seemed to have a stabilizing influence. The ancient among them often acted as wise advisors. Especially when Humans realized how old they actually were.

And now that the AgFlu was gone, some of the fear had left too. Already, more communities were starting to communicate and trade with each other on a regular basis.

Yes, things were looking up.

"We can make this world better, right? Not perfect, but better?" Skye asked tentatively.

"We can." He squeezed her tight. "We will—with some

help from our new friends. I reckon we can make it better than the one we lost. We gotta try."

"Yes. Let's try."

Kelsey, Sue Ellen, and Jesse ran past the window on their way to somewhere.

Skye and Dylan laughed.

"Let do it for us—but for them too," Skye said, snuggling closer to Dylan. "For their future, and their children's future, and generations on."

Dylan leaned down and tenderly kissed Skye's forehead.

"You got it, Darlin'."

AFTERWORD

This concludes the Sanctuary's Aggression Series. It will always have a special place in my heart.

Sharp-eyed readers will see that I have left loose ends throughout the series. That was on purpose. Over time, I may write some stand-alone books in this world.

But for now, I am moving on.

I sincerely hope you have enjoyed the special characters in this series.

I have ideas running around in my head for a new series. It will be (unless I get *other* ideas) strictly post-apocalyptic. Look for my newsletter to stay informed. :)

You, dear reader, are who these books are for. I enjoy writing them, but without readers, they would sit in some dusty drawer. Where's the fun in that?

So enjoy this and any other books that may come your way.

Reading breathes joy into our lives, enriches it in a way nothing else can. It gives us dreams, hopes, and wonders.

Books wrap us in their sturdy pages and sail us to new, exciting worlds. And we joyfully go for the ride.

Maira :)

ALSO BY MAIRA DAWN

Sanctuary's Aggression Series in order of release:

Sanctuary's Aggression

The Road: Sanctuary's Aggression 2

The Climb: Sanctuary's Aggression 3

Sanctuary's Aggression Box Set - Books 1-3

The Girl: Kelsey's Story - Sanctuary's Aggression Novelette

SeaBound: The Beginning Prequel 1

SeaBound: The Atlantis Cure Prequel 2

The Trial: Sanctuary's Aggression 4

The Rescue: Sanctuary's Aggression 5

∾

VISIT MAIRA DAWN

Stay up to date with new releases and more!

www.mairadawn.com

https://www.facebook.com/mairadawn.writer/

ABOUT THE AUTHOR

This is Maira Dawn's seventh book in the continuing *Sanctuary's Aggression Series*. Maira first wrote on Wattpad and quickly developed a large following. *Sanctuary's Aggression* hit #1 on Wattpad in Science Fiction, Pandemic and other categories. The series is now being released on Amazon.

If you enjoyed this book, I'd love to hear about it. Leaving a review on Amazon or Goodreads is a big help to indie authors. :)

You can also find me on Facebook . If you would like to sign up for my newsletter, you can do so at www.mairadawn.com. News of deals on my books will always be shared there, and I always share deals on other books too!

facebook.com/mairadawn.writer
twitter.com/MairaDawn
instagram.com/mairadawn

Printed in Great Britain
by Amazon